Searching for

The policeman stood behind her and ran his hands up over her hips and her waist, up the side of her chest, down across her shoulders and then round to her front. She drew back from his grasp in surprise as his hands cupped her breasts, and found herself pressing against him.

'I'd advise you not to resist, miss,' he whispered in her ear.

'I can assure you I have absolutely no intention of resisting,' she murmured.

Searching for Venus

ELLA BROUSSARD

Black Lace novels are sexual fantasies.
In real life, make sure you practise safe sex.

First published in 1998 by
Black Lace
Thames Wharf Studios,
Rainville Road, London W6 9HT

Typeset by SetSystems Ltd, Saffron Walden, Essex
Printed and bound by Mackays of Chatham PLC

ISBN 0 352 33284 0

Chapter One

Louise scratched the side of her nose with her pencil and sighed. From her vantage point high at the back of the lecture theatre, she could see her fellow students busily taking notes below her: a mass of bowed heads and furiously scribbling hands. She didn't know why they bothered. Dr Petersen was a pompous, misogynous bore, without a doubt the worst person imaginable to be lecturing on 'The Myth of Venus'. She couldn't understand how it could be possible to make a subject as interesting as the history of art so tedious, but Dr Petersen succeeded every time. Louise had endured nearly two years of his monotonous, nasal voice, his priggishness, his feeble attempts at off-colour jokes, and his favouring of male students over his female ones. She comforted herself that there was only one more academic year to go, and then she would be free of him. Once she graduated from university, she would never have to see him again. She couldn't wait.

She looked down towards the front of the lecture theatre, where Dr Petersen was standing in front of a lectern on the low stage. Behind him were three blackboards, partially obscured by the slide screen that had been drawn down in front of them. Dr Petersen was wearing a grey suit. How appropriate, thought Louise. Louise watched as he droned on, all the time tightly gripping the sides of the lectern with his long bony fingers. His face was long, lean, and sharp-featured; and it was the kind of face that made him seem of indeterminate age. He could quite easily be anywhere between forty and seventy. His hair was thinning, and he wore it scraped over the bald dome of his head. Louise thought back to the time she had seen him outside the central administration block in a near-gale, struggling to hold the long, lank strands down over his head. It amused her that his vanity about his hair loss made him adopt a ridiculous hairstyle instead. There would be no going bald gracefully for Dr Petersen, that was for sure. Dr Petersen cleared his throat noisily and continued.

'For the purposes of this lecture I will assume, I dare say correctly, that your knowledge of classical mythology is minimal. So who was Venus?'

Dr Petersen looked around the lecture theatre, and Louise grimaced in irritation. Of course the students all knew who Venus was, but no one was going to speak up and draw themselves to Dr Petersen's rancorous attention in the middle of a crowded lecture theatre. Predictably, he took the ensuing silence as one of ignorance rather than reticence.

'I will tell you, then. Venus was the Roman goddess of love, and much of her mythology was appropriated from that pertaining to the Greek goddess, Aphrodite. In turn, Aphrodite's cult had come to Greece from the Near East. Here we have a good example of the universality of certain themes in diverse mythologies. The concept of a goddess of love is found in many cultures over many thousands of years. But it is Venus in particular we are dealing with today. If you know anything at all of Venus, which I doubt, you may think of her as the goddess of love. However, I must qualify your perception. She was the goddess of physical love, rather than spiritual love. In fact, it would be more proper to describe Venus as the goddess of sex rather than the goddess of love. She bestowed physical beauty and sexual attraction, and was the personification of carnal passion and desire rather than fidelity and marriage.'

Dr Petersen narrowed his eyes and looked around the lecture theatre. 'Typical woman. Some things don't change much over the millennia, eh? I might add that the "venereal" of "venereal diseases" is also derived from her name. Diseases of love, named after a woman – albeit a divine one. How very fitting.'

Louise bristled. She would have a go at Dr Petersen about this at their next seminar, but she knew from experience that any protest at his sexism would be like water off a duck's back. Dr Petersen was so set in both his ways and his ideas that he seemed almost fossilised: a relic from an older, less advanced civilisation; a dinosaur. Slides flashed past on the screen in rapid succession as Dr Petersen continued his exposition.

'From the early fifteenth century, the intellectual movement in Italy known as the Renaissance rediscovered the riches of the classical world as source material for painting, sculpture, architecture and other associated disciplines. By about 1480, the first large-scale paintings based on classical mythology were being produced: the *Birth of Venus* and *Primavera,* by Sandro Botticelli. Venus is the central figure in both paintings.'

Slides of these paintings briefly illuminated the darkened room, and then were followed by another, this time of Botticelli's *Venus and Mars*. Louise studied the projected image, in which Venus watches a sleeping and near-naked Mars as four satyrs play with his armour. Dr Petersen became suddenly animated. He described at great length the particular type of armour depicted, the helmet and the sword and the type of lance; and Louise knew that Venus would barely merit a mention. Louise spent a lot of time undertaking her own studies, far removed from anything that Dr Petersen taught, and so she already knew that this was a richly allegorical painting, suggesting that love can tame the most aggressive and violent instincts. Louise lowered her head and doodled on the margin of the page of her notepad. The page was empty, apart from the date and the title of the lecture. Her long auburn curls fell across the whiteness of the paper.

'Titian,' said Dr Petersen, in such a peremptory manner that Louise looked up. Another slide of another Venus appeared on the screen, and Dr Petersen's droning commentary continued.

'Titian took Venus out of idyllic pastoral settings and placed her in the bedroom. Here she is, lying on a bed, gazing at us directly, her eyes full of invitation. Many of Titian's mythological works were commissioned by kings, and by the nobility. This is a prime example of high-class erotica, sanitised and made acceptable by its mythological setting. Such a portrait of a contemporary woman would have been unthinkable, but the social mores of the time were such that all Titian needed to do was paint a portrait of that same woman, throw in a few mythological references – maybe a cherub or two – and call her Venus, and it was suddenly all perfectly palatable. In time, the term "Venus" came to represent any naked woman in an enticing pose, rather than to be taken in its strictest sense as a depiction of the goddess herself.'

Dr Petersen sniffed disapprovingly. 'Hardly an edifying subject to have hanging on one's walls, I would have thought. Now we move on a hundred years, to about 1650. This artist had the good taste to paint only a single female nude during his career, and here she is.'

Another slide came on to the screen. Louise instantly recognised it as *The Rokeby Venus*, by Velazquez. A naked woman was reclining on her side on a silk-draped bed, with her back to the viewer. Self-absorbed, she was looking at herself in a mirror held up by a chubby-bellied cherub. Louise regarded the ripe fleshiness of the woman's bottom, and the swell of her hips swooping down to her waist. She could see how the gentle curves of a woman's body were pleasurable to the eye, and Velazquez had obviously enjoyed depicting them. He had even portrayed the small dimple at the back of the woman's knee and another just above her buttock on her lower back. It was a beautiful, glowing painting; and Louise could almost imagine herself in a similar pose, idly reclining on luxurious fabrics, waiting for a lover to arrive.

Louise gazed around her to see how her fellow students were reacting to the luscious acreage of naked female flesh displayed before them. For the first time, she noticed that Tom was sitting off to one side, two rows in front of her. The steep rake of the seating in the lecture theatre meant that she was looking right down on him. She studied his short cropped hair and tanned neck, and his broad shoulders. He was wearing a scruffy sweatshirt and, from the V of damp down the back of it, she guessed that he had come to the lecture straight from a practice session on the rugby pitch. As she watched, Tom leant back against the wooden bench seat, throwing his head right back. She could see his Adam's apple jutting out slightly from his neck, and the dark shadow of stubble on his face, but most of all she noticed that he was gazing at the slide of *The Rokeby Venus* from under half-closed lids. Louise watched as he coolly appraised the image of the naked woman. Did he like what he saw? Louise watched him for a while, wondering if he was affected by the voluptuous sensuality of the woman in the painting in the same way that she had been.

Louise's thoughts drifted away from the world of art history and into a more personal sphere. She idly ruminated about how much she liked Tom. She knew that, if she were totally honest with herself, she had to admit that it was more than a case of mere liking. She was drawn to him, yet she didn't want to be. He had that total self-possession that handsome men sometimes have: a slight hint of arrogance, and an expression that says, 'I know you like to look at me. Every woman does.' Louise didn't like men like that; and yet Tom's mere physical presence was enough to set her on edge, despite her reluctance to admit it.

Tom was in his final year, the year above Louise, and had never shown more than a friendly interest in her as a fellow student of the history of art. They attended some of the same seminars, and had swapped lecture notes a couple of times, but that was it. Their paths rarely crossed socially and, when they did, Tom always had a woman in tow. Louise suspected that, as a member of the university rugby squad, he almost certainly had hordes of rugby groupies after him, and could pick and choose as he liked. And besides, whenever she and Tom had met at parties or in the pub, she had always been with Jonathan.

Louise's musings were interrupted by a sudden movement. Dr Petersen fumbled with his notes on the lectern and, in doing so, he knocked the switching mechanism for the slide projector on to the floor. Louise watched as Dr Petersen scrambled to pick up the sheaf of papers and the switch. She knew from Bernice, their marvellously indiscreet departmental secretary, that he'd been giving this same series of lectures for at least twenty years; and Louise thought with a wry smile that he ought to be able to do it without his notes by now. Dr Petersen recovered himself, brushed down his suit jacket, coughed, and pressed the switch.

The painting that was projected on to the screen immediately captured Louise's full attention. Before her was a lush, colourful and sensual painting of a reclining female nude. It was painted in broad, confident strokes, so powerfully executed that Louise could almost feel the artist's energy still buzzing through the painting. Although the style of the painting was non-naturalistic, the woman in the painting was lying back on a bed with such unselfconsciousness and was gazing at the viewer so steadily – almost challengingly – that it seemed to Louise that the woman looked for all the world as if she was in a state of post-coital abandon but was still demanding more from her lover.

The slide didn't show only the painting. The old photograph from which the slide had been copied had been taken in a room – perhaps in an exhibition – and at some distance from the painting. The painting was partially obscured by three people standing in front of it, their backs turned to the camera as they regarded the portrait. From the style of their clothes, Louise guessed that the photograph might have been taken around the turn of the century. One of the viewers had been captured with his hand raised, and was pointing at the bowl of fruit on a table next to the nude. There was also a notice on the wall to the right of the painting, and Louise guessed that it probably detailed information about the work and its artist for the exhibition-goers.

Dr Petersen spoke. 'Now we move forward several centuries to see that the tradition of Venus portraiture continues, but only just. By the 1900s, ancient mythology formed a rarely tapped source of subject matter. Its relevance to the modern world was minimal. But some artists continued the tradition, if only in the naming of their paintings. Here we see Gustave de Valence's lost masterpiece, *The Venus of Collioure*.'

Louise's focus was total. For the first time during the lecture, she listened intently to Dr Petersen.

'This Venus was painted in 1905 by de Valence, a leading member of the Fauvist movement. We will deal with this, one of the first great aesthetic movements of the twentieth century, in more detail next year. A brief description of the movement will suffice for now. The Fauves, or "wild beasts", were so-called because of their calculated disregard for naturalistic depiction and their delight in the use of violent colour. Their name gives us an indication of the exuberance and savage energy of their work compared with what had gone before. The Fauves were primarily interested in the power of pure colour. Unfortunately, this photograph is hand-tinted. As you are all no doubt aware, colour photography had not been developed (if you will excuse the pun) at the time this photograph was taken, and the hand-tinting gives scant indication of the extreme intensity of the colour used in this painting.

'Gustave de Valence was one of the founding members of the Fauvist movement, although he never received the same recognition as some of his contemporaries in the movement, such as Matisse. Along with several other Fauves, de Valence's studio was based in the small French town of Collioure, on the Mediterranean coast. It is well documented that he used pure colours: paint squeezed straight from the tube on to the canvas. There was no mixing of pigments on a palette for de Valence. He knew that the emotional impact of pure, vibrant colour would be far greater. He exhibited widely, and this painting was acknowledged to be his finest work. It was shown at the Salon des Indépendents in Paris in 1906 to universal critical acclaim. Despite many lucrative offers, de Valence refused to sell it, and it remained in his studio. This is the only known photograph of the painting, taken at the Salon exhibition. The last recorded sighting of the painting was in 1910, and on his death in 1929 it was found to be missing from his studio, and has not been seen since. This is one of the great mysteries of the art world: does *The Venus of Collioure* still exist and, if so, where is she?'

The slide was replaced by another of Titian's *Sacred*

and Profane Love. It showed two Venuses side by side, one clothed and the other naked.

'Next week I will give the final lecture for this term and indeed for the academic year: "The Draped Figure and The Nude". I trust that you will all attend. Good day.' Dr Petersen stepped down stiffly from the podium and left by the narrow door by the stage. A relieved murmur went up from the students, and there was a flurry of shufflings and scufflings as they scooped up their notes and bags and trooped up the steps and out by the exit at the rear of the theatre. Tom caught Louise's eye as he walked past her, and winked. She was too surprised to react, and he was gone.

Louise sat for a while in the empty lecture theatre. On any other day, her mind would be in a turmoil, going over what Tom had just done and what it might signify. But not today. She couldn't get the image of the reclining nude figure of *The Venus of Collioure* out of her mind. Dr Petersen had talked about 'emotional impact' and, for once, she was in total agreement with him. If what she had seen was a pale, hand-tinted version of the painting, she could scarcely envisage how extraordinary the original must have been. The colours on the slide had seemed so bright and luminous, and the painting had such immediacy and was so full of life, that to think that such a beautiful thing was lost to the world saddened her deeply.

Louise remained, silently musing on *The Venus of Collioure,* until she was disturbed by the noisy arrival of the students for the next lecture. She remembered with a start that she had an important appointment. She collected her things together and hurriedly made her way to the departmental coffee room, where she had arranged to meet three of her friends from her hall of residence: Liz, who was a geography student; Charlotte, who was studying Russian; and Fran, who was a chemical engineer. They often met in the history of art coffee room, as the university campus was dispersed over a large area and Louise's department was the most central. Just as importantly, its coffee was also the best: percolated rather than instant.

The room was long and narrow, and surprisingly empty. After the four friends had poured themselves large mugs of coffee and bought some chocolate biscuits from the small range on display, they wandered up to the far end so that they could talk in privacy.

'OK, Louise. I want all the gory details,' Charlotte commanded.

'About what?' Louise asked, although she had already guessed what it was that the others were clearly keen to hear about.

'You and Jonathan. So, when did you split up with him?' Liz asked.

'Last week. How did you know?'

'Gossip gets around. Jack saw Jonathan in the student-union bar the other night, and Jack told Suzie, who told Ben, who told me,' Liz replied.

'Good news travels fast, eh?' Louise said, her words tinged with slight bitterness. 'Well, the split was inevitable; it had to happen. The whole thing was going nowhere, fast.'

'Hmm. I know what you mean. He's not exactly Mr Dynamic, is he?' said Liz.

Now that the news was out, Louise was relieved to be able to talk about it at last. She poured it all out in a torrent of words. 'Too right. Good old Jon. He was steady, dependable, predictable. All good qualities in a man, but somehow they added up to just one thing for me: stultifying boredom. I felt bad about it, but I had to do it. I had to get out. I felt so stifled, so trapped. He's a sweet enough bloke, but that wasn't enough. I need something more, but I'm not sure what.'

'How about more sex?' giggled Fran.

Louise laughed. 'Don't joke about it. Joan of Arc or any of the Vestal Virgins probably got more sex than I ever did.' She sat back, and sighed. 'Maybe I shouldn't complain but, on those rare occasions that we did make love, I was always left feeling unfulfilled by him. I can't understand it – a man who's not into sex. Not even interested in talking about it, let alone doing it. I've never met one of those before, I can tell you. Sexually, Jon was so conservative that whenever I suggested that we experiment or try something new, something different, he would refuse point blank. All I ever got was lights-out missionary position lovemaking. And as for foreplay – forget it. Food, outdoor lovemaking, a little bit of bondage: I suggested them all. Not that I've ever done those things, but I wouldn't have minded trying them: anything to spice up our jaded love life. I even bought a lover's guide and left it lying around, hoping he'd take the hint, but he got all embarrassed and ignored it. Some of the things in it made my eyes boggle, I can tell you. It did give me a few ideas, though!'

'I couldn't borrow it for Ben, could I?' laughed Liz.

Louise grinned, and then took a long, thoughtful swig from her coffee mug.

'God, I feel like I need to do something wild, to shake off the cobwebs. I can't believe I spent nigh-on two years in such a lacklustre, dead-end relationship. Why the hell didn't I realise it before now?'

'We wondered how long it would take you to see sense,' said Fran.

'You mean you've all been thinking the same thing, too?' asked Louise. 'Why didn't you tell me?'

Charlotte shifted uncomfortably on her seat. 'We didn't feel it was our business. Besides, for all we knew, you could have been deliriously happy with the situation. You never did say much about it, one way or the other. It was a bit personal, and you might have taken it the wrong way, thought we were criticising you.'

'That's what friends are for, isn't it? I wish you had. It might have helped to make me see sense and perhaps saved me a lot of wasted time. Oh well, I suppose we all learn from our mistakes.'

'How's Jonathan taking it?' asked Fran.

'Very well – in fact, too bloody well. He's just sort of accepted it without complaint, like he accepts everything else. It's not exactly flattering when you tell someone you want to finish it and they just shrug and say, "OK then," is it? A little bit of protest would have been nice.'

'So I take it that neither of you are pining too badly, then?' Liz asked.

'Yep. Sad, isn't it? We split up after two years and neither of us is particularly bothered about it. But then again, I suppose that it's indicative of our relationship. Couldn't be bothered.'

'So, have you got your eye on anyone else?' asked Liz with a mischievous grin.

'Let's just say I'm keeping my options open,' said Louise. 'All I really want right now is no commitments: just a damn good shag.'

'Don't we all?' chuckled Fran, and the four women laughed. They were so engrossed in their conversation that they didn't notice Tom walking down the length of the room to join them. He coughed gently to announce his presence, and Louise immediately felt her cheeks reddening. She wondered if he had overheard her last comment.

'Mind if I join you?' he asked; and Louise, Fran and Charlotte shunted round the bench seat so that there was room for him on the end. He put his mug of coffee down, sat next to Louise, and smiled. She smiled back, and couldn't stop herself from briefly glancing down at his baggy jogging pants and wondering what was hidden beneath. She had never seen him playing rugby, and so didn't know, but she was pretty sure he would be firm and fit. Just how she liked her men.

'Aren't you going to introduce us?' asked Charlotte, smiling at Tom but speaking to Louise.

'Oh hell, sorry. How rude of me,' Louise stammered, her reverie broken. She introduced Tom to the others, and she noticed with pleasure that he acknowledged them politely but also disinterestedly – flashing them that dazzling smile of his, before turning quickly to her again. It was always flattering to have the undivided attention of the most handsome man in the room, and it was not a position she was accustomed to finding herself in.

'What did you think of the lecture?' he asked her.

'Loved the slides; hated the talk,' she said with a grimace.

'Dr Petersen's an odd fish, isn't he? Quite how he ever managed to charm Mrs P into marrying him, let alone managing to produce a child with her, is beyond me. Mind you, she probably decided that once with him was one time too many. And as for not finding all those Venus paintings erotic – I can't understand it,' said Tom. He regarded Louise steadily, as if he were trying to gauge her reaction. Behind her, Fran, Charlotte and Liz exchanged glances.

'Shit, is that the time?' said Liz. 'I've got a seminar. Dr King will kill me if I'm late again. See you lot around.' She gulped down her coffee, grabbed her things, and hurried out of the coffee room.

Louise hardly noticed Liz's rushed exit. 'So did you find the Venus paintings erotic?' she asked, turning to Tom and looking at him enquiringly, with the slightest hint of a smile playing around her mouth.

'Yes, I did. Extremely. Who wouldn't? Well, apart from crusty Dr Petersen, that is,' Tom laughed.

Charlotte and Fran exchanged yet more looks and quickly drained their coffee mugs. 'We're off now – going clothes shopping,' said Fran. 'I don't suppose you want to come, do you, Louise?'

'Um, no thanks. Money's a bit tight at the moment, and I don't think dear Mr Wells at the bank is going to be quite so accommodating next time I go overdrawn.'

'OK, then. Bye.'

Fran and Charlotte gathered up their belongings and squeezed past Louise and Tom. Louise had to swivel around and pull her legs up on to the bench seat to allow them to pass and, as she did so, her back pressed against Tom. He didn't draw back from the contact as she expected him to.

When Fran and Charlotte were out of earshot, Tom leant close to Louise. 'I heard what you said earlier on,' he said.

'Oh?'

'About needing a damn good shag.'

Louise squirmed with embarrassment. 'Oh,' she muttered.

'Don't be embarrassed. I like to hear women talk plainly. They talk so differently when there are men about. Why is that?'

'I guess it's because there might be misunderstandings.'

'Misunderstandings about what?'

Louise was intrigued by the turn this conversation was taking. If she didn't know better, she might think that Tom was trying to chat her up. She smiled, and replied in a low whisper, 'Well, I find that when you have a conversation with a man about sex, he will almost always automatically assume that you are talking in specifics rather than in generalisations. He will take it that what you're really talking about is wanting to have sex with him.'

'And you're not?'

'Sometimes, and sometimes not. It depends.'

'On what?'

'On the man. On whether I fancy him.'

'And how would he know?'

'I'd let him know. Little signs: like laughing at his unfunny jokes, or holding his gaze for that little bit longer than necessary, or accidentally allowing my leg to touch his.'

'Or maybe your back? Accidentally, of course.'

'Maybe,' said Louise. He was keen, all right.

'I just want to say that, if you need any help, I would be more than happy to assist.'

'To assist in what?' Louise asked, pretending not to understand. She liked teasing men. She had often indulged in it to relieve the monotony of her relationship with Jonathan, in an attempt to inject some spice into a love life that was otherwise devoid of it. She found that playing with men like this always succeeded in making them even keener, although she never took it further. Out of some misplaced sense of loyalty to Jonathan, she now thought ruefully.

'In whatever it is you might want,' Tom said quietly.

'Now look who's not talking plainly! What is it you think I want?'

Tom moved closer to her. She was overwhelmingly aware of his leg, close to hers, and of his bulky proximity. She could smell the sharp tang of his sweat, clean and yet not quite clean. With one great pawlike hand, he gently pushed her auburn curls back behind her ear. Louise jerked back very slightly in surprise – she wasn't expecting this contact. Tom noticed her reaction and smiled, but he didn't remove his hand. Instead he let it drift down her hair until he caught her long dangling earring between his fingers. He rolled it lightly. She held her breath, all her senses focused on his hand. He was so close to her, millimetres away from the sensitive skin of her earlobe; and, as if he could read her mind, he slowly reached up and stroked the soft skin behind her ear and then the lobe itself. Louise involuntarily closed her eyes. She felt his touch on her flesh as if he had brushed against her with a branding iron. Her earlobes were among the most sensitive of all her erogenous zones. Tom leant even closer and whispered in her ear.

'I know what you want. I heard what you said to the others. Believe me when I say that I can make your wildest fantasies come true. I can make your body feel like it has never felt before. I can do whatever you want. You can ask anything of me – anything.' He stressed this last word. 'I want you to ask me. I'll do whatever it takes to satisfy you.'

Louise swallowed hard and tried not to give away her rising excitement at hearing Tom talk to her like this. But she was not going to allow herself to be beguiled by it. She looked at him sharply.

'Somehow, Tom, I don't trust you. I think that you dreamt up this spiel with your mates in the showers after a match; and I'm also pretty sure that you'll discuss whatever you get up to with them afterwards. You probably got a bet on with them. I know what you lot are like. Pick out a woman at random and see who can be the first to fuck her. I'm right, aren't I?'

Tom looked genuinely shocked. 'No. I promise you. You couldn't be further from the truth. I'm not like that. The others may be, but I'm not.'

'Then why should I believe you?' she asked.

He moved closer to her and whispered in her ear again. 'Because I love women. It's simple: I adore making love to women. I love the way they look, they smell, they feel; and most of all I love bringing a woman to orgasm. I love seeing that sweet look of abandon on a woman's face in the moments before her climax rushes over her.' He put his finger under Louise's chin and gently drew her face round so that she was looking directly into his eyes: his knowing, come-to-bed eyes.

'I want to see that look on your face. I don't want anything else, just to seduce you. And I know you want it, too. So why fight it?'

Louise could hear her heartbeat hammering in her ears. Her mouth had gone dry and her throat felt tight. She swallowed again, and whispered hoarsely, 'Do you talk to every woman like this?' She was intrigued by his forwardness.

'Just about. I find that, if you don't ask, you don't get. What they say is true: honesty really is the best policy. If I'm honest, and tell a woman what I want, then we can both go into it with no illusions; with the ground rules already set out.'

'And are you always successful?'

'Pretty much. And I've had no complaints. Listen, Louise. My particular thing is not what a woman can do for me, but what I can do for her. I don't even need to come. Just as long as *she* does, and again, and again. That's enough for me.' He looked at her and grinned. 'Despite what you might have heard about me.'

Louise scanned Tom's face closely, searching for a hint that might suggest that he was taking her for a ride. Something in his eyes told her that he was telling the truth. She slowly leant forward and kissed him. Her heart was pounding under her ribs, so hard that she was sure Tom would be able to see her shirt shaking with the pulse if he looked down. His lips tasted sweet, and she was surprised at how soft they felt. Somehow she had almost expected them to be hard and muscular, like the rest of him.

Louise felt Tom place his hand on her thigh, and could almost feel his touch burning through the material of her skirt. She felt a delicious shock as suddenly his fingers became busy, bunching and gathering the fabric, pulling it upward. The shock was almost instantly followed by a feeling of near panic, as she wondered whether anyone else in the coffee room could see what was going on. She tried to pull back from Tom, but he merely leant further forward and clamped his lips to hers again. This movement also allowed him to slide his hand further up her thigh, under her skirt this time. Louise was torn between the desire to let this continue and the concern that it ought to stop. Only she couldn't stop it. She hadn't felt the *frisson* of pure sexual attraction for a long, long time; and she realised how much she had missed it. She could feel herself opening up for Tom, and felt the gentle flood of her juices lubricating her sex.

Tom's fingers were slowly inching their way towards their goal. She felt his fingers brush the cotton of her panties, and was sure that he must be able to feel the rising heat that was emanating from her there. She opened her eyes wide as they kissed. She saw that Tom's were closed, as if he was concentrating all his senses on his busy mouth and his busier fingers. He slowly slid a finger, then another and another under the soft cotton of her knickers, searching and gently probing. All the time, his tongue was undertaking a similar search of her mouth, hungrily exploring her.

Louise jolted upright as he touched the soft flesh of her sex. It felt as if a thousand volts had passed through her. At that moment, Louise heard catcalls, jeering and whistling from the other end of the coffee room. She hastily broke free from their kiss, pushed his hand away and drew back from him. She looked past Tom and up to the other end of the coffee room. There she saw some of her fellow students – all male – gesturing crudely at them both.

'I've got to go,' Louise stammered, blushing furiously and smoothing down her skirt. She grabbed her bag, and rushed up the coffee room towards the exit. She hurried past the huddle of grinning men with eyes downcast, trying to avoid looking at them. They couldn't have seen, as Tom had his back to them, blocking their view; but she was still terrified that somehow they knew what had happened. She only started to calm down when she had reached her room in the halls of residence and made herself another mug of strong black coffee.

'Well, Tom, you certainly seem to have put me in a spin,' she said to herself.

Chapter Two

The next day, a Saturday, Louise woke early and went for a long walk. She had been preoccupied all the previous day by two things: Tom and *The Venus of Collioure*. She had gone over all that Tom had said and done several times, and had finally (although unwillingly) decided that it must have been rugby-club-inspired bravado. A handsome man like him wouldn't be interested in her, surely. She was better off out of it. She was still strongly affected by what had happened between them, though.

Louise felt as if she was suffering from some kind of sensory overload. As well as visions of Tom, she had also not been able to shake the image of *The Venus of Collioure* from her mind. She wanted to know more about Gustave de Valence and his striking painting. And so, after following her walk with a shower and some breakfast, she made her way to the university library.

The library was almost deserted, as Louise had expected. She knew only too well that weekends and work were an unknown combination to most students. The solitude of the library suited Louise. She didn't want any distractions from this particular piece of research. She decided that a good place to begin her search would be *The World Encyclopaedia of Art*, a thick volume concerning anything to do with art and artists. De Valence received a five-line entry, and no mention was made of *The Venus of Collioure*.

Louise frowned, and decided to try the library's computer index instead. She sat in front of the screen, and typed in some key words: de Valence, Collioure, Fauvism. The cursor blinked a couple of times and then a list of books and authors scrolled up on the screen. She copied down the six titles mentioned, plus their library accession numbers, and went off to find them.

With the six books spread in front of her on a table, the relevant pages marked with scraps of paper, Louise soon came to realise that very little seemed to be known about de Valence. The book that contained the most information about him carried three and a half pages of text and a full-page colour plate of *The Venus of Collioure*, plus some smaller reproductions of some of his other works. The colour plate of *The Venus* was the same photograph that Dr Petersen had shown in the lecture.

Louise scrutinised it for a long time. She was transfixed by it: the abandon of the woman's pose, the bluntness of her gaze, the brilliance of the colours. The woman was lying on a red sheet. Behind her was a blue wall and a window, looking out on to brown hills and the fiery dot of the orange sun. By the head of the bed was a table bearing a bowl of rainbow-coloured fruit. Covering the brown floorboards was a green rug with yellow splashes of colour. A single red shoe lay on the rug. Louise wondered what the woman in the painting was thinking. Was she waiting for her lover to come to her? Or was she in post-coital torpor, having already been visited by him? There was no doubt at all in Louise's mind that there was a lover: the painting almost oozed sex.

Also there in the photograph of *The Venus*, and

frustrating Louise by their permanent capture on camera, were the same three people viewing the painting at the exhibition. They obscured substantial parts of the painting. Louise squinted closely at the image, as if she might be able to see through these tiresome interlopers: the man pointing at the fruit bowl on the right-hand side of the painting; another man blocking out the area of the Venus's legs just above the knee; and next to him a woman who, together with her large feathered hat, was conspiring to conceal the Venus's feet and the bottom of the bed on the left-hand side of the painting. Louise frowned, frustrated that this was the only known photograph of the lost masterpiece. She knew that the colours were wrong, too – but how wrong? Had the person who hand-tinted the photograph even seen the original painting? Or had they worked closely from it?

Among de Valence's works reproduced in the book was a self-portrait. Louise studied it closely. Although painted indoors, de Valence was dressed in a heavy black coat, and was wearing a small black hat. He was holding a paint-stained rag in one hand and a brush in the other, and was gazing out of the painting past the viewer. He had a full dark beard and lively dark eyes. His curly hair reached his collar, and his cheeks were flushed with pink. He looked happy, healthy and well-fed; not quite the thin, tortured artist living in a garret that Louise had expected. So this was the creator of *The Venus of Collioure*.

Louise turned to the text. She learnt that the model for *The Venus of Collioure* was de Valence's favourite model, Estelle Gachet. It was rumoured that Estelle had been de Valence's lover, but this had never been proven. The text referred to a sequence of undated portraits of her which appeared to show her in the early and then more advanced stages of pregnancy, and two of these paintings were reproduced alongside the text. Louise looked at the paintings of Estelle carefully. Was de Valence's

Venus carrying his child? She read on. Nothing was known of Estelle Gachet after 1909, and no birth was ever registered under her name, but it was widely rumoured in the art world that she had indeed given birth to de Valence's child.

Also reproduced in the text was an entry in a journal. It had been made by Emile Louvain, de Valence's closest friend and a fellow artist.

> July 3rd, 1910
> Today I visited Gustave at his studio. I found him in good health and in surprisingly good spirits: we took several glasses of absinthe and talked of his forthcoming journey to Paris in pursuit of a commission. Despite his pressing financial concerns, he steadfastly refuses to sell his magnificent Venus. I have been reliably informed that the Metropolitan Museum of Art in New York offered Gustave 85,000 francs for her some three years ago, and that he refused their offer without even a second thought. Such stubborn and deleterious adherence to his principles! Now his beauty leans against the wall of his studio, half-hidden by other canvases and gathering a light coating of dust. Were she mine, I would display her to the world.

Deep in thought, Louise sucked the end of her pencil, furrowing her brow. So this was the last ever recorded sighting of *The Venus of Collioure*. What had happened to her? Where had she gone? Had de Valence destroyed her? Surely not, if it had meant so much to him. The painting was not in his studio after his death. Had someone come into his studio and removed her? Or had de Valence given her away before his death? If he could not bear to part with her for money, the only reason that made any sense to Louise was for love. It annoyed her that she would never know.

As she leant over the pages, busily taking notes, Louise felt a warm, soft touch on the back of her neck. She froze, and closed her eyes. She could smell a familiar mix of sweet sweat and musky maleness. He had an unerring knack: along with her earlobes, the back of Louise's neck was one of the most sensitive of her erogenous zones. She felt her rising arousal as slow, lingering kisses were gradually placed across her neck. When the tender ministrations finally ceased, she turned round. As she had already guessed, Tom stood behind her.

'So. I find you at last.' He smiled. He was wearing his rugby gear: a pair of sweatpants and a muddy rugby shirt. Of course. Saturdays were the main practice day for the rugby team, thought Louise.

Tom continued. 'I've looked everywhere for you. Where did you get to yesterday? We had some unfinished business.'

Disconcerted and aroused at the same time, Louise turned back to her notes. She wasn't sure what to do. She could feel Tom's presence behind her, and then she felt him lazily trace the line of her spine through her shirt with his finger.

'Leave that,' he whispered. 'Come with me.'

'No,' she said. 'I've got work to do.'

'Come with me,' he said again, more insistent this time. 'You know you want to.'

It was true. Louise couldn't deny that she wanted more than anything to go with him, and to be made love to by him. It didn't take her long to come to her decision. She put down her pen, stood and silently placed her notes in her bag. Then she turned to him and smiled.

'Let's go.'

As they walked past the tall rows of books back towards the central staircase, Tom placed his arm round Louise's waist. Gradually, she felt his hand slip lower and lower until it was resting over her left buttock. He started to caress the soft globe of flesh through the material of her skirt as she walked. Then his hand slid back up to her waist again and, exerting a gentle pressure, he guided her from the corridor and into one of the long bays between the high bookshelves. Louise stopped and looked at him, knowing what was going to happen and not wanting to stop it. Tom stepped up to her and took the bag from her shoulder and dropped it to the floor.

He stood in front of her and kissed her slowly. She responded, tasting again the soft sweetness of his lips. Gradually, their kisses became greedier, their tongues meeting and pressing and forcing. Tom pressed her back against the books. She could feel him against her, hard and solid.

'Remember what I said? Your pleasure rather than mine?' he whispered in her ear. With that, he sank to his knees in front of her and caught the hem of her ankle-length skirt in his hands.

'Are you crazy?' she whispered, trying to pull him up on to his feet again.

'No, just horny,' he whispered back, easily resisting her lesser strength.

'What if someone comes by? This is madness,' she whispered. But already her protestations were becoming weaker, and her efforts to pull him up less urgent. Despite the danger, the delicious inevitability of what was happening to her was too great to resist. She wanted to experience this illicit lovemaking; and the possibility of discovery tinged it with the thrill of the forbidden. She reassured herself. It was the weekend. The library was near-empty. And she could feel Tom nuzzling against her thighs, his breath hot on her flesh. She looked down. Tom had pulled her long skirt right up, and was holding it up on either side of her waist. He looked up at her.

'Do you want me to?'

With mounting excitement, she nodded, and watched as his head sank closer and closer to her crotch. He kissed the cotton-covered swell of her pubis, and Louise could feel his hot breath through the thin material. Then he slid a finger under either side of her panties, and stripped them down in one quick movement. Louise stepped out of them, and Tom stuffed them into her bag, before lifting her skirt once more. This time, he put his head up inside her skirt and let it fall back over him. Louise looked down on to this strange, moving mound beneath her clothing, and then she felt the wet dab of Tom's tongue against her flesh. First he slowly licked and kissed his way around her labia, and then moved inward, searching for her damp crevice with his tongue. She quaked with the urgency of desire as his tongue found its ultimate target, her clitoris. Taking it gently between his lips, he sucked, very lightly, on her aching bud. It swelled and hardened between his lips. Louise could tell that Tom knew this was the centre of all her pleasure, as he paid full attention to it, kissing and nibbling and sucking until she could feel the sweat gathering behind her knees. Her legs were becoming weak with the strain of supporting her when all she wanted to do was collapse on to the floor in a quivering heap.

She briefly wondered what would happen if anyone came by, but her rising lust soon pushed those concerns aside. Then Tom raised one of his hands and she could feel his strong fingers pushing into her, filling her and exploring her. This was the trigger she needed to come. She rode out her orgasm with Tom's mouth still clamped to her pulsing clitoris, and she bit her lower lip to prevent herself from calling out in her ecstasy.

When she was spent, Tom stood up and let her skirt drop down again. Louise slowly opened her eyes. She was slumped back against the bookshelf, but had hardly noticed the hard spines of the books digging into her back.

'There. That wasn't so bad, was it?' Tom said, grinning slyly at her.

Louise opened her mouth to reply, but could barely speak. It was as if the strength of her orgasm had paralysed her momentarily. She smiled at Tom, and slowly drew the back of her hand across her mouth, which felt dry and parched.

'I'll see you around,' said Tom, and then he bent forward and kissed her briefly on the mouth. She could taste herself on his lips: tangy and slightly acid. She watched Tom walk away. He certainly knew how to give a woman pleasure.

A few moments later, Phyllis Grant, the chief librarian, came by with an armful of books for reshelving. She glanced into the bay and saw Louise, and frowned. Still leaning against the shelves, Louise smiled back, relieved that Mrs Grant had not come by even a minute earlier. She thought to herself that Jonathan would never have dared to do anything like this. She still could barely register the thrill and the outrageousness of what Tom had just done to her. Nothing like that had ever happened to her before. She wanted more.

It was seven-thirty when Louise walked into the student-union bar, looking out for her friends among the throng of students noisily enjoying the start of another Saturday night's wild carousing. Over in the corner, she saw Fran, Charlotte, Liz and Ben, and Jack and Suzie sitting around a table. She wove her way through the crowd of people, and joined her friends.

'So, what are we going to do tonight?' she asked.

'How about going to the cinema?' asked Suzie. 'There's that new blockbuster – you know, the one about aliens landing on the moon. It's supposed to be pretty good.'

'Sounds good to me,' said Ben, and the others agreed. They finished their drinks, gathered their coats, and headed off to the multiplex.

It took a little time for the group of friends to get organised once they had bought their tickets. A variety of refreshments had to be bought; visits to the loo had to be made; and only then were they ready to join the queue. It was the second night of the film, and it was clearly a very popular choice. Once inside, they made their way up to the back row of seats, and settled down in eager readiness for the wonky, amateurish advertisements for local curry houses and garages that preceded the main feature. Connoisseurs of kitsch and unintentional comedy, they enjoyed seeing these adverts almost as much as the film itself. Then the lights dimmed, the Muzak ceased, and the screen curtains drew back with a low swishing sound.

About half an hour into the movie, Louise realised that something odd was going on in front of her. She had noticed that the couple sitting immediately in front of her had been necking during the adverts; and now the man was sitting with his head tilted right back, so that he was staring at the ceiling rather than the screen. Louise could see in the dim reflected light from the screen that his eyes were closed. The girl had her head close to his, and was whispering in his ear; and Louise could see that her right arm was making a slow, regular up-and-down movement. Louise blushed as the realisation of what the woman was doing struck her, and she turned to Liz, who was sitting next to her.

'Oh my God, can you see what they're doing?' Louise whispered, furtively pointing at the couple.

Liz looked down from the screen, and grinned as she too realised what was going on. In turn, she nudged Ben, who alerted the others. They all got the giggles, which were made worse by their attempts to stifle them.

'I can't believe anyone would do something like that

in public,' Liz whispered to Louise. Louise was about to agree, when she remembered what had happened in the library. Smiling to herself, she said nothing. When they came out of the darkened theatre into the brightness of the foyer an hour or so later, the others were full of talk of the film. Louise found that she could not contribute much to the conversation: she had been too busy watching the off-screen action instead.

Louise was back in the university library again. She loved the quiet, studious peace in the library. The low whisper of voices was punctuated only by the scuffing of a chair leg on the carpeted floor or the papery flutter as someone turned a page.

She was doing some background reading for her final essay of the academic year. She thought with relief how nice it was not to be facing examinations this year. Instead, her second-year work was graded by continual assessment throughout the year, and this was the last piece of work to be assessed. The first and third years of her course were more traditional, capped by examinations at the end of the summer term.

Louise was in the journals section of the library, chasing up some obscure references to an artist called Brazzini, the subject of her essay. As her research progressed, she found increasingly more and more obscure references to his life and work: articles in magazines or newspapers or learned journals, footnotes in other works cited, and quotes from someone else's autobiography that mentioned Brazzini. They all had to be followed up.

Louise loved chasing references. There was something of detective work about finding out as much as she could about someone's life in this way and piecing together the various scraps of information to create a coherent whole. She thought if she hadn't chosen to study history of art she might just as easily have turned her talents to becoming a private detective, or a forensic pathologist, or an archaeologist – all disciplines with similar methods of painstaking clue-gathering.

She read an article about Brazzini's willingness to experiment with new techniques throughout his career, and of his championing of new artists. A footnote mentioned that he was visiting young artists in their studios up to a month before his death at the age of ninety-three, and referred to a photograph on page fourteen, volume nine of *New Horizons in Art*. Another reference to chase up, she thought to herself, and added it to the list. She knew from discussions in her seminars that *New Horizons in Art* was a British journal which had been going for a couple of years in the late eighties and early nineties, before it had folded due to lack of finance. Its circulation had never reached above the high hundreds, largely due to its specialised subject matter. Its articles had been exclusively devoted to young, underexposed artists. From what Louise knew of these artists, it seemed to her that most them were underexposed due to a lack of talent, more than anything.

Two hours later she had worked her way down her list of references. She went over to the bay marked NA–NI in the journals section, briefly scanning the shelves before pulling out a box file which had *New Horizons in Art* written on the spine. She had not referred to this particular journal before. She took the box file over to her table and opened it up, intrigued by what she might find. Inside were twenty or so poorly produced magazines, little more than photocopies stapled together under a card title page. They were ragged and dog-eared and had become slightly faded over time. She hoped that the volume she was looking for was in the file, and then reflected that to grace any of them with the title 'volume' was something of an aggrandisement.

She quickly went through the various issues and, to her relief, found that volume nine was indeed present. She consulted the contents list, and found that the reference was contained in an article on 'Young Provençal Artists' by someone she had never heard of. She turned to page fourteen. Half the page was taken up by a photograph which was captioned: 'The grand old man of the art world, Gianni Brazzini, visiting Milo Charpentier in his studio. Sadly, Brazzini died shortly after this photograph was taken.' She already knew that Brazzini had died in October 1990, so the photograph was securely dated at least.

The photocopying process meant that the photograph had reproduced very badly. As well as being in black and white, it was smudged and indistinct. Louise glanced at it only briefly before scanning the text to see if Brazzini got a mention. She wasn't surprised to find that he didn't, and so pushed the journal to one side and crossed it off her list. Nothing useful there, but this weeding process had to be gone through each time with each reference, just in case.

She turned to the next book on her list, and found this one much more helpful. She diligently made notes for the next twenty minutes, before sitting back and stretching to ease her cramped shoulders and neck. Her buttocks were numb from the hard library chair, so she got up and paced up and down by the shelves a couple of times. Returning to the table, she glanced down and saw again the photograph of Brazzini in the young artist's studio. Strangely enough, she found it clearer from a distance, the smudges resolving into distinct and interpretable features.

In the photograph, Brazzini was talking to the artist, who had dark curly hair and was smoking a cigarette. Hanging on the wall behind the two men was a large painting of a nude woman, and beneath it was a stack of canvases. Something struck Louise with a shock as jarring as if a bucket of ice-cold water had just been thrown over her. One of the canvases at the back of the pile was only partially exposed. Its left-hand side stuck out a foot and a half or so beyond the others. She knew with an absolute certainty that what was blearily visible in black and white could be only one thing. She rushed up to the history of art section on the next floor of the library, and in her haste bumped into Mrs Grant, who was coming down the stairs.

'No running,' Mrs Grant called after her, but Louise was deaf to all admonishments. She was on a mission. She knew she was right, but she still had to check. She raced round to the section in which she had been studying the previous week, hurried over to the shelves, and gave a triumphant, 'Yes!' when she saw that the book she sought was still on the shelves. She grabbed it and ran down the stairs again. Back at her table, she flicked through the book. She was all fingers and thumbs in her haste. After a few frustrating moments she found what she was searching for: the colour plate of *The Venus of Collioure*. She grabbed the journal with the blurry black-and-white photograph and held it next to the colour plate.

'It must be. It *must* be,' she muttered to herself. What she could see in the black-and-white photograph could only be the part of *The Venus of Collioure* that was obscured by the woman with the hat. There, in the photograph of Brazzini and the young artist, on the canvas sticking out from the back of the pile, was the bottom of a bed, and a pair of feet. The size of the canvas, the lines and the style were the same – or at least, as far as she could tell in the smudgy photocopied photograph. Of course, Louise couldn't compare the colours; but the tones seemed similar, with corresponding areas of lighter and darker paint.

Louise hurriedly read the photograph caption again. Milo Charpentier. The name meant nothing to her. She was working fast now, spurred on by pure adrenalin. She felt as certain of her discovery as she had ever felt about anything. She ran down to the reference section two floors below, and grabbed the *Directory of Modern European Artists*. She was about to take it back upstairs when Mrs Grant came striding over to her. She stood right in front of Louise, blocking her path.

'Reference books may *not* be removed,' Mrs Grant hissed. 'I've got my eye on you.' She stalked off back to the desk and glowered at Louise as she date-stamped a pile of books handed to her by a student. Louise shrugged, and quickly flicked through the pages of the thick directory.

'Charleston . . . Charmes . . . Charolles . . . Chârost . . . Charpentier . . . Bingo!'

Louise eagerly read the entry. 'Milo Charpentier (b. 1965). Self-taught, working in Provence, France. Specialises in erotic portraiture.'

Louise read the entry again, just in case she had missed something in her haste, but there was no other information. After the elation of only minutes ago, she now felt suddenly deflated. But it had been unreasonable to expect any more. Had she really thought that the entry might read, 'Milo Charpentier (b. 1965). Self-taught, working in Provence. Specialises in erotic portraiture. Keeper of *The Venus of Collioure*'?

And 'working in Provence' was frustratingly inexact. How on earth was she going to track him down?

Louise had been mulling over the problem of finding Milo Charpentier. It was while she was flicking through *Private Eye* in her room, a couple of days later, that she got an idea. In among the small advertisements in the back of the magazine was one that read:

> LOVERS OF EROTICA! The James Bower Collection specialises in erotica, both antique and contemporary. Paintings and sculptures, prints and photographs, originals and reproductions. Write or

telephone for fully illustrated colour brochure: £10, redeemable on first order.

Contemporary original paintings, subject matter: erotica. It could have been custom-made for Milo Charpentier, and it had to be worth a try. Louise didn't know anything about the world of erotic art, but she reckoned that it must be a fairly specialised market. Artists creating this kind of work might find it difficult to find sufficient clients purely by word of mouth or by exhibiting their work in a gallery. Signing up to an agency like this would surely be a good move. Had Milo Charpentier come to this decision, too? And, if so, had he chosen this particular agency?

Ten pounds was a lot of money to Louise, but she reckoned it was worth it. There was no way she would be able to track down Monsieur Milo Charpentier through the phone books – how many Charpentiers must live in Provence? She could scarcely afford one telephone call to France, let alone the hundreds that it might take to find him. It was a long shot, but it was worth it. She closed her eyes and willed Milo Charpentier to be on James Bower's books; then went over to her desk and quickly typed out a request for a brochure.

Four days later, the brochure arrived. Louise was relieved to see that it was in a plain brown envelope when she collected it from her pigeonhole. She didn't want the porters getting the wrong idea about her. She hurried back up to her room in the hall of residence, locked the door as a precaution – her friends were used to coming in unannounced – and sat down on the bed, holding the envelope to her chest.

'Please let him be in here. Please,' Louise whispered. Then she tore the envelope open. The brochure was thick and glossy, and printed on good-quality paper. The cover was black, apart from the words 'Erotica from the James Bower Collection', which were printed in vivid red lettering. She decided that she had to be systematic and work methodically through the brochure from cover to cover. She opened it, not quite sure what to expect.

What Louise saw took her by surprise. She was no prude, but the engravings illustrated on the first page were explicit in the extreme. Couples were depicted engaged in a variety of sexual activity; some of it acrobatic and energetic, judging by the unnaturally positioned limbs and the dislodged wigs. As a history of art student, she could tell from the style of the engraving, and from the costumes and hairstyles and the furniture depicted, that the pictures dated from the early part of the eighteenth century, and that they were probably French. As a young woman who had not had nearly enough sex recently, she found them extremely stimulating.

Louise turned the pages. The variety of styles and media and the periods represented within the brochure surprised her. There were casts of Stone-Age 'Venus' figurines, which showed women with grossly exaggerated breasts, hips and buttocks; Indian erotic sculptures, probably looted from temple façades in previous, less-enlightened centuries; exquisitely painted Persian miniatures of couples making love in perfumed gardens; Regency-period engravings of scenes of debauchery; original pen-and-ink drawings of Salome and the last of her seven diaphanous veils by Aubrey Beardsley.

After the section of various antique artworks and historical reproductions, she came to the section on contemporary artists. There were brief biographical notes on each artist. She held her breath as she turned the pages, scanning the titles at the top of each one, looking for Milo Charpentier's name.

The brochure contained page after page of pictures of naked women, of naked men, and of couples making love. She stopped at one page where the pictures were particularly arresting. One was of a woman masturbating dreamily, one hand between her legs and the other massaging her breast, while a man sat near her on the bed and watched. This was something Louise had always wanted to do in front of Jonathan, but had never dared, for fear that he would get up and leave rather than watch. Louise thrilled to the idea of pleasuring herself while a man watched. But she wouldn't let him touch. He'd just have to sit there and not touch, not say a word, until she had done all she wanted to do. For once, a man would have to wait on her demands.

Closing her eyes and mentally elaborating on this favourite fantasy of hers, Louise felt herself becoming aroused. That familiar sensation was returning once more, warm and slick and urgent. She went over to the curtains and drew them, and then undid the zip on her jeans and pulled them down slightly, until they were just over her hips and allowed her enough room to slip both hands down the front. She lay back on the bed and slid her hands under her panties, feeling her sticky, moist heat.

Just as Louise started to touch herself, there was a knock at her door. Suddenly panicking, she pulled up her jeans and hurriedly licked her fingers, before wiping them on the bedspread. She went to the door, wondering who it might be. Her friends would have simply tried the handle without knocking. She unlocked the door to find Tom standing there. Further down the corridor behind him, she could see Fran leaning out of her room, trying to see who this male visitor was. Suddenly embarrassed, Louise grabbed Tom and pulled him into her room before she had even said anything.

'Now that's what I call keen,' said Tom, looking at her with bemusement.

'Just didn't want the university grapevine to be buzzing with the news of your visit; not just yet, anyhow.'

'Why? Are you ashamed to be seen with me?' he asked.

'No. I'd just like a little privacy sometimes, and it's pretty much impossible in this place. So, how are you?'

'Don't I get a kiss?' he asked.

She kissed him briefly. He licked his lips. 'You taste nice,' he said. Louise wondered if he had recognised the taste.

Tom looked around the room. 'What's with the closed curtains? Were you sleeping?'

She shook her head, relieved that her door had been locked. She wasn't sure she could have coped with the embarrassment if he had walked in. Tom followed Louise's anxious glance, and saw the brochure on the rumpled bed.

'Hello, what's all this, then?' he asked, cocking his eyebrow at her. 'Been reading a dirty mag? I thought only men did that.' Louise was about to explain, but Tom seemed more interested in looking through the brochure. 'Actually, all this is a bit artier than the stuff I'm used to. I mean, the stuff I've seen the others looking at. So, do you like this?'

Before she could reply, the brochure fell open at the painting of the woman masturbating.

'Very nice,' said Tom. 'I've always wanted to watch a woman do that, but so far I've not found one who'd let me.'

Louise took the brochure from him and put it on the desk. 'Maybe you just have,' she said. Tom looked at her, unsure if she was joking or not. She took his hand and slid it down the front of her jeans. His fingers soon found her moist openness. 'That's all you get for now,' she said. 'I take over, from here. Sit down. On the armchair. Pull it round to face the bed. Don't say a word. And don't touch. Me or yourself.'

She lit the candles scattered around her room, and turned off the overhead light. She put some music on her CD player, and then slowly started to perform a striptease for Tom. The more turned on he became, the better it would be for her, because she was in control. She wasn't going to let him have any say in what happened.

First she peeled off her jeans, slinking them down over her hips. She was wearing an outsize man's shirt, and she knew that Tom would only be able to glimpse her underwear beneath it every now and then. Gyrating to the music, she slowly pulled her shirt up, first showing her panties, then her navel, then the smooth skin of her torso, and then the black lace of her bra. Tom's eyes were fixed on her body. Louise pulled the shirt up over her head and off. She stood facing him in her black underwear. He was sitting in the chair, still and rigid. His hands were grasping the arms of the chair, and she could see a faint glistening of sweat on his brow. He licked his lips quickly.

He's wondering if he's going to get any, Louise thought to herself with a smile. Well, I might just let him. But then again . . . I might just make him sweat it out a bit longer.

She ran her hands over her body, delighting both in the feel of it and in the effect it was having on Tom. The control she felt over him was an undeniable spur. She cupped her breasts, feeling the soft lace of the bra and the hot flesh of her breasts under her palms. Then she slid both hands down her stomach and under the front of her panties.

'Oh God,' murmured Tom thickly. He reached out for Louise, but she jumped back.

'Back in your chair. I move. You stay still. That's the deal.'

Warned, he sat back, and Louise began to move again, swaying in time to the music as she reached round to the clasp at the back of her bra. She unclipped it and let it fall forward, catching the straps on her upper arms so that the cups didn't leave her breasts. She moved closer to Tom, and leant down slightly in front of him. The bra seemed to be held over her breasts by friction alone, and she knew that the slightest further movement forward would cause it to fall. Tom obviously knew this too, and craned forward, as if he were willing it to drop.

She moved away from him and turned her back. She let the bra fall. Then she moved her hands down, running them over the pleasing curves of her waist and hips. She slowly wriggled her way out of her panties, pulling them down bit by bit until more and more of her rear was revealed to Tom. She could hear his muffled groans, and she turned to face him once more. She could see with satisfaction that under his jeans he was sporting a massive hard-on. She advanced on him slowly, and he couldn't take his eyes from her body. He glanced at her breasts, then down to her curls and back again.

'Stay still and say nothing,' she ordered. This wonderful sensation, of being in control and being able to do whatever she wanted, was so new to Louise. She wasn't going to waste this opportunity.

She went over to the bed and lay down with her legs apart, her sex pointing directly at Tom. His eyes were locked on that most intimate spot. Louise's feet were planted flat on the bed, with her legs bent slightly at the knees. She slid her hands down to her mound. The thought of what she was going to do was stimulation enough for her; and she was wet and ready before she had even touched herself. She lazily slid a finger down over her curls, searching out the part of her which needed satisfying the most. Her fingers found the hard bead of her clitoris first, and then slipped lower, sliding effortlessly into the slippery warmth of her sex.

Tom moaned as her fingers disappeared almost up to the knuckles, and Louise smiled to herself. She would make him squirm. She began to work busily, flicking her fingers in and out of her quim, and moving upward every now and then to caress her clitoris in a lazy, circling motion. Soon her desire was so great that thoughts of her audience gradually disappeared, and she was overcome by the overwhelming need for release. Her stomach muscles tensed, and the sudden welling rush of her orgasm overtook her. Her body trembled uncontrollably. Her fingers worked frantically until the last tremors had subsided.

Recovering herself, Louise looked across at Tom. His eyes had a glazed expression and, from the size of it, his crotch looked as if it were close to bursting.

Louise got up, walked over to Tom and reached down to unbuckle his belt. She could feel his hardness under her fingertips. Then she slowly undid the buttons of his fly, popping them open one by one. She was secretly pleased to see that Tom wasn't wearing any pants. His dark wiry fuzz tickled her fingers, and beneath nestled the solid shaft of his cock. She reached in and gripped his prick in her hand, making a fist around its thick girth. She gently drew it out of its lair. Tom gave another groan, and she could feel his cock hardening yet more in her hand. She bent her head down into his lap and kissed the dome of his circumcised cock, running her tongue over it. Tom groaned, urging her to continue.

But this wasn't about Tom: it was about her. She removed her mouth, and could sense his straining frustration. She straddled the chair, so that her sex was barely an inch or so away from Tom. She knew that he could see, but wanted to see more; that he could smell her, but wanted to taste her, too. He would have to wait. She gripped his cock again with one hand, and slowly lowered herself over it. She could feel his manhood pressing against her, and she allowed herself gradually to engulf his prick. She could feel him filling her and stretching her. It was time to let him do the work.

'Fuck me,' she whispered in his ear, her arms draped lazily over his shoulders. Tom needed no second bidding. He grasped her round the waist and began to thrust into her, lifting her up and down over his cock at the same time. His rhythm increased, and he fucked her faster and faster. She knew that it wouldn't take him long to come: the poor man can only take so much stimulation, she thought. Sure enough, she felt Tom thicken inside her, and then came the unmistakable groans which heralded his orgasm. She felt him plunge into her for the last long, shuddering strokes, and then he kissed her neck before collapsing back into the chair. Louise smiled with satisfaction. He was good, but she was better. What a pity she hadn't tapped this unrealised potential before now.

After Tom had left, Louise blew out the candles and then lay back on the bed, wondering if it would be as easy as this to fulfil all her fantasies. Sated by sex, she fell into a dreamy, blissful sleep.

When she woke, an hour later, she remembered that she hadn't finished looking through the brochure. She picked it up and carried on her search for Milo Charpentier. She turned a page, and then another, and then another. Nothing. Turning to the last pages in the brochure, she felt with crushing disappointment that she had failed. Where would she look now?

She glanced down at the last pages. There, on a two-page spread, above large reproductions of four paintings of naked women, was the name she had been searching for. She looked again in disbelief. She had been hoping against hope that this would be what she would find, but she hadn't really expected to be successful. Feeling almost dizzy, she read Milo Charpentier's biographical notes:

> We think you'll agree that we've saved the best until last. Milo Charpentier is in his mid-thirties,

and is one of our most sought-after artists. He gains much inspiration from the lush and sensual landscape around his remote rural studio near La-Roche-Hubert in Provence, and he often incorporates these elements in his work by portraying his nudes in outdoor settings.

Louise couldn't believe it. She'd tracked Milo down; and that brought her another step closer to finding *The Venus of Collioure.*

Chapter Three

The end-of-year results had been announced, and Louise had been awarded a high upper second for her work: an excellent grade. She was not expecting any congratulations from Dr Petersen, however. She and all her fellow second-year students had been summoned to see him one by one. Waiting outside his office, Louise had not been surprised to find that Dr Petersen had seen all his male students before his female ones.

'Come,' a thin, querulous voice ordered sharply from behind the door.

Louise quietly entered Dr Petersen's office.

'Ah, Miss Sherringham. Take a seat, tell me the title of your proposed final-year dissertation, and then outline to me the research that you will be undertaking.'

Louise took a deep breath. She felt she already knew what Dr Petersen's reaction would be, but that made her all the more determined.

'My dissertation will be titled "Lost and Found: The Search for *The Venus of Collioure*". I propose to study Gustave de Valence's life, with particular reference to his painting *The Venus of Collioure* and its known history, and to investigate its present whereabouts.'

'"Its present whereabouts"? Am I to take it, Louise, that you are in possession of information that the rest of the art world is not privy to?' Dr Petersen asked, his voice barbed with derision.

'I know where *The Venus of Collioure* was in 1990. That's not so very long ago. I'm sure I can track it down.'

Dr Petersen laughed, making no attempt to disguise his disbelief and scorn. 'You know where it was in 1990? And may I ask how you know this, Louise?'

'I've seen it in a photograph. It's in an artist's studio.' Louise did not want to say any more. Somehow, she did not trust Dr Petersen, and she knew enough about the fiercely competitive academic rivalry between art historians to know that such information should be guarded carefully. She was quite sure that Dr Petersen would be unscrupulous enough to make use of her information for his own purposes. A reputation, not to mention a considerable amount of money, could be made from such a discovery. She had to protect her sources.

Dr Petersen leant back in his leather armchair, and inspected the fingernails of his right hand. Louise could sense what was coming, as she had often seen this particular example of body language during her seminars with him. It was a favourite gesture: one that inevitably preceded a derisive or withering comment. He sucked his breath in between his teeth.

'My dear, I feel that you should know by now, a full two years through your course, that when artists are learning their trade and searching for a style of their own, they frequently learn by copying the work of other, greater artists. This artist of yours has obviously copied *The Venus of Collioure*. The greatest art historians have been on the trail of that painting for nigh-on ninety years and have found nothing – how can you possibly hope to come up with anything when they have tried and failed? It is a ridiculous proposition, and quite out of the question. You must choose another topic.' Dr Petersen spoke with a finality which he obviously expected to be obeyed.

'I don't think it is out of the question at all,' Louise answered.

Dr Petersen smiled at her with mock sympathy, and spoke as if he were having to explain something very simple to a simpleton. 'Don't forget that your dissertation marks comprise a high percentage of your final exam result, and if your research is unsuccessful you will get a poor mark and will almost certainly fail your degree. This coming summer vacation is your only real opportunity to conduct research for your dissertation. I suggest that you use the time wisely and do not fritter it on this hare-brained project.'

Dr Petersen's bullishness only spurred Louise's own. 'Can you prevent me from undertaking this research?' she asked.

'No, Louise. All I can do is strongly recommend that you should not. If you fail, and I can assure you that you will, there will be no time left for you to research another dissertation topic. I trust that you are aware that your final academic year will be an extremely busy one, and that you simply won't have the time to undertake any research during term-time.'

Louise nodded. 'I understand. I wish to make my formal submission, Dr Petersen. The topic of my final-year dissertation will be "Lost and Found: The Search for *The Venus of Collioure*".'

Dr Petersen stared at Louise and pursed his lips in disapproval. He did not like being defied, especially by a woman.

Louise continued. 'Am I correct in thinking that there are departmental travel bursaries to assist the funding of dissertation research?'

'You are. You can obtain an application form from

Bernice. The awards will be allocated in a week's time. Good day, Louise,' Dr Petersen said testily.

Louise left the room with a wide smile. Dr Petersen was a bully, but she could stand up to him.

The university campus was empty. Most of the students had already gone home or gone abroad for the summer vacation, and Louise was killing time until the announcement of the travel bursaries. She had seen a poster in the student-union bar advertising the university rugby club tour of Ireland that summer. She knew that the team were having a final practice before leaving the next day, and so wandered over to the university sports ground. She wondered what Tom would be like on the field.

From a distance she could hear the shouts of the players and the encouraging yells of the supporters. She walked round the pavilion and on to the grass playing field. The rugby squad were playing against the second team, and small huddles of onlookers stood around the field. She joined the nearest group, and scanned the players, trying to spot Tom. Louise didn't know much about the rules of rugby, but she could guess from his build that Tom was likely to play out on the wing. He didn't have the heavy, blocky build of the players who took part in the scrummages. She scarcely recognised Tom when she finally saw him. He was covered in mud, both front and back, and his face and hair were plastered with it too. He was wearing a headband, and his gum-shield made his mouth appear a different shape. His knees were strapped, as was one of his elbows.

She watched as the game progressed, admiring the fluid skill of the running play. She also admired the rough physicality of the players themselves, as they threw themselves into a tackle or a maul. She drifted off into a reverie about being among them, being pursued and grabbed and pulled down by a muscular player and then covered by a heap of sweaty, writhing bodies, all trying to get to her. She knew the reality would be very different, with painful bruises and cut lips and broken limbs but, in her fantasy anything could happen. She dreamily watched on for another few moments, until Tom hollered to be passed the ball and Louise's trance was broken. Then Tom had possession, and he charged up the field, easily avoiding a couple of tackles, and threw himself over the line to score a try.

Minutes later the final whistle blew and, after a short talk from the coach, the players turned to walk back to the pavilion. Tom must have noticed Louise in among the onlookers, as he came straight over to her. This pleased Louise. She could smell the same mix of sweat and muskiness that she had noticed on him in the library, but it was much stronger this time. Despite his headband, beads of sweat were gathering in his eyebrows and dripping over his face, and he was breathing swiftly and deeply after the hard work-out.

'Hi there,' he said. 'I wasn't expecting you to be here.'

'Neither was I, to be honest. I just sort of wandered over. Thought I'd watch you in action.' She grinned, and looked him slowly and deliberately up and down. A pair of black lycra athlete's shorts were showing from under the legs of his looser drawstring rugby shorts. His legs were even better than they had appeared from a distance: well-muscled and hairy.

'Want to come for a walk?' he asked.

'Don't you want to get cleaned up?'

'In a bit. Come with me.'

Louise started to walk alongside Tom. His strides were so long that, for every two steps he took, she had to take three.

'Where are we going?' she asked. She already had an idea about what might happen when they got there. Since breaking up with Jonathan, her long-desired sexual education was progressing better and faster than she could have hoped.

'You'll see,' he replied enigmatically. They walked across the playing fields and into the woods beyond. Louise expected Tom to make a move for her at any moment: maybe to press her up against a tree or throw her down into the bracken. But, to her disappointment, he seemed more interested in merely walking with her and chatting about his upcoming tour. After about twenty minutes he looked at his watch.

'That should do it,' he said. 'Come with me.'

Louise could scarcely conceal her mystification as they retraced their steps through the woods, back across the playing field and towards the pavilion. Tom led her up the wooden steps, but she paused at the door. Louise knew that the pavilion was considered a strictly male domain and its sanctity was jealously guarded by the players.

'Come on,' Tom urged.

'Aren't they still in there?' she asked, thinking of the rugby players who by now would be sitting in their deep communal bath, hollering bawdy songs, drinking beer and scarcely well disposed towards an interruption by a woman.

'No, don't worry. It only takes fifteen minutes to shower and leave – especially when the big match is on. They've all cleared off to watch it at our unofficial HQ.'

Louise looked at him blankly.

'The Cow and Calf. You know, the pub with the huge TV screen in the corner.'

Louise knew of the pub. It had a reputation for being a rough dive where fights frequently broke out. She entered the pavilion behind Tom, sheltering behind him should any stray rugby players be around to challenge her. The pavilion was split into two parts: the bar, which was closed up; and the changing rooms. Tom pushed open the door to the changing room.

'Come in here,' said Tom.

'I'm not sure,' said Louise, dithering. Tom cut short any discussion by grabbing her by the arm and pulling her inside. Louise was expecting to be greeted by an overwhelming odour of jockstraps and bad feet; instead, the changing room smelt of soap, shampoo and deodorant. She could even detect faint traces of aftershave. Dirty kit hung from a row of pegs along one wall, and under the bench seat beneath were piles of rugby boots, carelessly flung aside with laces undone and mud everywhere. A tiled partition blocked off half the changing room, and behind it were the showers.

Tom stepped up to her and looked down at his mud-spattered kit. He unlaced his boots and peeled off his socks.

'I think it's time to get cleaned up,' he said, disappearing into the showers for a moment. Louise heard the rapid pattering stream of water start up, and almost immediately clouds of steam were billowing out from behind the tiled partition. Tom came out and looked at her. 'Want to help me?'

Louise nodded, and watched silently as Tom peeled off his kit, throwing his strapping and his headband and his rugby shirt to the floor. All the time he kept his eyes fixed steadily on her. Then he reached down, undid the drawstring on his shorts, and let them drop. He stood before her in his black lycra shorts. He wasn't wearing a jockstrap – she could see the shape of his stiffening cock beneath the tight, clinging material. His prick was so clearly defined by the lycra that she could even make out the ridge of his glans. Louise could feel herself reacting to this sight, and Tom stood still for a moment, letting her admire him in his shorts, before pulling them down. His cock sprang free. It was almost fully erect now. Tom gave it a couple of long slow strokes. Then he moved towards her. She could smell him strongly now, but it wasn't unpleasant: a clean sweaty smell from all his exercise.

Then Tom reached for her and pulled her to him. Louise stood meekly and let him undress her. He paused when he had stripped her down to her bra and panties, and reached out to cup her breasts. Burying his face in her cleavage, he nuzzled the soft skin. Then he reached round and undid her bra, then slipped it down her arms and off. Her breasts were pale, creamy globes, capped by two small pink nipples which had tightened into hard points. He bent to take a nipple in his mouth, then switched to the other breast. She cradled his head as he nursed on her, stroking his mud-encrusted hair. Still nibbling and sucking on her breast, he slid his hands down to her panties and pushed them down over her hips. She wiggled free of them and kicked them aside.

Kissing her, Tom put his arms round her and carried her into the shower. The steam was so dense that Louise could scarcely see, but she could just about make out that he had turned on all four shower heads, so there was a sheet of water jetting down. Bottles of shampoo and shower gel lay about on the floor. Tom carefully put her down, and pulled her into the hot streams of water. He cupped her face in both his hands and kissed her, as the droplets of water rolled down their faces. Louise's hair was soon soaked through, and coiled into snaky wreaths of dark auburn across her white skin. She looked down to see the muddy water running away by their feet.

'Here,' she said, reaching for the soap. 'I'll clean you off.'

She lathered the soap in her hands then reached up and started to rub his neck and shoulders. She massaged him with the soapy suds, easing his bunched muscles, before tracing her hands lower down his back. She felt the steely hardness of his muscles sliding under her hands, and traced down his spine. Then she played her gentle, tantalising touch over his gluteal muscles, feeling the jut of his buttocks, cupping first one and then both in her hands. As she did this, he automatically clenched them, pulling the tensed cheeks closer together.

This gave Louise an idea and, with a mischievous smile, she reached out for the Vaseline jar lying on a shelf. Doubtless it was used for preventing chafing within the rugby players' jockstraps, but she had another use for it. Something she'd read about in a magazine a while ago. She quickly popped off the top of the jar and took a generous dollop of the lubricant on her middle finger. Reaching round with her left hand, she grasped Tom's cock and began to masturbate him very slowly. He groaned and pressed back against her. Louise worked his penis with long slow strokes, feeling it harden. She could even feel the veins bulging against her palm. In only a few, swift strokes, she knew that he was reaching the point of no return.

That was her cue. She reached down with her right hand and pressed at the soft puckered opening of his anus with her lubricated finger, all the while masturbating him steadily with her other hand. There was a moment's resistance, and then her finger slid in. By the time Tom realised what she was doing, it was too late. She pushed in her finger all the way to the knuckle, and she started to move it around inside him. She could feel a spongy gland deep inside him, and she rubbed against this, hoping it was the magical prostate. This in turn triggered Tom's orgasm, and he bucked and reared and shuddered as he came. She waited until he was fully spent before removing her finger.

'I want to make you come now,' Tom murmured as he turned to face her. But Louise shook her head. She didn't want it right now. And so they soaped each other slowly under the shower, washing away the sweat and the smell of sex.

'I can't believe what you just did, but it was fantastic,' he said afterwards.

'If I'd asked you, you'd never have said yes, would you?' she replied.

He nodded. 'Just think what I would have missed.'

As she walked back to her hall of residence from the pavilion, Louise reflected on her brief liaison with Tom. It had been wild and adventurous, by her previous standards. Tom was a good lover, but he was young and Louise felt that he was a little . . . well, unrefined. What he lacked in finesse and experience, he made up for with stamina, and his staying-power was exceptional. It was frustrating that she had got together with him so late in the day. He had taken his finals, was leaving for Ireland tomorrow and was not coming back next term. And now Louise had started, she wanted more. She wondered what lovemaking with an older, more experienced man would be like. What delights could he teach her? She knew that, given the opportunity, she would prove a willing pupil.

It was the day that the allocation of the travel bursaries was announced. Term had formally ended, and Louise would already have left had it not been for the delay in the timing of the announcement.

At half past eight, she knocked on the door of the departmental secretary's office. She could hear Bernice unlocking it, mumbling, 'My God, you're keen,' from behind the door as she did so. When she saw that it was Louise, Bernice smiled and said, 'Hi there, Louise. Come on in. I've got your envelope.'

She handed it to Louise, who hastily tore it open. Louise scanned the short letter quickly, but the second word was enough to let her know what had been decided by the departmental board. 'We regret to inform you that you have been unsuccessful in your application for a travel bursary. We wish you the best of luck with your studies this summer.'

Bernice handed Louise a mug of coffee. 'Bad luck, Louise. That Dr P certainly has got it in for you.'

'Oh, you know already?' Louise said flatly.

'Sweetheart, I'm the secretary. I typed the letter. Besides, that little twerp came in here one afternoon, ranting and raving about your choice of topic. He was in an extremely unpleasant mood, even by his standards. He said that he was going to recommend to the board that your application be turned down as it was not a sensible use of funds. A wild-goose chase, as far as he was concerned, he said. I was pretty relieved when he went off to shout at the prof instead. At the meeting of the board, everyone else was keen to let you have the money, especially as you'd done so well this year, but he vetoed it. He was adamant, absolutely set against it. I've got the minutes here somewhere, if you want to see. It won't hurt anyone if you have a little look. Hush-hush, of course.'

'No thanks, Bernice. I can imagine what he said. I think I'd prefer not to know the reality.'

'Cheer up, love. Have you thought of a bank loan?'

Louise laughed ruefully. 'I've thought about it, but I doubt my bank manager's going to listen to me very sympathetically. Still, I suppose I've got nothing to lose.'

'That's the spirit,' said Bernice. 'Ring him up and make an appointment. You can use the phone here.'

To her surprise, Louise was able to make an appointment with Mr Wells, her bank manager, for an hour later. Walking along the high street to her bank, Louise became angrier and angrier by the minute. If it had not been for Dr Petersen, she felt sure she would have been awarded the bursary. That mean-spirited, malicious man. So what if she failed in her research? It was her decision; her risk to take. But she would not be put off. If Petersen didn't want her to embark on her search for *The Venus of Collioure*, then that was all the more reason to go ahead with her project. She would never allow herself to appear to be influenced by what he said, such was her lack of regard for him.

But the board's decision would have dramatic financial repercussions for her. She would have to fund it out of her own money – or rather, the bank's. She wasn't sure whether Mr Wells would agree to another loan. Kindly old man that he was, he had a business to oversee rather than a charity.

She arrived outside the imposing granite-fronted building in the high street, and rummaged in her bag for a hairbrush. She quickly tidied herself up, and then pushed open the swing door. The lady at the reception desk smiled professionally at her, and directed her to a corner with a couple of chairs and a table to await her appointment. 'Mr Wells will be with you in a moment.'

Louise looked around the foyer. People were queuing to see the tellers, and a man was arguing vociferously at the Bureau de Change about the commission charged on his transaction. Louise exchanged sympathetic looks with the harassed clerk.

Time crawled by. Louise had tried to feel fairly upbeat when she had entered the bank, but this delay was causing her to become more and more unsure of her chances. She flicked through the brochures laid out on the table. They tantalised her with talk of big loans: for that special holiday, a car, whatever. She didn't dare to think what she would do if Mr Wells turned down her application for a loan. If he refused to arrange an overdraft for her, then her chances of going to France were scuppered. There was no way she could raise enough money herself in time.

The door leading from the bank foyer to the upstairs offices opened, and Mr Wells looked around briefly before his gaze settled on Louise. He smiled, and Louise had the sudden, incongruous thought that he looked just like Father Christmas, minus the shaggy white beard and red outfit. He had twinkling, smiling eyes, rosy cheeks and a rotund figure; and he radiated geniality.

'Miss Sherringham. How nice to see you again. Would you like to follow me up to my office?'

Louise gathered her things, and followed him up the stairs and into his office. Ever the gentleman, Mr Wells pulled out a chair for her in front of his desk. The desk was fairly empty, bearing just a couple of piles of paper and a silver-framed photograph of his wife and four grown-up children. He shuffled the papers, and then looked at Louise.

'Now, how can I be of assistance?'

Louise swallowed hard. Here goes nothing, she thought. 'I need to borrow some money.'

Mr Wells smiled as widely as before. Maybe things aren't going to be so bad after all, thought Louise, and she continued: 'I need to go to France this summer to research my final-year dissertation. I haven't been awarded a departmental travel bursary, so I need to take out a loan. Please.' She hoped that she didn't sound too desperate.

'I see. How much were you thinking of?'

Louise dropped her hands to below the desk where Mr Wells couldn't see, and crossed her fingers. 'Two thousand pounds,' she half whispered.

'Two thousand pounds,' Mr Wells repeated. 'That's a lot of money, if you don't mind me saying.'

'I know. But I don't know how long I'll be over there. Maybe a couple of months or more. There'll be living expenses: my food and board, petrol and such like. Of course, I'll try to find somewhere cheap to stay, but I think I'll probably have to do quite a lot of travelling, and it'll be the peak tourist season.'

Mr Wells leant forward across the desk. 'Can you tell

me the reason why you haven't been awarded a bursary?' he asked.

Louise bit her lower lip. 'My tutor thinks I'll be wasting my time. He doesn't think it's a sensible topic.'

'But you do?' Mr Wells asked.

Louise nodded, and started to explain about Gustave de Valence and *The Venus of Collioure* and Milo Charpentier and her absolute conviction that she had located the lost masterpiece. Her enthusiasm was such that her speech got faster and faster, and she started to bang her fist on Mr Wells's desk to drive her points home. He watched her with a wry smile. When she had finally run out of steam, he spoke.

'Well, I'm no expert on such matters, but I can tell that you certainly believe in this project. I may get into trouble with head office for this, but I've decided to authorise your loan.'

Louise couldn't contain herself. She got up, leant across the table, and planted a big kiss on Mr Wells's cheek.

'Steady on, Miss Sherringham,' he laughed. 'You will understand that I'm afraid that I can't make the loan unconditional. The loan, plus the interest, must be fully repaid by eighteen months from now.'

Louise had known that there would be conditions, but in her excitement and haste she hadn't thought through the consequences of such conditions. Eighteen months from now was not long. She would graduate in late June next year, so that gave her a mere six months after that to find the money. There was no chance that she could save enough to repay the loan while she was still a student, so she would have to find a job pretty promptly once she graduated. She knew that was no small undertaking for a history of art graduate. Good jobs that her qualifications suited were hard to come by. Mr Wells's condition would put extra, unexpected pressure on her, but Louise knew that she had to accept. There was no alternative. She had to go to France. She reached across the desk and shook Mr Wells's hand.

'It's a deal,' she said.

Liz stood on the pavement holding a large stuffer bag while Louise arranged yet more luggage inside the battered orange Volkswagen camper van.

'Hurry up, Lou, this thing's heavy. What have you got in here? The kitchen sink?'

Louise stuck her head round the door of the camper van and grinned. 'Just about everything but. Let's see. I want to make one last check that I've got everything I need, just in case.'

She hauled the bag off Liz and plonked it heavily on the floor of the van, which sagged noticeably on its suspension. She unzipped the bag, and took a quick inventory of its contents.

'Notebooks, pens, pencils, laptop, box of disks, spare batteries, lead and travel plug, hired video camera, a box of five blank tapes, two camera bodies, three different lenses, flash unit, two portable studio lights and batteries, tripod, colour slide film, black-and-white print film, reference books. I think that's the lot. Have I forgotten anything?' She looked questioningly at Liz.

'Don't ask me. I wouldn't have a clue what you're going to need, apart from a road atlas of France.' She paused. 'Hang on. Have you got enough clothes? You might not be able to get to a launderette very often.'

'Don't worry. I've catered for every eventuality,' said Louise, gesturing at a large suitcase on the floor of the van. 'Smart, casual, beach and boudoir, posh restaurant and cheapo truck stop. I've got an outfit for them all. It's one of the bonuses of having such a spacious vehicle that I don't have to travel light. And, should the worst come to the worst, I've even got a tube of concentrated travel wash.' She grinned at Liz.

'God, you're so sickeningly organised,' said Liz.

'Got to be,' said Louise, making one quick last check of the contents of the van. She seemed pleased with the results. 'Right,' she announced, hopping out of the van. 'That's me sorted, then, I reckon. I've got a camping stove, a sleeping bag, high-protection suntan lotion, sunglasses and, most important of all, soft loo rolls. Ready for the off to *la belle* France. Sunshine, wine and a lost masterpiece, here I come.'

'So it's not going to be all work, then?' Liz laughed.

'I'm definitely going to find the time for play,' Louise said. 'It's too good an opportunity to miss.'

'Are you *sure* you're going to be all right?' Liz asked. 'It's a hell of a long way to drive on your own, all the way down to Provence. And on the wrong side of the road at that ... But I suppose at least you've got the advantage that you can speak the language fluently, which is something.'

'Stop fretting, Liz. Honestly, you're worse than my mother. There's no worries. Besides, I'm stopping off at Jean-Pierre's. Remember me talking about him? He's been my pen pal since we were both nine, and he lives conveniently near the halfway point in my journey.'

'Jean-Pierre? But I thought you'd told me that you hadn't seen each other for years?'

'Not since that ill-fated trip when I went to stay with him when we were in our early teens. The awkwardness of puberty was just setting in, and consequently we couldn't stand the sight of each other. He was a spotty immature youth to me, and I think that I must have been a severe embarrassment to him. He was still at that stage where girls are regarded as soppy creatures, best avoided. He was always worried that he might ruin his street cred with his friends if he was seen around with me. Consequently, the trip wasn't a great success. Still, we made it up by letter over the years, and even though I haven't seen him for so long I feel that I know him well. I'm looking forward to it, and who knows?' Louise laughed and winked at Liz.

'God, you're terrible. Since your split with Jonathan you've been on the prowl virtually nonstop,' laughed Liz.

'Merely making up for lost time,' Louise grinned.

Louise had booked a place on an overnight Dover to Calais ferry, which was scheduled to arrive in France at one-thirty in the morning. She ate a late supper in the ferry's self-service restaurant, and reflected afterwards that the food she would be eating over the next couple of months would doubtless be considerably better than the rubbery omelette and overcooked vegetables that she had just eaten. She then picked her way past the prone bodies which had settled down for the night on just about every available seat or floor space, and made her way up on to the deck.

She was surprised to find herself all alone. Everyone else seemed to be trying to get some rest. Louise was too excited, too full of anticipation to think of sleeping; and she ignored the sensible voice in her head that was telling her to get some rest. She knew she had a long drive facing her, but the adrenalin buzzing through her made sleep impossible. She walked round the side of the boat, holding on to the railing, until she reached the bow. She turned, and looked back at the ship. She could see that the curtains had been drawn across the windows on the passenger decks, and the only light was that coming from the bridge. There she could see several white-uniformed figures moving around. She assumed that they were checking on the radar and sonar and whatever else it was that nautical types did. She gave them a cheery wave and was pleased when two of the crew waved back at her.

She turned again and leant over the rail, and watched the plough-like prow of the boat below her throwing up a white spume as it cut through the black water. There was a strong, chilly breeze, and she could feel the salty air riming her skin. She pulled her thin cardigan round her, wishing she had thought to wear something warmer than her long cotton dress. She wasn't in balmy France quite yet. She gazed out into the blackness lit only by the faint pinpricks of the stars and the occasional light from other boats. She wondered how her search would go and whether, by the time she was making this journey in the opposite direction, she would have seen *The Venus of Collioure*.

She heard a cough, and turned to see a young man standing a few feet off to her right.

'Hello,' he said, smiling at her, and she could immediately tell from the way he pronounced this one word that he was French.

'Hello,' she said back to him, smiling. He was tall and well-built and, from his crew-cut hairstyle, she guessed that he might be a soldier. He was clean-shaven, and his nose looked as if it had been broken at some time in the past.

'It is very beautiful here, in the night, no?' he asked. She smiled to herself. Only an incurable romantic or a man on the pull could call this chilly and damp blackness 'beautiful'. She sensed that this might well be an attempt at a pick-up. In her Jonathan days, she would have bridled at such an approach, but not now, not this time.

'Yes, it is,' she lied, going along with his pretence. He approached her, and stood at her side, looking at her as if trying to read her thoughts.

'You are English?' he asked, and she smiled. She knew the reputation that her fellow countrywomen were supposed to have on the Continent; and whereas such stereotyping would usually have annoyed her, now she found that it could well be working to her advantage.

'Yes, I'm English,' she said.

'Are you alone?' he asked.

'Yes.' She smiled back at him. 'Quite alone.' Apart from the guys up on the bridge, she thought, with a wicked twinkle in her eyes.

'Good,' he said. They stood silently side by side for a while. The man said nothing, and did nothing. Just when Louise had started to think that nothing more was going to happen, and that perhaps he was simply an incurably romantic Frenchman after all, the man made his move. Holding on to the rail with his right hand, he swung round behind her and grabbed the rail to the left of her with his other hand, effectively pinioning her between him and the rail. Louise looked down and saw that he had tattoos on the backs of his hands.

Louise stood still, wondering what he would do next. She was also hoping that the crew up on the bridge were watching. This would brighten up their dull night watch, and give them something to talk about in the mess room. She could hear the man breathing behind her, and could feel him pressed hard against her, forcing her up against the rail. He leant close to her, and whispered in her ear.

'I love beautiful things. And you are very beautiful.'

Louise raised her eyes heavenward. She could do without the commentary. She knew what she wanted, and small talk wasn't on the list. She pressed her buttocks back against his erection in an open, brazen invitation. The man had no trouble in interpreting her body language. She could feel his hand fumbling against the small of her back, and knew that he was undoing his belt and flies. Simply knowing this caused her to dampen almost instantly, her internal muscles clenching with the expectation of what was about to happen.

Louise moved her legs apart and leant forward on tiptoes to aid the man in his efforts, and he swiftly pushed her dress up until it was round her waist. She caught the loose flapping material and held it against the rail. He slipped a hand under the edge of her panties, pushing them to one side, and quickly ran his fingers up and down over her sex, testing her wetness. Then he withdrew his hand and she could feel him grasping his erect penis and guiding it towards her.

Its stubby head pressed against her sex. Almost instantly, the man's thick prick sank deeply into her, and he started to move in and out with a slow, pumping movement that rapidly increased in speed. Louise had to keep a firm hold of the railing. He was plunging into her so powerfully that he lifted her right on to the very tips of her toes with each upward thrust. She hoped that the crew was getting a good look.

At the same time, the man spat on his hand and slipped it under the front of her knickers and started to rub the engorged bead of her clitoris. This, to Louise, was much dirtier, much ruder than simply being fucked. She was being masturbated by a complete stranger, and he was doing this solely for her pleasure. It was too much, and the sudden rush of her orgasm came on her before she was ready for it. She sank back against him, and he came immediately, grunting.

They stood up against the rails, locked together, for a while afterward. When the man withdrew, Louise expected him to walk away, in keeping with the style of this short, anonymous coupling; but instead he sank to his knees behind her. Pushing her dress back up round her waist, he lifted his head to her soaking furrow and pressed his tongue against her, sucking and lapping, drinking her clean. She went back on tiptoes, and shifted her feet further apart to allow him better access. She leant forward on to the rails to bring her clitoris closer to his mouth, and soon he found it and understood what she wanted. She felt her clitoris swelling again, and the pulsing sensation starting once more, first deep in her belly and then more localised in the fiery nub of her clitoris, before another orgasm swept over her. There was a rushing, pounding noise in her ears, and for a moment Louise wasn't sure if it was the sound of her orgasm or the noise of the ship ploughing through the water beneath her.

The man waited for her pulsing orgasm to ebb away before removing his hot wet tongue and standing up. He carefully adjusted her panties into their former position and pulled down her dress, checking that the hem was straight; then he kissed her on the back of the neck and left. All the time, Louise had remained fixedly staring out to sea, tasting the salt on her lips.

When she eventually turned around, she shyly looked up to the bridge. All seven crew members were standing at the window, binoculars to their eyes, looking down at her. They let their binoculars drop on the straps round their necks, and started to applaud her. Then one of them reached across and up, and pulled something out of Louise's view. Three loud bursts on the foghorn rang out. Louise grinned, and waved at them as she walked back inside.

Start as you mean to go on, she thought to herself with a self-satisfied smile.

Chapter Four

Louise had deliberately chosen a night crossing on the ferry. It meant that the roads were more or less empty for those first few hours when she was adjusting to driving on the right, taking roundabouts the wrong way and familiarising herself with the French road signs. From Calais, she quickly made her way on to the *péage*, the toll motorway which would speed her journey southward. She had chosen a route down the eastern side of France, avoiding Paris. She didn't think her navigational skills were good enough to get her through the capital without giving herself a near heart attack. Besides, she had already been to Paris several times, and wanted to see as much of rural France as possible.

Louise made good progress on the first part of her journey, putting a fair distance between herself and the coast by the time dawn broke over the undulating countryside of the Champagne region. From the *péage*, she could see the green serried rows of the vineyards flashing past, and regretted that she did not have time to stop and investigate more fully, and maybe even try a tasting at a champagne cellar. She decided that she would make the time to do so on her return journey.

The daylight also allowed her to appreciate more fully the contrasts between the two countries: little things like the different style of paint markings on the road; the distinctive outlines of the electricity pylons that marched across the countryside – unfamiliar, yet not too dissimilar from those in England – and the almost omnipresent shutters on the doors and windows of the houses. Then there were the larger differences, such as the type of landscape and the architectural style of the buildings. The greatest difference of all, even at this early hour, was the strength and brilliance of the sunlight.

At about half past eight, Louise pulled off the *péage* and drove into the nearest small town. She stopped at a roadside café for some breakfast, and got out and stretched like a lazy cat, trying to loosen her cramped and sore muscles. She sat at a table outside the café in the heat of the morning sun – it was already far warmer than it would be back in England – and waited for someone to come and serve her. It was not long before a young woman appeared and took her order; and she soon returned with a tray bearing a large cup of coffee, a wicker basket with three croissants, some fruit preserve in a small pot and a couple of pats of butter.

Louise ate her breakfast slowly, watching the world go by. Schoolchildren with heavy satchels walked past in groups, chatting noisily; women carrying baskets full of fresh market produce stopped to greet each other; and old men sat in the shade of the leafy trees that lined the road, observing her as closely as she observed them.

Louise looked up as a young man walked past her table, and they made eye contact. He was appraising her in an obviously sexual manner, openly and quite unabashed. She had not fully realised what the phrase 'undressing someone with one's eyes' had meant until now, and it struck her once more how at ease the French seemed with their sexuality. Louise could not imagine many of the men of her acquaintance back home behaving like that, sizing a woman up so blatantly. Construction-site workers maybe, she thought with a grin, but such behaviour was not habitual, as it seemed to be here in France. She watched the young man go into the café and lean across the bar and kiss the young woman who had served her earlier. Louise watched their conversation; and unable to hear what they were saying, she interpreted their flirtation through their body language.

When Louise finished her breakfast, she went into the café to pay, and saw that the young man was now on the other side of the bar, and had his hand on the girl's rump as she bent over the sink and washed out some cups. Louise grinned. It was evidently never too early for *l'amour* in France.

At lunchtime, Louise turned off the *péage* once more to find her way into a nearby small town to buy some food. She bought a roundel of goat's cheese, a baton of bread, some peaches and grapes and a bottle of spring water, and then drove into the countryside to find a picnic spot. She ate her lunch in the shade of a huge Spanish chestnut tree on the banks of a river. She needed a rest from driving, and so after she had eaten she lay back and dozed in the dappled shade.

Refreshed and back behind the wheel, Louise made steady progress. The camper van was not capable of going very fast, but that suited Louise as she wanted time to look around her. France seemed so much greener than England, and much less intensively farmed, and the roadside verges were covered with masses of brightly coloured wild flowers.

She drove through vast areas of woods and forests which appeared untouched by human intervention, even though Louise suspected they were probably carefully managed. Here and there the wild tracts were punctuated by wheatfields speckled with brilliant red poppies, by fields of sunflowers with the yellow discs of their flowerheads all turned towards the sun, by smallholdings with a few rows of vegetables. Then there were the ubiquitous vineyards. Wide rivers flowed steadily by, and poplar-lined canals cut a straight watery path through the countryside. Every now and then, Louise would stop the van at a particularly stunning view and stretch her legs while enjoying the scenery; or halt at a roadside stall selling peaches or melons and chat to the stallholder as she ate the messy, juicy fruit.

As she drove on, slowly but surely heading south, Louise passed signs for places with familiar names. Familiar not because she had visited them, but because she had seen the names on wine labels: Gevrey-Chambertin, Nuits-Saint-Georges, Beaune. By the early evening, she was not far from Mâcon. Jean-Pierre lived in a large village near to the town of Cluny, a little to the north-east of Mâcon, and so Louise turned off the *péage* and followed the signs for Cluny.

A week previously, Louise had spoken to Jean-Pierre on the telephone to organise her stay with him, and he had sounded excited at the prospect of her visit. They had not met since that ill-fated trip, and she knew that he had changed much since then. He had moved away from his family, and now worked part-time in the vineyards and cellars of a local chateau, and part-time as a tour guide in the area. He had sent her a photograph of himself a couple of years ago, and Louise had mused that he had indeed changed. He bore scant likeness to the skinny beanpole of a youth that she remembered.

Louise finally arrived at Jean-Pierre's village, and drew up alongside an old man who was standing by the side of the road. He directed her to Jean-Pierre's house, and five minutes later she was parking the van outside a small house with a vine growing over the peeling paint of its walls. She nervously walked up to the front door, apprehensive at exactly how this reunion was going to go. It had been a long, long day, and she didn't exactly feel at her scintillating best.

Two hours later, all Louise's worries were well forgotten. Jean-Pierre had greeted her as if they had last seen each other only days before, and had made her so welcome that she felt she already belonged in the small, comfortable house. And she was secretly pleased by Jean-Pierre too. If anything, he was even more attractive than he appeared in his photograph. His hair was an unruly mop, brown but bleached lighter on the top by the sun, and it had the becoming habit of flopping down over his eyes every now and then. His eyes were a dark brown, speckled with lighter golden flecks which gave him an almost leonine air.

But, above almost everything else, Louise found his accent one of the most appealing things about him. Jean-Pierre insisted on talking in English to her. He often had to give tours in English and, even though he seemed perfectly fluent to Louise, he felt he needed to practise it whenever he could. Louise felt that she could close her eyes and listen to him for hours on end: his lilting tones and the charming mispronunciations which only heightened his appeal to Louise; the melodious sound that English acquired when spoken by a non-native speaker. His voice alone was sexy. When combined with the rest of him, Louise knew that he was going to prove hard to resist.

Jean-Pierre asked Louise if she would like to go out for a meal at his favourite restaurant. He explained that it offered a fine range of local specialities; and besides, he wasn't much of a cook. Despite her tiredness, Louise agreed enthusiastically, as she was hoping to try as many types of French cuisine as possible during the summer. He showed her to the guest room, and then pointed out the bathroom, saying that he would wait downstairs while she freshened up.

The bedroom was compact, and thus was dominated by the double bed which seemed to take up nearly all the floor space. Louise pulled back the coverlet. The bed linen was freshly starched; and a long, single bolster was stretched across the width of the bed, lying where she was more used to seeing two smaller pillows side by side. She smiled. Another little cultural contrast. The French had a saying for it, after all: *vive la difference.*

She put her suitcase down on the bed, and unpacked her washbag and a towel. She wondered about this coming evening, and how it would go. Should she make the first move? Or wait for Jean-Pierre to? She knew he was interested, but wasn't sure of the extent of his interest, so if she made the running she might be in for a disappointment. On the other hand, he might be too shy to do anything. But no, that didn't seem likely, given the way he had been looking at her earlier. That decided it.

I'm going to seduce him, Louise thought to herself with a smile. She laid out her slinkiest dress on the bed. It was a simple, classic little black number, made of chiffon and cut so expertly that it clung closely to her curves. It was her one and only extravagance, bought during her first term at university: a designer dress for which she had paid a walloping designer price. Louise placed a pair of black hold-up stockings next to it on the bed, and some black lacy panties. The combination of the black clothes and her glossy, glowing Titian hair would be spectacular, and she knew it. A pair of black high-heeled shoes completed her ensemble.

The bathroom contained a lavatory and a bidet, a wobbly basin that appeared to be coming free from the wall, a shower stall and a massive cast-iron bath. The mixer tap and plughole were placed in the centre of one of the long sides of the bath. Louise thought playfully that, with both its rounded, sloping ends, it would be ideal for two people to bathe in at once.

Looking around on the shelves, she saw a razor and a

bristle shaving brush, some bottles of aftershave and shampoo, a can of shaving foam, and a small pot of hair gel. She knew that she ought not to, but she couldn't stop herself from taking a sneaky look in the mirrored cabinet above the basin, wondering if it might give her any clues about Jean-Pierre, or reveal any hidden secrets. The cabinet contained plasters, ointment, a couple of bottles of pills, some mouthwash, a comb and a spare toothbrush. Nothing out of the usual. Even though she knew it was none of her business, Louise was pleased that there were no female toiletries around. She knew she had no claim to Jean-Pierre, but nevertheless she felt jealously possessive about him – for tonight, at least.

Louise mentally tossed a coin between the invigoration of a shower or the relaxation of a bath, and plumped for the latter. She sprinkled some bath salts in the bottom of the tub and ran the taps. She kicked off her shoes and stepped out of her crumpled and stale dress with relief, before slipping down her knickers. She had managed a quick strip wash in the toilets on the ferry after her unexpected liaison with her French squaddie, and had put on a fresh pair of undies, but the uncomfortable stickiness of a day's worth of travelling meant that she was looking forward to her ablutions with relish.

She stepped into the bath as it was still filling, and lay back. The water only just covered the slight mound of her stomach, and she gazed down fondly at the soft curves of her belly, idly stroking the shallow dimple of her navel with her fingertips. Louise liked the way her body felt. The hot water from the tap was splashing down on to her right thigh, and she closed her eyes, enjoying the spreading warmth and feeling of complete abandon. The incessant pressure of the water on her leg and the warmth creeping up over her body triggered another sensation, the desire for release.

Louise shifted slightly, sliding down the bath a little and positioning her crotch so that it was directly below the running water. The force of the water surprised her and, despite the muffling effect of the finely coiled curls which covered her sex, she could feel the water beating strongly down on to her hooded clitoris. The movement of the water soon elicited a response, and she could feel her clitoris hardening and her arousal increasing. Louise shifted again, throwing her left leg out over the side of the bath and hooking her right leg up around the taps. This placed her now open and exposed sex directly below the gushing torrent and, by making gentle adjustments, Louise moved herself so the water fell at first on her clitoris; and then, when she felt she was coming too close to orgasm, on to her outer lips for a moment. When she had recovered from the imminence of her climax, she redirected the water on to her bullet-like bud once again.

The hot water felt like a hot, agile tongue, caressing and pleasuring her with its watery touch. She turned down the flow of the water so that it fell in a more erratic patter. This only heightened her arousal, as she could not predict where it would fall, or how hard, or for how long. She had to constantly shift and change her position, searching to master what was not completely within her control. When her orgasm finally flowed over her, the strength of her response was such that she gasped with surprise. She splashed and writhed in the water, and could not stop herself from calling out. Finally, she lay still, before reaching up and turning off the tap.

As she towelled herself dry, Louise wondered with a flush of guilt whether she had run the hot-water tank empty, leaving nothing for Jean-Pierre. She also wondered if he had guessed why she had spent so long in the bathroom, and hoped that he hadn't heard her cries of ecstasy.

When she finally walked down the stairs and made an entrance into the living room, Jean-Pierre looked up from his book and the amazement on his face made Louise flush with pleasure. She had spent a long time dressing, arranging her hair and applying a light covering of make-up. Her beauty was so pure and natural, and her skin so flawless that she didn't need much assistance: just a hint of mascara and a light smear of lipstick.

'You look fantastic,' Jean-Pierre said with feeling. To Louise's delight, he appeared genuinely thrown by the transformation that she had effected. She waited while he ran upstairs, quickly washed and threw on some clean clothes. He came down again, looking good in a charmingly dishevelled way. Ironing was obviously not his forte; and Louise took it as a further, reassuring confirmation of the lack of a female presence in the house.

It was very late, but Jean-Pierre assured Louise that it didn't matter, as most people liked to eat later in the evening, and the restaurant stayed open until whatever time the last diner chose to leave. The patron welcomed them warmly, and ushered them to a small table in a private corner of the dining room. He lit the candles on the table, took their wine order and, after telling them about that evening's special dishes, left them in peace to decide what food to order. Jean-Pierre made some suggestions about what she might like to try, and Louise was quite happy to follow his advice, although she did blanch slightly at the thought of the vine-leaf-fed snails. However, she reminded herself that this was to be a summer of new experiences and acquiesced with as much enthusiasm as she could summon.

A young waiter came to the table with their wine, and as he filled their glasses he gave Louise a long, piercing look. She automatically glanced down at her dress, worried that she might be exposing more of herself than was proper and, as she looked up, she caught his eye again. He smiled, and flashed his eyebrows at her as if to say that he had been enjoying the view, too.

Jean-Pierre was aware of this exchange: he leant over and whispered in Louise's ear. 'That's Edouard. I think he likes you.'

Louise blushed. 'So? He can see that I'm with you.'

'That doesn't mean you can't enjoy him as well.'

Louise looked up sharply. There was something loaded about Jean-Pierre's use of the word 'enjoy'. He leant forward, and she felt his hand on her thigh under the table. He slowly slid his hand back and forth over the sheer material of her dress, gently caressing her. Louise coloured, as it was obvious from his posture and the movement of his shoulder what Jean-Pierre was doing. In fact, she reckoned that any onlooker might think that he was behaving even more indecently than he actually was. Louise was mortified that he could be doing this in public, and so blatantly at that. She looked around the restaurant anxiously. She was relieved to see that all the other diners were too intent on their own companions and their food to have noticed.

Edouard returned with their first course, just as Jean-Pierre sat back. The young waiter gave Louise another loaded look as he carefully placed her napkin on her lap for her, adjusting it so that it was straight and covered her fully. She was electrified by his touch, and felt sure that his hands had remained there for a little longer than the operation demanded. Now she was acutely aware that both men were interested in her.

As they ate their meal, Louise and Jean-Pierre discussed their first, disastrous meeting.

'Of course, I was so mean to you all those years ago because I fancied you. I know it seems stupid now, but that was the way it manifested itself,' Jean-Pierre told her, between mouthfuls of food. 'But I'll make it up to you.'

Jean-Pierre reached down beneath the table with one

hand, and Louise wondered what he was doing. Then she felt a warm sensation on her calf. Jean-Pierre had kicked off his shoe, pulled off his sock and was massaging her stockinged flesh with his bare toes. He rubbed his foot up and down her calf, before slipping his foot between her legs and sliding it up the inside of her thigh under her dress. Louise clamped her thighs together, but Jean-Pierre twisted and probed and insinuated his toes further and further up, until he reached the bare flesh at the top of her stockings. There he massaged her burning flesh, all the while eating his meal as if nothing untoward was happening. Louise closed her eyes, feeling herself respond with growing excitement.

Louise excused herself to go to the lavatory. She told Jean-Pierre that she wanted to check her make-up, but there were other reasons. Louise wasn't sure she could let herself go enough to continue with this in a room full of people. What if she couldn't control her cries, or if they saw what was happening to her? Despite her recent experiments in exhibitionism, she had never had such a close audience. And there was another, more prosaic reason. She was so aroused that she was worried that the damp patch in her knickers might show through her dress, and she wanted to check. That was something else she didn't want a restaurant full of people seeing: the telltale sign of her arousal undermining her apparently sophisticated appearance.

As she turned the corner in the narrow corridor leading past the kitchen, she bumped – quite literally – into Edouard. A few drops of the chilled soup he was carrying on a tray spilt on to her thigh. Edouard was aghast at what he had done and apologised hastily. Although mildly annoyed, Louise was thankful that at least the soup had not been hot. She reckoned she was equally at fault. She hadn't been looking where she was going, as she had been too wrapped up in thoughts of Jean-Pierre's unusual seduction technique.

'Please, I am so sorry. Let me help you,' Edouard offered, taking her hand and leading her into a small room. It was clearly the staffroom, and contained several wooden chairs, a rack which held clothes on hangers, a few cupboards on the wall and a basin in one corner. Edouard ran some water into the basin and took a clean, folded handkerchief out of his pocket. Then he knelt in front of her.

'Excuse me,' he said, and reached up her skirt. Taken aback, Louise stood stock still. Using the palm of his hand as a support under the material, he dabbed at the soup with the hanky. Louise watched as the stain gradually disappeared, but she was more keenly aware of the occasional touch of the back of his hand against her thigh. She knew that he would be able to tell she was wearing stockings, as he had brushed against the lacy top of her hold-up. However, his face registered nothing.

'There,' he said, removing his hand, standing up and surveying his handiwork. The stain had indeed gone, but had been replaced by a much larger wet patch, which caused her dress to cling even more closely to her thigh.

'I think there is a hairdryer here somewhere,' he said, looking in one of the cupboards. 'I'm sure Marianne keeps one for when she has showered after work.' Louise looked on in bemusement as he rummaged through some poor woman's personal belongings before pulling out a small hairdryer.

'It needs to be on the coolest setting. The chiffon is pretty delicate,' Louise said. She didn't think it polite to add, 'And also very expensive.' Poor Edouard was clearly upset at what he had done. And besides, she thought, he's French. He probably doesn't need to be told that the dress is a designer one and therefore expensive. Edouard plugged the hairdryer in, altered the setting, and switched it on.

Louise held out her arm, wrist upward. 'Try it on me first,' she said. 'I want to be sure.'

'Of course. It is a beautiful dress and you do not want to spoil it,' said Edouard, directing the jet of pleasantly warm air on to her skin.

'That's fine,' she said. Louise could as easily have added, 'I'll do it,' but she was enjoying this close attention, and so she said nothing more. Edouard dropped to his knees again and began to dry her dress, playing the warm stream of air over the damp patch. After a few moments, he looked up at Louise.

'I must dry it from the inside as well.'

Louise smiled her consent. She knew that the material was so sheer that he could dry it perfectly well from the outside, but she was intrigued and aroused by this obvious ploy.

Still kneeling in front of her, Edouard reached up inside her dress again. She could feel the warm wafts of air playing about on her calves, then her knees, and then her thighs. As Edouard directed the warm air on to the fast-disappearing damp patch, his hand brushed against Louise's thighs. She shifted involuntarily, and he took this as all the encouragement he needed. Still holding the whirring hairdryer, he lifted his hand until the back of it brushed against the soft lace of her panties. She moved again, this time parting her legs slightly to allow him better access. Edouard grazed the back of his hand down the front of her panties and between her legs. She felt the back of his hand encounter another damp patch: the sodden material which indicated her arousal. Louise knew she was far wetter now than she had been sitting at the table with Jean-Pierre.

Edouard looked up and smiled. 'Maybe I had better dry this, too,' he said. 'Lift your dress.'

Louise was too swept away with desire to do anything but obey. She slowly raised the dress by its hem, revealing her stockings, then her stocking-tops, and then her panties to Edouard. He sat back on his heels and swore gently under his breath. Then he moved forward again, and brought the hairdryer up to her knickers. Louise could feel the exquisite rush of hot air on the material, warming her already feverish sex. She threw her head back and moaned.

'You like?' asked Edouard, though he needed no answer. Louise's pleasure was displayed all too clearly. Edouard slipped a single finger under the side of her panties, and gently pulled them to one side, exposing her flushed and pouting sex. He swore again when he saw the russet-gold tendrils of her pubic hair. Then he lifted his hand and deployed the hairdryer once more, only this time he aimed it directly on to her slick, throbbing sex.

Louise opened her eyes with surprise, but the sensation was not unpleasant. Far from it: the warmth of the air only mirrored the internal warmth she felt. Edouard played the warm air over her with fast, impatient sweeps, and after a while she felt his other hand sliding up her inner thigh, over the stockings and the lace, to meet her urgency. Edouard teased her, first bringing the hairdryer closer and increasing the temperature, then withdrawing it before it became uncomfortably hot. She wondered how he could be judging it so finely, and then realised that he could feel the hot air on his other fingers, which he was stroking very gently along her swollen labia. Louise was relieved he was touching her, as the insubstantial drifts of air were frustrating her with their ephemerality. She needed something more substantial, and it seemed that Edouard was about to provide it. But Louise was to be frustrated even further, for there was a sudden knock at the door, and Edouard hastily withdrew his hands.

'Edouard, what are you doing in there?' a man's voice called out.

Louise dropped her dress just as the door opened and

the patron entered. He paused to take in the tableau of Edouard kneeling with a hairdryer in his hand in front of a flushed and trembling Louise. Then he spoke.

'Back to your work now, Edouard.'

As Louise walked past him out of the room, the patron grinned and winked at her. 'Jean-Pierre told me not to bother you, but I've got a business to run. Sorry.'

When she got back to the table, Jean-Pierre was leaning back in his chair, smoking a fat cigar.

'Did you enjoy yourself?' he asked.

'Very much,' Louise replied.

'Tell me all about it, in detail,' said Jean-Pierre. 'But not here. Back home.'

Early the next morning, Louise was woken by a cockerel crowing. The noise was so loud that it sounded as if he was perched right below the window. The sun was already streaming into the room through the slats in the shutters, and Louise looked over at Jean-Pierre, incredulous that he could sleep through the deafening racket. But of course he's used to it, she thought. She reached over and gently pushed back one of the curls from his eyes. He stirred, mumbling something that Louise couldn't make out, and turned over so that he was lying on his back. Louise gazed down on his body, nut-brown against the crumpled white sheets. She thought again of all that had happened between them the previous night (and well into the early hours of the morning) and smiled. How different from the last time she had been with him, when her presence had seemed to be solely an intense irritation to him.

She pushed the sheet back down Jean-Pierre's chest, so that she could see more of his perfect body. Not that she hadn't seen plenty the night before, but that had been by candlelight. She ran her finger lightly over the corrugation of his stomach muscles, and played it lazily in the hollow of his navel. She was entertaining ideas of massaging him into a priapic wakefulness, but then reflected that she had a long journey to make, and once she began lovemaking all over again with Jean-Pierre she would find it hard to stop.

Louise looked up at Jean-Pierre's face again. He was still deep in sleep. His eyelids were flickering, and she guessed that he was dreaming. She didn't want to wake him, but she had to leave if she was going to get to her destination in daylight. She leant across and gently kissed him on the lips, and then slid silently off the bed. She gathered up her scattered clothes and padded through to the bathroom. The shower blasted away what vestiges of sleepiness remained. Afterwards, Louise went into her own, unused room and quickly pulled on a long sleeveless summer dress. With an impish smile, she neglected to put on any knickers. She towelled her hair dry roughly, knowing that the warm breeze through the van window would soon dry it off.

Louise packed her few clothes back into her suitcase, and then remembered something that Jean-Pierre had given her the previous evening, just before they fell asleep in each other's arms. 'A little something in case you get lonely,' he had said, and had handed her a package that contained a pair of small silver balls joined by a short cord. She had no idea what they were. Jean-Pierre had been amused by her ignorance, and had explained that they were called love eggs, and she should wear them inside herself. The metal would soon warm to her body temperature and, as she moved, they would move inside her, stimulating her. Louise had wondered then what Jean-Pierre was doing with them, but said nothing. Now she placed them on top of her clothes in the suitcase, and carried it down to the kitchen. She made herself some breakfast, and as she ate a piece of brioche with some jam she scribbled a note to Jean-Pierre on the back of an envelope, explaining the reason for her early departure and thanking him for his hospitality.

'We must do this again,' she wrote with feeling. She got up to leave, and then thought of something with a smile. She reached for the envelope, and added: 'Thank you for the present. I shall think of you whenever I use them . . .'

Louise had a long way to drive, and to an as-yet-uncertain final destination. She was banking on the villagers of La-Roche-Hubert being able to direct her to Milo Charpentier's house. She knew that this was something of a gamble, but she had no alternative. As she started up the van, she looked up to Jean-Pierre's shuttered window to see if he had woken, but nothing stirred. She smiled, put the van into gear, and headed off.

Unlike Jean-Pierre, the rest of the town was coming awake. Children wandered back from the boulangerie with large sticks of bread under their arms; others wove precariously on their bicycles, with crusty loaves balanced in wicker baskets; and the roads were already busy with noisy mopeds and small, high-sided Citroën delivery vans. Louise saw the old man who had directed her to Jean-Pierre's house the previous evening, and waved gaily at him. The old man grinned, raised one arm in salutation, and lifted his cap with the other.

I could live here, she thought to herself as she drove through the twisting cobbled streets, searching for a road sign that would direct her back on to the main road for Lyons. The people were so friendly, and she loved the mellow, laid-back pace of life. But most of all, Louise knew that her high spirits were largely due to something as simple as the sunshine. The intensity of the light was so different from that in England, and she found it impossible to feel gloomy or depressed in such brilliance. England already seemed so far away, and France so full of promise.

Chapter Five

Back on the *péage*, Louise had ample opportunity to take in the ever-changing landscape around her, as the road was wide and straight and surprisingly empty for the time of year. She headed southward, past Lyon, past Valence, past Montélimar. Her steady progress on the *péage* caused Louise to fall into a kind of reverie. She was just about aware enough to concentrate on her driving, but no more. After all, motoring along at fifty miles an hour in the slow lane, with no need for gear or lane changes, and no call for overtaking, wasn't exactly taxing driving. She drove past broken-down cars on the hard shoulder; a discarded, shredded tyre from a lorry; a police car parked up on a ramp. Passing by, she could see men toiling in the fields by the road, pulling vegetables or tending to the vines.

The warm sun seemed intensified as it passed through the windscreen and settled on Louise's pale flesh, and she undid the top few buttons of her dress to expose more of her skin to its glorious caresses. But after a few minutes she was still too hot; and so she wound down her window part of the way, allowing the cooling breeze to play over her skin.

Glancing in the rear-view mirror, she saw that a police car was following her in the slow lane, at some distance. She wondered if it was the one that she had passed a few kilometres back. She carried on, glancing in the mirror every now and then. The police car was following steadily, getting no closer, but it was not dropping back either.

It can't be me he wants, she thought, glancing in the mirror. She wasn't worried. She knew that at fifty miles an hour she could hardly be pulled over for speeding. She guessed that the policeman was on routine patrol, and had fallen in behind her as she was driving at a low enough speed to allow him to check out the other traffic as it passed them both.

After about twenty minutes or so, Louise saw the sign for her turn-off from the *péage*. She checked in her mirror and then indicated, and noticed with a slight frown of irritation that the police car was doing likewise. For the next half-hour, the patrol car remained behind her as she drove further and further into the heart of Provence. The roads became even quieter as the views became more and more spectacular, but Louise was concentrating on her driving now. She knew it had to be exemplary when there was a policeman following her.

As she looked in the rear-view mirror once more, Louise saw the blue light on the roof of the police patrol car start flashing. The car was right on her tail now, and its headlights were flashing repeatedly, just in case she hadn't got the message. She could see that the driver was alone in the vehicle, which was so close that it entirely filled the view in her mirror. The policeman was gesturing at the side of the road with a deliberate and repeated pointing movement. Well, I guess it's definitely me that he wants to stop, she thought sarcastically.

Louise indicated and pulled on to the side of the road, watching in the side mirror as the police car drew to a halt behind her. The driver's door opened and a uniformed police officer got out. He slowly approached the van, looking at the rear lights as he passed, and came to the window. Louise wound it right down, and smiled up at him. He had a lean, tanned face; short, dark hair; and very blue eyes. Louise just knew she was going to enjoy being detained by this handsome young officer. He nodded an acknowledgement at her, but did not return her cheery smile. He leant in, scanning the interior of the van. She noticed that his gaze passed over her body rather more slowly than was necessary.

'Driving licence, please,' he said. He had a low, gravelly voice, surprising in one who looked so young.

Louise fumbled in her bag for her international driving permit and her own British driving licence, and handed them to the policeman. He took them and scanned the paperwork. Louise noticed how tanned his hands were. Short dark hairs covered the backs and went part-way up his fingers. She wondered if he was similarly hairy all over.

'Registration and insurance documents, please,' he said, holding out his hand. She handed these over too.

'Is there a problem, officer?' Louise asked politely with a wide smile. She had found in the past that it paid to keep officials as sweet as possible. Besides, it wasn't hard to smile for this man: he was certainly very easy on the eye. The officer smiled briefly and said nothing. Louise guessed that he had stopped her because he was bored. She wondered whether he had seen her British number plate and decided to amuse himself by hassling a foreigner.

'Show me your reflective warning triangle, please.'

Louise almost laughed at this request. However, she knew that it was a compulsory legal requirement in France to carry such a piece of equipment in case of an emergency. Laughing at an officer as he discharged his duty probably wouldn't go down too well.

Louise fished around under the passenger seat until

she found what she was after. She pulled it out and showed it to the officer. He took the warning triangle from her and pulled it out of its plastic cover, assembled it and set it down on the tarmac.

Officious little sod, she thought. Make that officious, handsome little sod, she corrected herself. Louise had a weakness for men in uniform. She noticed the long baton under his belt and the handcuffs dangling from his waist, and smiled to herself as some very rude thoughts crossed her mind.

There was a clatter as the warning triangle toppled over on the road. Louise leant out of the window, looked down and saw that one of the supporting legs was broken. She hadn't thought to check it before she left England. The policeman tutted.

'Open your vehicle, please,' he ordered. Louise undid her seat belt and went round to the sliding door. She opened it and stood back to allow the policeman to step inside the van.

'What are you looking for?' Louise asked.

'Just a routine search, miss,' the policeman replied.

He lifted up some of her bags, and peered around. He pointed to her stuffer bag, and asked her to open it.

Oh hell, thought Louise. He's so suspicious that there's no way he's going to believe that all this expensive equipment is mine. However, the policeman glanced at the contents, including the video camera, the laptop computer and the cameras, and then gestured at her to close the bag again. He then pointed at her suitcase. Louise flushed. She could feel her ears tingling and getting hot, and knew that her cheeks would also be giving away her embarrassment. The policeman sensed that he was on to something, and repeated his request. There was a hardness in his voice this time, suggesting that he did not expect to be disobeyed.

Unwillingly, Louise opened the suitcase. There, on top of all her neatly folded clothes, were the love eggs, the parting present from Jean-Pierre. The policeman slowly raised his eyebrows in surprise, and then looked at Louise.

'Yours, miss?' he asked.

Louise nodded. She decided to try to brazen this out. 'They're a present from a friend. I'm not sure what they are. Are you?' she asked the policeman.

'Oh yes, miss.' The policeman looked at her and smiled. She thought how very attractive he looked in his smart uniform and cap. He picked up the silver balls and placed them in a small plastic bag, which he then sealed and put in his pocket. 'I think I shall have to ask you to give me some more details. Please come to the patrol car with me.'

Louise wanted to laugh. Surely he wasn't going to arrest her for possession of a sex toy? It seemed vaguely ridiculous, but she followed him anyway.

The policeman led Louise to the patrol car. There he stopped her and told her to spread herself against it so that he could search her. This is getting better and better, she thought. She hesitated deliberately, hoping to provoke him. He reacted by pushing her roughly towards the car. He grabbed her hands and placed them on the roof of the car, and then kicked her legs apart so that she was spread-eagled.

Then he bobbed down beside her and clasped her left ankle between both his hands. He ran his hand up her leg beneath her dress, swiftly and firmly. Louise had never been frisked before, but she was sure it wasn't normally done like this: the policeman's hands slowed down as they reached higher up her thigh, until he was sliding them up at a snail's pace. She felt his fingers nearing her bare crotch, and was exquisitely aware of her nakedness under the dress. But the policeman frustrated Louise's mounting excitement by breaking his grip and repeating the performance on her other leg. This had the effect of arousing Louise so much that she shifted slightly, moving her legs even further apart. She hadn't intended to do this: it was an unthinking, carnal reaction.

Again the policeman broke his grip before reaching her quickening centre. He stood behind her and ran his hands up over her hips and her waist, up the side of her chest, down across her shoulders and then round to her front. She drew back from his grasp in surprise as his hands cupped her breasts, and found herself pressing against him.

'I'd advise you not to resist, miss,' he whispered in her ear.

'I can assure you I have absolutely no intention of resisting,' she murmured back, turning her head so that her lips were almost brushing against the collar of his uniform. She could see the pulse pounding in his neck, a fast, regular quivering beat beneath his tanned skin.

The policeman carried on his methodical search, running his hands over her arms, and then down her back, before sweeping them slowly over her bottom. Louise leant back against him again. This was too delicious.

At last the policeman seemed to acknowledge her obvious desire, because now he acted quickly. Reaching behind him, he took his handcuffs from his belt and pulled her hands behind her. Before she had time to react, he had clamped the handcuffs over Louise's wrists. She winced slightly. The handcuffs were tight and the metal hard and cold against her tender skin. It wasn't exactly painful, but it wasn't comfortable, either.

The policeman opened the door, put his hand on the top of her head and forced her down into the back of the patrol car. With his other strong hand on the small of her back, he got in beside her.

Louise scrabbled on the seat, quickly turning and looking at him with a challenging invitation. This was getting better by the minute. They had an understanding: he knew what she wanted and was more than happy to give it to her. He roughly pushed her back against the leather seat, so that her head was leaning against the far passenger door. Louise felt vaguely awkward, with her arms handcuffed behind her, but she barely noticed this discomfort as she was so focused on the policeman and his intentions. She also suspected that she was supposed to feel discomfort. It was all part of the game.

The policeman leant over her, breathing quickly. She could sense the aphrodisiac effect that his power over her was having, and she struggled weakly in a transparently half-hearted attempt at defiance.

'It's no use. You can't get free,' he said, looking down at her. His nostrils were flared, and he reached up and undid the top few buttons of the jacket of his uniform.

'No, leave it on,' Louise whispered before she could stop herself. She was past caring, past bothering about keeping up the pretence of being an unwilling detainee.

The policeman flipped her over on to her stomach, and Louise was disappointed to feel him undoing the handcuffs. He rolled her over on to her back again, crossed her hands at her waist, and then clipped the cuffs round her wrists once more. Louise closed her eyes as she experienced the force of another flush of arousal. She felt her stomach fluttering and her sex moistening yet more. The policeman pulled her arms upward, fished in his pocket for a second pair of cuffs, and used them to fix her manacled arms to the grab rail above the door. Then he sat back and regarded her. She was stretched out beneath his gaze, prone and exposed and defenceless: exactly how she wanted to be.

'Now, how am I going to discipline you?' he mused out loud. 'A defective warning triangle is a very serious matter.'

'Cut the chat and get on with it,' Louise muttered under her breath.

'Silence,' he shouted at her. Louise grimaced and

pulled lamely against her restraints. The policeman was clearly enjoying watching her struggle, and Louise was pleased to feel that her movements had the effect of sliding her dress up against the slippery leather seat, exposing a long length of her thigh.

The policeman knelt above her, and then fumbled with his belt. Louise watched with keen anticipation. She could feel the wetness of her arousal, slowly running out of her and soaking into the material of her dress. The policeman unzipped his flies and released his cock, rigid and imperious. Gazing down at her, he stroked it fondly a couple of times, each time drawing the foreskin a little further back and exposing the turgid pinkish-red bulb of his glans. Louise could see the clear bead of lubricating fluid gathering at the eye of his cock. She could smell his arousal: a musky scent that she adored.

'This will silence you,' the policeman said. He shuffled forward on his knees, straddling her. He placed his cock at her mouth and pressed against her closed lips. This, too, was part of the game: she struggled, and wildly shook her head from side to side, trying to evade the pressure of his penis. The policeman reached forward with one hand and grabbed the back of her head to hold it still. He was gripping her tightly, pulling her hair so that it made her wince. Louise struggled and he jerked his hand a little, pulling her head even further back and thereby indicating his displeasure at her resistance. It was mildly painful, but the intensity of the moment converted the pain into pleasure. She ceased her struggling. Then the policeman let go and stroked his hand round over her throat. Louise could feel her pulse pounding against the palm of his hand. Still with his hand on her neck, he pushed against her lips once more with his engorged prick.

'Open up,' he said. Louise obeyed, and he slid his thick length into her mouth. Louise knew that now he was in the vulnerable position, as she could easily halt this game by biting down on him. But she didn't want it to end. The policeman gazed down at her as he moved his cock in and out of her mouth. He was so excited that within only a few strokes she could feel him thickening and then the hard, salty spurts of semen jetted on to the back of her throat. Louise swallowed eagerly. The policeman withdrew, and buckled his trousers again.

'Let that be a lesson to you,' he said. 'Ah, but there's one last thing.' He fumbled in his pocket and pulled out the bag bearing the love eggs. Louise instinctively slid her legs wide open on the slippery leather seat. She wanted her share of fulfilment from this encounter. The policeman took the silvery balls and pressed one against the wet, accepting opening of Louise's sex. He pressed slowly, and the egg slid into her. Then he pressed the second one into her, gently pushing it and the other right up into her, leaving just the cord hanging outside. As Louise shifted on the seat, she could feel them moving against each other inside her, setting off rippling waves of pleasure.

Then the policeman released her from her manacles. He helped her out of the back of the patrol car, and pulled down her dress. 'Bon voyage,' he said, as she walked back to her van. 'Enjoy your visit.'

Oh I will, thought Louise. There's no doubt about that.

Louise made good progress after her short period of detention with the law-enforcement officer. The countryside gradually became wilder and more rugged, changing from the gentle green rolling scenery into a craggier, rockier landscape. It was striking in its severe beauty. The light seemed brighter, harsher; the ground dry and less fertile. She could see bands of rock strata jutting out from the hillsides; and, beneath them, villages built of the same stone, almost camouflaged in their surroundings.

It was late afternoon, and Louise was now in the

depths of Provence, far from the tourist trails. She was tired: the strain of driving was starting to tell on her, but she knew from her map that she wasn't far from La-Roche-Hubert.

Louise scanned the horizon, and saw a small village perched on a hilltop in the distance. The houses were clustered on the top of the rocky promontory. They were all built of the same honey-coloured stone that seemed to glow in the warm afternoon light, and all were unevenly capped with terracotta tiles. She wondered if this could be her goal. The road started to head upward, twisting steeply up the wooded hillside, and her question was soon answered as she drove past the road sign announcing the name of the village. She had reached La-Roche-Hubert, and now was only one step away from finding Milo Charpentier, and, with him, *The Venus of Collioure*.

Louise parked the camper van just off the dusty village square, beneath a large plane tree. She walked past the large stone fountain in the middle of the square towards the bar. It seemed the obvious place to start her enquiries. Outside the bar were several tables shaded by parasols, but no one was sitting out in the light. She could hear the low drone of voices coming from inside the dark, smoky bar. She pushed the door open, and almost on cue the murmuring hubbub ceased. Feeling awkward, she looked around, trying to adjust to the gloom.

She saw that all the customers were men. Some sat at tables, playing cards; a couple were playing table football; while a few others were sitting on stools up by the bar. Smiling nervously, she walked over to where the patron was standing behind the bar. She was aware that she was being closely watched, and the lascivious looks on some of the men's faces showed that they were taking more than a passing interest in this new and attractive arrival. Louise suddenly wished that she had put on some undies that morning; and was keenly aware of the sinuous movement of the love eggs inside her. Could they tell?

'Yes?' the patron drawled from behind the bar.

'Hello. I'm looking for Milo Charpentier. Do you know him?'

Behind her, she could hear a few of the men whispering. The patron smiled. 'Yes, I know Milo.'

'Could you tell me where he lives, please?' she asked. 'I have some business with him.'

Everyone laughed. Louise was confused and wondered why they should think this funny. The patron leant across the bar, and gave her the instructions to find Les Oliviers, Milo's house. As she left, he called out after her, 'That old goat. You want to watch yourself, missy.' The other men in the bar laughed heartily at these words, and Louise frowned with foreboding.

She started up the van again and drove out of the village. The road leading down the other side of the hill was even narrower than the one by which she had approached the village, and it took her along a twisting route, climbing and then falling again. Louise drove carefully, concentrating equally on following the patron's instructions and on avoiding the potholes and fallen rocks in the road. 'Only eight or nine kilometres,' he had said, and Louise was convinced that she had already travelled that far, but still there was no sign of Milo's house: or any house, for that matter. She guessed that the notion back home of a country mile must have its equivalent in a French rural kilometre. Besides, the patron had said that the road petered out when it reached Milo's, so she could hardly miss his house.

The landscape became more rugged as the road climbed. White limestone crags towered over the landscape and nearly all signs of civilisation apart from the road seemed to have disappeared. The hillsides were covered with a rough scrub. Then the road dropped again into a wide, wooded valley. The patron had said that Milo lived by a river: Louise felt that she must be close now.

As the sun dipped slowly towards the craggy horizon, the shadows cast by its orange light were lengthening almost perceptibly. Louise followed the road down into the valley; and sure enough, the tarmac terminated at a rough track which led off past some trees. She slowly drove down the trail, worried about the suspension and the tyres on the van. She didn't fancy getting a flat out here. She could swap the wheel for the spare easily enough, but the nearest garage where she could get a puncture repaired must be miles away. As the track brought her past a rocky outcrop and then a group of olive trees, she saw the house.

It was an old stone building, with shutters on the windows and doors, and a roughly paved terrace sheltered by a vine-covered canopy. On the terrace were a few pots of bright-red geraniums. Had it not been for the flowers, she might have thought the house derelict, such was its condition. The paintwork was faded, blistered and peeling; the shutter on the door was banging lazily in the breeze; and there were tussocks of grass, now bleached by the summer heat, growing amongst the terracotta roof tiles. Some of the guttering was missing, adding to the general air of neglect. There were no vehicles, no washing on the line: nothing to indicate habitation, apart from the open shutters.

Louise drew up the camper van in the shade of a large fig tree and turned off the engine. She stepped out of the van and listened. Over the ruffling breaths of wind, she could hear the gentle swirling rush of the river running past the olive grove below the house. The olive trees looked old and venerable, with gnarled, thick trunks, and she could see the brown ovals of the ripening fruits among the silvery-green leaves. She thought that these must be the trees from which the house took its name.

As she listened, hoping to hear voices, movement, or anything to suggest that she hadn't come all this way in vain, a bird mewed high above her. She looked up, and saw the dark silhouette of an eagle spiralling on one of the last thermals of the day.

She wandered over to the house, and caught the banging shutter in her hand to still it. She fixed it back on its hook against the wall, and cautiously knocked on the door. Nothing stirred. She tried the door: it was open. She stepped into the house, and found herself in the kitchen. It was a low-ceilinged room, floored with large terracotta tiles, some of which were cracked. The walls were painted with an uneven ochre-coloured wash. There was an old cast-iron range stretching along almost the entire length of one wall, and against the opposite wall a set of rough wooden stairs led upward. In the centre of the room there was a large table, with bench seats along both sides and a chair at either end. The table was bare apart from a vase of flowers. This at least heartened Louise. She could tell that they were freshly picked – they were wild flowers and she knew from childhood experience that these wilted quickly. She was encouraged, and called out into the echoing silence.

'Hello?'

There was no reply. She turned and walked outside again, and as she did so she thought that she could hear the distant sound of voices: high, laughing, female voices. Looking in the direction of the sound, she noticed a worn path winding down through the olive trees. She followed it, and the voices became louder. The path brought her down to the river.

The scene that greeted Louise was so surprising that she almost turned to go back to the house. She did not want to be thought a voyeur; and yet some irresistible urge forced her to remain and look. A small waterfall tumbled over a rocky outcrop in the river, and the force of its ten-foot drop had created a deep pool beneath it. Downstream, the river became shallower again, and was scattered with boulders. But it was not the river or its large and clear pool that drew her attention.

Two women were in the pool. Both were naked, their long brown hair flowing behind them as they swam in the water. A third woman was paddling at the river's edge, a little further downstream. She too was naked, the light reflecting off the wet gloss of her bronzed skin. The women were extraordinarily beautiful. All three shared the same dark, sultry looks that made Louise instinctively think of gypsies, of Carmen, of fiery Mediterranean passions.

It was only then that Louise noticed a man sitting on a large boulder on the other side of the river, sketching the women. The sketch pad was balanced on his knee, and he was gripping a small hand-rolled cigarette between his teeth, puffing away as he drew with fast, certain strokes of his charcoal stick. A half-empty bottle of wine was propped against the base of the boulder. The man was wearing light linen trousers and a loose unironed cotton shirt, and he sported a couple of days' worth of dark stubble on his chin. Louise could see dark curls peeping out from the neck of his shirt, and longer dark hair curled out from under the rim of his frayed straw hat. The cigarette, the curly hair: this must be the man in the photograph with Brazzini, surely. Louise felt certain that he could only be Milo Charpentier.

No one had noticed her presence, and so Louise coughed. The man looked up, and Louise was strongly aware of his bright-blue eyes appraising her with interest from across the river.

'Well, what have we here? Perhaps a water nymph?' she heard him say to himself. He threw the cigarette away, put his sketch pad down on the rock and scrambled to his bare feet. Louise watched as he hopped with an easy agility from boulder to boulder across the river.

He hurried up to her, and stretched out his hand. She took it, and they shook silently. Louise felt this formality made a strange contrast to the informality of the scene in the river below her. She was about to introduce herself, but the man put a silencing finger over her lips, and looked her up and down.

'So very pale. Quite remarkable. You're not French. I can tell that straight away.'

Louise wondered if her dress sense had given her away. The man continued, talking to himself rather than to her. 'Pale, ivory, creamy skin. It appears almost translucent, and it seems to glow in the afternoon light. And those freckles. Very appealing. But most of all, look at this hair. Such a colour.'

The man lifted his hand to touch her hair, and then stopped and cocked his head to one side as if to ask permission. Bemused, Louise nodded. He raised his hand again and gently ran his fingers through her hair. She was acutely aware of his touch. It was flattering to be the object of such a careful and close examination. Toying with the curls between his long, elegant fingers, he smiled at her.

'Soft, delightful. What an extraordinary colour. Like liquid, spun amber. Like burnished copper threads. Titian hair on my pale water nymph. Superb.'

Louise wondered at this strange reception. No 'who are you?' or 'what brings you here?', no indication of surprise at her unannounced entrance. 'Are you Milo?' she finally collected herself enough to ask.

He smiled, as if amused by her question. 'Yes, I'm Milo.'

'I'm Lou –' Once more he silenced her by placing his finger gently across her mouth. He slowly stroked his finger from side to side over Louise's lips, sending unexpected surges of desire through her.

'Hush. I don't want to know your name. I shall call you Loulou,' he said. 'In Arabic, it means "Pearl", and it can be the only name for one with such milky, pearly skin.' Milo traced his finger down the length of Louise's bare arm. 'And pearls come from the water, my little water nymph.'

Louise tried not to show her bemusement at Milo's manner. Artists were expected to be eccentric, after all.

'Of course, I shall have to paint you. Have you ever posed before? Seen yourself as others see you? Opened yourself up to someone's intense, probing scrutiny?' Milo smiled as he said this, and Louise wondered if more was being conveyed by his words than she might at first be expected to understand. She blushed.

'Something about you tells me that you have not: all the better. I can teach you. And you are so different from my dusky-skinned naiads here,' Milo continued, gesturing over to the river, where the three women were still idling in the water. 'I shall be glad of a diversion.'

Before Louise could ask him what he meant by this, Milo called down to the women.

'Solange, Isabelle, Colette: come and greet our visitor.' Louise watched as the women rose out of the water like three magnificent Venuses and approached her up the narrow path. They were completely unabashed by their nudity, and behaved as if they greeted complete strangers in a state of nakedness every day. But who knows, perhaps they do, thought Louise. She was starting to think that nothing was ever likely to be prosaic or predictable *chez* Milo.

The three women stood in front of Louise, smiling. They had stunning bodies: athletic and toned, full and sensual; and all three had the same rich honey-coloured skin. They must spend a lot of time without any clothes on, Louise thought, to achieve that all-over tan. But then again, she knew that Milo liked to paint his nudes outdoors, so it was no great surprise.

'Ladies, meet Loulou,' said Milo.

'Hello, Loulou,' they chorused sweetly.

'Loulou will be staying with us, won't you, Loulou?' Milo asked.

'But . . .' Louise said in confusion. She had been prepared to introduce herself to Milo and then drive back to La-Roche-Hubert and find lodgings there for the night; or even to sleep in the camper van if she had to. She hadn't meant to impose on his hospitality.

'Well, stay for tonight at least – and longer, if we can persuade you,' Milo said.

Louise looked at the four of them, scanning from face to face. They were all smiling, friendly, and welcoming. 'That's very kind of you. Thank you,' she said.

'You look hot and bothered,' one of the women said. 'Come for a swim, Loulou.'

'Um,' Louise paused, uncertain what to do.

The women gathered around her, laughing. 'Take your clothes off and come for a swim.'

'I'm going up to the house. Come up when you're done,' said Milo. 'We'll have some wine and you can tell us all about yourself. Apart from your name, of course,' he added with a laugh.

Louise watched as Milo walked barefoot up the rough path. Once he had disappeared, she pulled her dress off over her head. She hoped, with a flush of shame, that the women had not noticed the cord of the love eggs dangling down between her legs; but they were already back in the pool. They called out to her and pointed to where she could dive in: a rocky ledge near to the waterfall. Louise hurried down the path to join the women, kicked off her sandals, took a deep breath and plunged into the inviting water.

She surfaced spluttering and coughing with surprise. The water was cooler than she had expected, but it was wonderfully refreshing. The women swam over, and the three dark beauties trod water around her, questioning her and chatting. Through the shifting reflections on the surface of the water, Louise could see their bronzed bodies and her own pale one. She could feel the tensions of the journey ebbing away, and a calm, relaxing torpor coming over her.

After their swim, the four women walked back up to the house. The three Frenchwomen disappeared upstairs briefly and reappeared, dressed this time, but only just. All three were wearing white cotton dresses, which showed off their tans beautifully; and which were also near-transparent when the women stood with the sun behind them. At the same time, Louise had slipped behind the camper van and changed into a clean dress.

Now Louise and her four new friends were sitting on the terrace, drinking a local red wine and eating fat olives from an earthenware dish. Louise was trying to work out the arrangement between Milo and the women. The ease and familiarity with which they addressed him and each other, and with which they moved around the house and surroundings, suggested that they lived here. But surely not? They were miles from the nearest village, and with no visible means of transport. How did they live? What did they do for food? It seemed a strange set-up, no doubt about it.

'So, Loulou. To what do we owe the honour of your visit?' Milo asked, rolling another cigarette.

Louise wasn't sure where to begin. Suddenly it all seemed so unlikely that this scruffy artist could be in possession of *The Venus of Collioure*. He would think her foolish for thinking such a thing, let alone travelling all the way down to see him in Provence on such an outlandish hunch. She decided to get it over with quickly.

'I'm studying history of art at university in England, and I want to do my final-year dissertation on Gustave de Valence and *The Venus of Collioure*. And I think – I mean, I hope that you can tell me where she is.'

Milo threw back his head and laughed. His shoulders

heaved up and down and Louise could see tears gathering in the corners of his eyes. He laughed so hard that he started to cough, and he gasped to catch his breath.

'Excuse me, Loulou. I can't help it. My God. You've honestly come all the way from England because you think I know where *The Venus of Collioure* is? You're a wonder, that's for sure.'

Louise was crestfallen: she hadn't expected to meet disappointment so soon. She was also slightly piqued by Milo's gentle teasing. 'So you don't know where she is?' she asked.

'I didn't say that, Loulou. I'll make a bargain with you. I might tell you what I know. But I'm not one to hurry things, so it could take a few days. You will have to be patient. I won't be rushed. I won't be bullied. I'll tell you if and when I'm ready to tell you – but I can't tell you when that will be. You'll just have to stay with us, and wait and see. How does that sound?'

Louise felt she had little option. But at least Milo hadn't denied all knowledge of *The Venus* outright. There was still hope. And looking around her, she could think of a lot worse places to stay than this idyllic farmhouse deep in the heart of Provence.

Dusk was gradually falling over the hills, and the cicadas intensified their chirping into a full-blown evening chorus from the nearby trees and bushes. Milo went into the kitchen and came out with a lit oil lamp. Louise watched as moths and flies were soon attracted to it, beating themselves with futile persistence against the glass shade.

As she talked to Milo and the women about her journey, Louise became aware of the distant sound of an engine, its rumbling throb reverberating off the hills and valley sides. She looked over in the direction of the road, and could see the faint yellow glow of headlights weaving towards the house. The noise became louder and louder, and eventually an old green Citroën van drove down the track and parked right next to Louise's camper van. A man got out and waved at them, before going round to the back of his van. Solange and Colette got up and ran over to him. They greeted the man warmly with embraces and kisses, before helping him to carry boxes of fresh fruit and vegetables into the kitchen.

Milo called the man over when he was on his way back out of the kitchen door. He approached them with an easy-limbed, loping grace, carrying himself with a cocksure confidence. He was as brown as the three women, and his short hair was bleached blond by the strong sun. He was younger, taller and broader than Milo, and yet Louise was intrigued to see that he treated Milo with slight deference. She was briefly reminded of wildlife documentaries she had seen, where there would be one dominant male reigning over the other subservient males in a pack. It seemed that Milo was the alpha male here at Les Oliviers.

'Antoine, say hello to Loulou. She will be staying with us for a while.'

Antoine looked at Louise and smiled, a rakish smile that suggested that his interest in her was more than purely social. He took Louise's proffered hand, and then bent down and kissed her on both cheeks, not once but twice. Louise caught a hint of scent as he kissed her, but couldn't place it. She watched as he walked back to the van and hefted up a heavy sack of flour as if it weighed nothing. He threw it over one shoulder, and picked up a large demijohn of wine in the other hand. He carried them into the kitchen, and Isabelle got up from the table and went indoors to join the others, leaving Louise and Milo alone.

'I can see that you are trying to figure us out. Colette, Isabelle, Solange and Antoine are my family. We all live together. They model for me, and in return I look after them. I'm a painter, if you hadn't already guessed.'

'I know,' said Louise. 'I read about you in the *Directory*

of Modern European Artists, and in the James Bower Collection catalogue.'

Milo grinned. 'Ah. So you also know what it is that I paint.'

Louise grinned back. 'Yes.'

'And what do you think of that?'

'I saw some of your paintings in the brochure. I liked them.'

Milo narrowed his eyes at her, scrutinising her closely. 'Are you being honest or are you being polite?'

'Honest,' she replied.

Milo seemed pleased with her answer. He sat back in his chair, and lit another cigarette.

After an hour or so, Solange called them into the kitchen to eat. Louise hadn't realised how fast time had passed as she talked to Milo. She wanted to broach the subject of *The Venus* again, but decided not to; not just yet, at least. She didn't want to risk irritating Milo by carping on about it. It was obvious that the pace of life here was slow and easy: she would have to learn to adapt to it, to give herself up to the relaxed rhythm and not pester Milo unnecessarily.

She followed Milo into the kitchen. The room was lit by candlelight and by the warm glow of the fire in the range. A fine feast was laid out on the table: a huge dish of cassoulet, some salads and fresh vegetables, an onion tart and other appetising dishes which Louise could neither identify nor name. A large carafe of wine sat in the middle of the table, next to the vase of wild flowers. By now they had wilted badly, and their colours had faded to more muted hues.

During the meal, Louise watched with fascination as Milo fed titbits of food to Solange and then to Colette on his other side, before reaching across the table and popping a tasty morsel in Isabelle's mouth. He flirted with them all as if they were his lovers. At one point, Antoine leant across and stroked Colette's cheek, brushing the hair back from her eyes. Louise noticed the intimacy of this gesture and looked at Milo, to see what his reaction would be. But Milo merely smiled, and continued to caress Colette's arm. Louise thought that it might take her some time to puzzle out the exact nature of the set-up at the old farmhouse.

After the meal, Milo announced that Antoine would make the coffee. Louise noticed that Antoine did not baulk at being ordered about like this. Milo gestured Louise through to the room opening off from the kitchen. It was a large living room, simply furnished with a few fat armchairs and a couple of sofas. Solange, Colette and Isabelle came in with her, but Milo hung back in the kitchen. Over the noise of the three women's chatter, Louise could hear Milo talking in a low, cool voice.

'Stay off her. House rules. You can have the other three, as before, but leave her alone.'

Then Milo reappeared, smiling and carrying a bottle of brandy. Antoine appeared a few minutes later, carrying a tray with some small cups of strong black coffee. He then made his apologies, saying he was ready for bed. Louise was disappointed that he was leaving so soon, but tried not to let it show. She wondered if his early retirement was anything to do with her. She watched as Antoine kissed the three women good night, and observed how they all followed him with their eyes as he left the room. Milo chatted on. He drained his coffee in a single gulp, and then filled the cup with the cognac and downed that quickly too. Louise was impressed by Milo's prodigious intake of alcohol, which hadn't seemed to affect him in the slightest. He had been drinking steadily through the meal, and was on his third brandy refill by the time Louise had finished her coffee. He was talking animatedly about his latest painting: a portrait of Isabelle.

Despite the caffeine, Louise was finding it a struggle

to keep her progressively heavy eyelids open. She was unable to stifle a yawn. Milo appeared not to notice, and continued chatting away about his painting. Then he grilled her thoroughly about what she thought of her course at university. Had it taught her well? Did she feel that she could understand art the better for it? Louise tried hard to concentrate and answer his rapid questions, but the dull wooziness of sleep was taking over, and she could no longer hold it back. It had been a long couple of days. Her lids fluttered closed, and stayed that way. She slowly tipped over until her head was resting on the arm of the sofa.

'Oh, the poor dear,' said Solange. 'We must put her to bed. She's tired out. Shame on you, Milo; you shouldn't have kept her up like this.'

'Where is she going to sleep?' asked Isabelle.

'We'll put her on the sofa tonight, and sort something out tomorrow. You girls see to her,' said Milo, getting up and leaving the room. He paused in the doorway. 'Goodnight, my dears. I'll see you later.'

Chapter Six

When Louise woke the next morning she immediately experienced the befuddled confusion of one awakening in strange surroundings. It took her a couple of moments to recollect where she was. The shutters outside the windows were closed, but they fitted so badly that enough light came into the room to allow her to see clearly. She saw her dress draped over the back of one of the armchairs. Lifting up the tasselled cotton blanket that was covering her, she checked what she already knew to be true. She was naked. She wondered who had undressed her and put her to bed.

Holding the blanket about her, she went over to one of the windows and pushed the shutters open. The van in which Antoine had arrived the previous night was gone, and there seemed to be no one about. Just as she was starting to think that she was suffering from *déjà vu*, a repeat of the deserted-house scenario of the previous day, Louise heard a noise in the kitchen next door. She wandered through, to find Colette kneading a large lump of bread dough on the table. Colette looked up and smiled.

'Good morning, Loulou. Would you like some breakfast?' Colette wiped her flour-covered hands on her apron and went over to the range. She took a battered old enamel coffee pot off the hotplate and poured Louise a large bowlful of coffee. Then she gestured at Louise to sit at the table, and fetched a couple of small cakes and a bowl of fruit.

'What time is it?' Louise asked, pulling the blanket around her.

'Midday.'

'That late?' said Louise.

'We didn't want to disturb you. And besides, there's no rush, is there?'

'Where's everyone else?'

'Solange has gone to the market at La-Roche-Hubert with Antoine, and Milo is painting Isabelle.'

'I see,' said Louise as she sipped gingerly at the piping-hot coffee, her hands cupping the deep bowl. She broke off a piece of one of the cakes and dunked it in the bowl. The cake was so light that it dissolved almost instantly.

'How long have you been here with Milo?' Louise asked.

Colette paused from her kneading to think. 'Let me see. I met him for the first time at Collioure: it would be two years ago now. There's a candlelight procession held there each year on Good Friday. Milo borrowed my candle to light his own, and told me that he wanted to paint me. I came back here with him the next day.'

'Just like that?' said Louise, surprised at how easily Colette had fallen in with him.

'Why not?'

Why not indeed? thought Louise. She had just spent the night in Milo's house, and he had been a stranger until barely eighteen hours ago. It wasn't so different from what Colette had done. And she could easily see how Milo could have that effect on a person.

'And the others?'

'Solange and Antoine were already here when I arrived, and Isabelle joined us earlier this year. Milo had gone off on one of his jaunts, and she was serving in a bar where he was drinking. Like me, she didn't take much persuading to come back here with him.'

'Is Milo painting Isabelle down by the river?' Louise asked.

'No. He's in his studio, for once. It's round the back of the house, beyond the terrace. Go and see him, if you want.'

Louise nodded, and drained the last of her coffee, leaving the sludge of dissolved cake at the bottom of the bowl. She took it over to the sink and washed it up, then went back to the living room. She saw that someone had brought in her suitcase. She picked out her washing gear and went back into the kitchen.

'Where's the bathroom, Colette?'

'Up the stairs, at the end of the landing,' Colette replied, pointing with a dough-covered finger at the rough open-tread stairs.

Louise stepped cautiously up the stairs, holding the cotton blanket around her and mindful of the possibility of encountering nails or splinters under her bare feet. At the top of the stairs there was a narrow landing, with two doors opening off the left-hand side and another door at the end. Walking towards the bathroom, Louise couldn't resist glancing in through the other two doors. She wondered about the sleeping arrangements. There didn't seem a great deal of room for five people up here. She couldn't see into the first room very clearly, as the door was only just ajar. She could see a rug on the floor, and nothing else. In the second room she saw a huge bed. It appeared to be made of three single mattresses pushed together on the floor. The bedding was rumpled and disarranged, and items of discarded clothing lay about.

Louise was intrigued by the possibilities. Did the men have one room, and the three women the other? Did they all sleep together? And, she wondered, did they love as communally as they lived? Judging by Milo's words to Antoine the previous night, it seemed that they might.

When she came down to the kitchen again, freshly bathed and dressed in a pair of shorts and a loose strappy top, Louise was struck by the welcoming yeasty smell of baking bread. Colette grinned at her.

'I think I'll go and see Milo,' Louise said.

'He'd like that,' replied Colette. 'Especially if you take him this,' she added, handing Louise a bottle of pastis.

Louise went outside and was immediately dazzled by the brilliance of the Provençal noon. Even in the shade of the vine-draped canopy, she still squinted into the sunlight. The sun cast short, strong, dark shadows, and the ground almost hissed with the baking heat. She could hear the intermittent grating call of cicadas in the nearby bushes. Louise became aware of movement behind her. She turned and saw Colette standing at her side.

'Isn't it beautiful? Our own private Garden of Eden: that's what Milo likes to call it.'

Louise nodded her agreement, and was about to walk out into the sunlight when Colette called after her.

'Hey, you'll need this,' she said, holding out a bottle of suntan oil. Louise reached out to take the bottle, but instead Colette flipped the lid open and poured a generous pool of the oil into her own cupped palm.

'Here, let me,' Colette said.

Louise stood passively and allowed Colette to rub the oil into her skin. Colette knelt in front of her and carefully covered her legs with the warm, slick oil; and, as Colette's hands slid further and further up her leg, one hand around either side, it vividly reminded Louise of her encounter with the policeman the previous day. She flushed with flustered embarrassment, grateful that Colette could not read her thoughts. Colette looked up at her and steadily held her gaze as she massaged the oil into Louise's leg. Louise felt that she was being tested: gently probed to see what her reaction would be.

Colette stood up in front of her and began on Louise's arms, and then turned her round and treated the back of her neck and her shoulders. Colette then spun her round again and surprised Louise by squirting the oil directly on to her skin above her top. Louise could feel it dribbling down her front and between her breasts. Colette laughed. 'I'll leave you to rub that in.' She blew Louise a kiss and went back into the kitchen.

Louise was surprised to find that among her many confused reactions was frustration. She had wanted Colette to caress the oil into the soft tender skin of her breasts. She was perplexed. She had never had this kind of feeling for another woman before. She could look at pictures of a woman's body and find it appealing – in fact, she had frequently done so during her studies at university – but to find a woman in the flesh so erotically stimulating and so sexually attractive was a new experience to her. Previously, she had enjoyed looking at a woman's body without wanting to explore it further, or to feel it pressed against her own. Her desires now were changing. She wanted to pleasure another woman. And maybe even be pleasured by one.

After all, this was to be a summer of new experiences, so why not this one, too? Thinking of Colette, Louise brought her hand to her chest and dreamily massaged the oil into her skin, feeling the soft, fleshy warmth of her breasts. When the oil had finally disappeared, she sighed and stepped out into the sunlight. She walked round to the far side of the house, looking for the studio. A little further down the slope, she could see a small stone building. She guessed that it might have originally been a cow shed or an outhouse of some sort. One side of the roof was completely glazed over, whereas the other side retained the original, uneven terracotta tiles.

Louise walked down to the building and, on a whim, peered in through the open window.

The building comprised a single room, with wooden floorboards. The room was flooded with light. On the opposite side of the studio was another large window which looked down to the river and a door, which was flung wide open. Everything was painted white: the stone walls, the floorboards, the underside of the unglazed half of the roof, even the roof beams. The effect was sparse and bare.

At one end of the room stood a trestle table, covered with tubes of oil paint, jam jars full of paintbrushes, and a slab of glass on which dabs of paint had been squeezed and mixed. Milo was standing by the table, carefully cleaning a brush with turpentine. Next to the table was a paint-spattered wooden easel, which bore a large canvas. From where she was standing, Louise couldn't see what was depicted on the canvas. On the wall behind the easel hung a large painting of a nude woman, and leaning against the wall was a stack of canvases. With a rush of euphoria, Louise recognised this as the same view that she had seen in the photograph of Milo and Brazzini – and the stack of canvases not ten feet away from her was the stack that had contained *The Venus of Collioure*.

At the other end of the room was a large couch. It was covered with an ivory-coloured silk throw and there were several large cushions scattered about, some on the floor and others on the couch. Isabelle was sitting on the edge of the couch. She was naked. The contrast between the pale silk and the darkness of her skin and hair was striking.

'So, Isabelle, what do you think of our new visitor?' Louise heard Milo say to his model as he loaded his brush and turned to the canvas. Neither Milo nor Isabelle had noticed Louise at the window.

'She's very beautiful,' said Isabelle. She lay back on one of the cushions and closed her eyes.

'She is, isn't she? I intend to paint her soon. I wonder how successful I shall be in persuading her to pose like this for me.'

'As successful as you always are, my love,' said Isabelle. 'We all adore posing for you. You make it so easy.' Isabelle slowly parted her legs and brought her right hand down to her groin, laying it across her pubic hair, with one finger dipping slightly into her downy cleft. She cupped her left breast with her other hand, brushing the nipple with her fingers. Louise watched as it hardened into a dark-brown tip, surrounded by the paler brown of the areola.

'I love doing this for you,' Isabelle whispered.

Milo stood regarding his model for a moment, and then put down his brush. He walked over to the couch and gazed down at Isabelle, who responded by moving her legs further apart in a clear invitation.

'What do you hope the viewer will be thinking as he looks at your portrait?' Milo asked her.

'I hope that he will be aroused; that he will look at me and want me; that he will wish that he could crawl right into the painting and make love to me.'

'Good,' said Milo. He reached into his pocket, pulled out a handkerchief, and dabbed his forehead. Louise wondered if it was the heat of the glasshouse-like studio; or the effect of Isabelle.

'I think I want you to pose like this,' Milo said after a pause, moving over to kneel on the couch next to Isabelle. He reached down and, hooking his hand under one knee and then the other, brought them up so that her legs were bent and the soles of her feet flat on the couch. Then he took her hand from her breast and moved it down to her sex to join the other.

'Touch yourself,' he said in a low voice.

Isabelle languidly looked up at Milo, and then spread

herself with one hand, stretching the lips away from the moist red core of her sex. She lifted her other hand up to her mouth and licked her middle finger very slowly. Then she returned it to her crotch, and started to stroke her slick opening in a deliberate up-and-down movement. All the time, her eyes were fixed on Milo.

'Good, good,' he whispered, slowly backing away from her without taking his eyes off her busy fingers. He reached out for his brush, and turned to work on his canvas with a new vigour.

Louise put the bottle of pastis under the window, turned, and headed back to the house. She didn't want to disturb Milo right now. She felt a hot flush of shame at what she had just witnessed. But part of her knew already that it was only a matter of time before she too would be lying like that in front of Milo, open and exposed.

Instead of going straight back to the house, Louise wandered off to explore the surrounding countryside. The cicadas were still beating out their irregular, zigzagging rhythm, and after a while Louise ceased to notice their noise. She wandered along the river for a while, following it on its gentle downhill course. The valley was lushly vegetated, and provided a haven for the birds which sang noisily in the cover of the trees. Louise could see that, higher up, the dry rocky hillside was much barer. She headed upward, wondering what the view would be like from the jagged crags she could see towering above her.

She walked along a path that was fringed with lushly leafed shrubs and trees. These gradually gave way to pine trees and tall, thin flame-shaped cypresses on the fringes of the river valley. As she climbed ever upward these in turn gave way to tussocks of parched grasses and low scrubby bushes of broom. The path petered out, and Louise continued to scrabble upward, determined to reach the top of the crags and survey the view from such a spectacular vantage point. The ground was dry and stony, but the perfume carried on the breeze was unbelievably strong for such an arid, unfertile-looking landscape. Louise looked around, searching out its source. Her leg brushed against a low grey-leafed plant and the sudden burst of aroma told her that she had found one of the culprits: a wormwood. She picked a couple of leaves, crushed them between her fingers, and sniffed. The perfume was incredibly strong. Looking around, she could see wild herbs growing in among the rocky outcrops: low spreading mats of thyme, taller rosemary and sage plants, and clumps of marjoram. These were familiar plants to Louise but, for every one she recognised, there were many more that she did not know.

She climbed up, higher and higher, scrabbling over the rocky ground until at last she reached the top of the highest crag. By now she was sweating, and wished that she had the suntan oil and some water with her. There was no shade, and the sun seemed stronger and harsher at this height. A sudden breeze swept over the crag, and Louise could feel it cooling the sweat on her skin. She sat on a rock and took in the glorious view. Below her, the valley stretched like a green ribbon through the brown, stony landscape. She could just make out the red roof of Les Oliviers, and she thought that she could see someone moving through the olive grove down to the river. She waved, but no one looked up.

A few days later, Louise was sitting with Solange on one of the large boulders overlooking the river. The two women were enjoying a companionable silence, both wrapped up in their own thoughts. Louise had got no further with Milo and her search for *The Venus of Collioure*. She wanted to have a look in his studio, and search through the stack of paintings leaning against the wall, but had not yet had the opportunity. Milo was so busy with his portrait of Isabelle that he barely left the studio during the day, and her absence would be noted in the evenings. Besides, she didn't want to abuse the trust of her host. She was hoping that Milo would choose to reveal *The Venus* himself.

'We've been talking about the sleeping arrangements,' Solange said, tossing some pebbles into the pool. 'It seems from what Milo has said that you're going to be with us for quite a while, Loulou.'

That didn't seem a good omen. Louise frowned, but said nothing.

'It can't be comfy for you on the sofa in the living room,' Solange continued. 'You need a proper bed. We're normally pretty fluid: we sleep wherever we want to. Would you be happy with that? If you're not – and we'll understand it – feel free to carry on sleeping in the living room.'

Louise thought for a moment. It wasn't ideal, sleeping in the living room, as Milo was a night bird and liked to stay up until the small hours, talking, smoking and drinking. She was curious to find out how this strange tribe slept together, and what better way than to join in?

'I'll fit in with your arrangements, if that's OK. But I don't want to put anyone out,' Louise said.

Solange laughed. 'Oh, you won't. Don't worry about that.'

That night, after the evening ritual of a large meal and plenty of wine followed by coffee in the living room, Louise excused herself. She wanted to be the first into bed, to see what would ensue. She went into the first bedroom off the landing, which she had not yet been into. In the room was a chest of drawers, an old wardrobe and an iron-framed double bed. The bed was tidily made, with an embroidered white cotton bedspread and pretty lace-trimmed pillowcases. Louise decided this would be her bed for the night. She wondered who else might make the choice.

She showered quickly and got into bed. She was as she normally slept, naked. Half an hour later, she heard light footsteps coming up the wooden stairs. They passed her door and went along to the bathroom. Ten minutes later, the footsteps returned and the bedroom door opened. Solange tiptoed into the room. She pulled back the sheets and climbed into bed next to Louise. She leant over and kissed Louise gently on the cheek.

'Good night, Loulou,' she whispered, and then settled down, rolling over so that her back was turned to Louise. Louise felt vaguely disappointed. She had been expecting more than this, somehow. She closed her eyes, and drifted off to sleep.

Later that night, Louise was woken by a strange noise. She lay perfectly still, and listened hard. She then became aware of a slight rocking motion next to her, and realised with a shock that she was not alone with Solange in the bed. She turned her head, very slowly, towards the source of the repeated noise, which she now recognised as a stifled moan. Illuminated by the bright silvery moonlight pouring in through the curtainless window, she could see that, next to her, Solange was lying on her back, her right hand across her mouth. She was biting the back of her hand to prevent herself from calling out. Antoine was crouched above her, slowly moving backward and forward over her. He was pushed up over her on the palms of his hands, and the covers had been thrown right back. They were both naked. Louise watched silently as Antoine moved into Solange, his buttocks clenching and quivering with each thrust. There was a slow deliberateness about his movements, and Louise guessed that it was in an attempt not to wake her.

Louise could feel herself become more and more excited as she watched the couple making love right next to her. Careful not to give her wakefulness away, she slipped her hand down her stomach and slid her thighs apart with infinite slowness. She watched as Solange's full breasts shuddered with each of Antoine's thrusts, the brown nipples taut and erect. Every so often, Antoine would lower his head and take one in his mouth, sucking and playing with it; then he would break away to kiss Solange again. Their lips crushed together with a bruising force and passion, and Louise licked her own lips as she watched, trying to imagine the feel of Antoine's lips on her own.

At the same time, Louise's hand felt for her own downy furrow, and she began to work her practised fingers over her yearning sex, smearing the juices of her desire up on to her clitoris. She gently pulled back the soft skin and, with her other hand, began the light feathery dabs on her clitoris that would bring her to orgasm. She knew how to measure out her stimulation so that she did not achieve climax too soon; she knew from long years of practice that, the more she could tease herself and the longer she could last, the better the orgasm would be when it finally came.

Antoine, too, seemed to fully understand the delights of delay. He paused in his thrusting, and withdrew his penis. He lowered himself over Solange so that it lay, slick and glistening in the moonlight, against her stomach. Louise watched with fascinated awe as it twitched and jerked.

'Put it back in me,' Solange whispered desperately.

Antoine shook his head, and then slowly shuffled on his knees up the bed until he was straddling Solange at the shoulders. He held his penis around the base and brushed it against her, smearing the sticky tip across her mouth. She licked her lips, tasting their mixed juices, and then opened her mouth to take him in. Antoine slowly fed his penis into Solange's mouth, pushing it in inch by inch as her lips stretched round its veiny girth.

Louise lay silently, working her fingers with a frenzy as she stimulated herself. She couldn't believe what was going on right beside her: this was more explicit than any blue movie she had ever seen, and ten times more erotic. Not only could she see, but she could feel their movements, hear their muffled cries of passion, and she could smell their arousal.

Antoine was now fucking Solange's mouth almost as vigorously as he had earlier been plunging into her sex. She was grasping both his buttocks in her hands, as if she was trying to force him still deeper into her. Antoine's hands were flat against the wall at the head of the bed, and he looked down with satisfaction as he worked his engorged manhood in and out between Solange's eager lips.

Then Antoine paused again, and slowly withdrew his cock. Solange pressed hard against his buttocks with her hands, but he easily overcame her efforts to keep him in her mouth.

'What now, Solange?' he whispered.

She responded by slowly scrabbling to her knees so that she was facing him. He sat back on the bed, his knees still bent under him, and his heels touching his buttocks. His cock was pointing towards the ceiling, and it twitched and brushed against his belly. Solange moved up to him, and shifted first one knee and then the other over his. She threw her arms round his neck. Antoine took her weight off his thighs by cupping her round buttocks in his hands. He lifted her upward with ease, positioning her over the hard tower of his prick. Louise could see that Antoine's biceps were fully flexed as he took Solange's weight; and the long, lean muscles in his forearm were tensed like steel hawsers. Slowly, he lowered Solange down over his cock. Louise watched as his swollen prick was gradually engulfed by Solange's hungry sex. Solange moaned as Antoine entered her and began his thrusting rhythm once more. He lifted her up and down over his cock as if she were weightless.

Louise was reaching the point of no return. She watched as the two lovers rocked, clasping each other in a close, fervent embrace like drowning souls; and she felt the heat of her own orgasm steadily rising. Her clitoris, already tender, felt as if it might burst at any moment; and, before Louise could hold it back once more, her climax thundered over her. She closed her eyes with the force of the onslaught, and pressed her head back into the pillow. Her eyes were shut, but she could see stars.

Next to her, she heard the moaning and the guttural groans which told her that Solange and Antoine had reached their orgasms together, too carried away to think of stifling their cries.

As she lay back, ready for sleep and enjoying her body's tender release, Louise heard Solange whisper in the dark. 'Sweet dreams, Loulou.'

Louise fell easily into the relaxed rhythm of life at Les Oliviers. Lulled by the calm and the quiet, the brilliant sunlight and the easy living, she gradually began to forget the whole reason for her visit to Provence. Milo had drawn her into his communal lifestyle with seductive ease. Almost all thoughts of life back in England, of university, of her search for *The Venus of Collioure* were suspended. All that mattered was the moment. Louise wanted new experiences, and she sensed that, here at Les Oliviers, they were waiting for her.

Some days she would accompany Antoine on his walk to check the traps he had set for rabbits; on other days she would spend her time with the women, swimming naked in the pool or lying in the shade of the olive trees, talking about nothing in particular. Every few days she would drive with one or other of Milo's models into La-Roche-Hubert to shop at the small daily market there.

There they would choose from the beautifully fresh and succulent vegetables of the region: plump, glossy purply-black aubergines, huge globe artichokes, wild mushrooms, yellow and green courgettes and fat, sweet tomatoes; or purchase fish caught fresh in the Mediterranean early that morning; or select from a crowded selection of smoked meats and sausages and game birds. Louise loved the bustle of the market, and the mixture of smells: ripe cheeses, fresh breads, flowers, the tang of the olives in their vats of brine, the smell of fresh hide on the shoe stall, fresh fruit, and the rich, musty smell of truffles and other fungi. She felt as if all her senses had been sleeping until now, or working on half-power. Milo and his entourage, Les Oliviers and Provence had energised her unlike anything she had ever felt before.

'Loulou. I finished the painting of Isabelle yesterday. I want you to pose for me now,' Milo said one morning over breakfast.

Louise looked up and blushed. Despite her ease and familiarity with everyone in Milo's strange household, she still felt uncomfortable when confronted with the proposition of taking her clothes off for Milo. He had an effect on her that she couldn't rationalise or explain. She felt completely relaxed with the others, and yet she still hadn't managed to fully shake off her reserve with Milo.

'If you are embarrassed, we can do it in my studio, if that would help,' Milo said.

Louise glanced across to the others. They all nodded encouragingly.

'OK,' she said quietly.

Once in the studio, Milo set about propping a new canvas on the easel. 'Take off your clothes, Loulou. I can hardly paint you clothed, now can I? I have my reputation to think of.'

Louise looked around for a screen or somewhere to

shield herself as she unrobed. Now that the possibility of posing for Milo had become an actuality, she was starting to have doubts. To be exposed like that to a man's gaze was one thing; to be painted in such a pose, available for eternity to everyone who saw the painting, was another.

A pang of conscience and guilt came over her, as she thought for the first time in a long while about the reason for her visit here to Les Oliviers. It was not to be painted; it was to find a painting. But she had to do this. Louise had a nagging feeling that, if she refused to pose for him, Milo might renege on his promise to tell her about *The Venus of Collioure*. He had not said as much explicitly, but she did not want to give him any excuse to go back on his agreement.

And so Louise quickly took off her dress and underwear. She folded them neatly, and carefully placed them in a pile on one of the rush-seated chairs – anything to delay the inevitable. She stood before Milo, suddenly very shy indeed, one hand covering her breasts and the other her pubic mound. Despite her various sexual explorations since breaking up with Jonathan, Milo had a curious effect on her, reducing her to a state of nervous confusion. Ridiculous as it seemed, with Milo she felt like a virgin all over again. She thought back to her first evening at Les Oliviers, when she had overheard Milo warning Antoine off her; and yet it hadn't been in order to keep her for himself. Milo had not shown much interest in her. At least, not sexually. He seemed far more interested in her potential as a model than as a lover.

Milo finished arranging the canvas and organising his oils and brushes. He looked up, and clapped his hands on seeing Louise.

'My God, if it isn't my very own Venus, emerging from the waves! The exact same pose as Botticelli's goddess. Extraordinary. But I require you in a different pose, dear Loulou. Lie on the couch, please.'

Louise turned and went over to the couch. Milo came over and stood over her as she settled back among the silken cushions. He looked down at her, and then sat on the edge of the couch next to her.

'Apart from *The Venus of Collioure*, what do you want from your time here, Loulou?' Milo asked.

Louise was pleased that he had mentioned the painting, but wasn't entirely sure what he was getting at.

'You must want something out of life, apart from that mouldy old painting,' he prompted. Louise looked up at Milo, trying to work out why he was teasing her. She was sure that he didn't really think that de Valence's masterpiece was a mouldy old painting.

'Do you have a boyfriend?' Milo asked. Louise shook her head. Tom didn't count.

'Why not? You're beautiful.'

Louise explained about breaking up with Jonathan, but didn't give the full reasons. She thought that 'it wasn't working out' was a sufficient explanation for Milo.

'Why not? Sex?' Milo asked, sharp as a ferret after a rabbit.

Louise's reddening cheeks were enough of an answer for Milo. 'Did he not want enough? Or perhaps he was too demanding?' he asked, a wicked glint in his eye.

Louise snorted at the latter suggestion. 'If only,' she said with a sigh, and then explained all about her problems with Jonathan. She had known that Milo would worm it out of her eventually.

Milo smiled. 'I think you'll find that we'll be able to help you, here at Les Oliviers. Now, to work.'

He explained the pose he wanted her to adopt and, when she had difficulty in achieving exactly what he wanted, he helped by arranging her limbs for her. Placing a hand on either inner thigh, he pushed gently, so that her legs slid apart. He carried on exerting the pressure until her legs were splayed. He looked down at her thoughtfully. She couldn't tell if he liked what he saw, or if he was viewing her with a coolly professional regard.

'You have a pronounced *mons veneris,*' he said. 'I have always loved that phrase, "mound of Venus". It's the part of a woman's body that always draws my eye. I love to see it under the stretched material of a bathing costume or silhouetted by a pair of tight leggings. That beautiful swell, that mound beneath which the secret delights of a woman are hidden.'

Louise reddened some more, and drew her hand over her pubic mound to cover it from Milo's gaze. Milo brushed her hand aside.

'I decide the pose. The pose I want is that which you might adopt should you be inviting your lover to give you cunnilingus.'

Louise blushed furiously at the word but, if Milo had noticed, he gave no hint.

'You want him – or her – right there, right at your very centre. You have to make access as easy as possible. And, to help them, you are preparing yourself, touching yourself.'

Louise blushed yet more.

'Do it,' Milo commanded. 'Touch yourself.'

Louise complied, timidly placing her hand back over her pubic hair. She couldn't refuse Milo.

'No. You know what I mean. Touch yourself.' There was an edge in Milo's voice.

Louise closed her eyes, and brought both hands to her sex. With one hand, she slowly spread the fleshy petals of her lips, exposing the bright pinkness of her inner self to Milo. With the other, she brushed lightly against her clitoris. Despite her discomfort and embarrassment, she knew that doing this, to Milo's command, would have only one outcome. Already she could feel the familiar spreading warmth, the gathering slickness.

'Good. Stay like that. Exactly like that. Don't move.'

Louise groaned inwardly with frustrated desire. If she couldn't move to touch herself more, there was no way she could experience the release she already craved. She lay there, with a hand on either side of her labia, spreading herself open.

She watched as Milo squeezed paint out of tubes, throwing them carelessly over his shoulder when they were empty. He worked furiously, as if he had to capture the moment immediately, before his inspiration disappeared. Every now and then he would step out from behind his canvas and walk up to her, concentrating so hard on her that he was almost squinting. Then he would disappear behind the canvas again, and Louise could see his arm moving rapidly and yet deliberately over the canvas. He knew exactly what he wanted to portray. Periodically, he would take a long draught from the wine bottle standing amid all the paints and brushes.

After twenty minutes or so, Milo stepped out again from behind the easel and walked up to her.

'You're not completely comfortable with this, are you, Loulou? I can tell from your pose: it's stiff; coiled and tense.'

Louise nodded her agreement.

'I can't have that in an erotic painting. Everything must seem fluid, natural, abandoned. I need to loosen you up a bit. One moment.'

Milo disappeared out of the studio door, and Louise could hear him walking back up to the house. A few minutes later she heard him returning. He re-entered the studio, with Colette in tow. Louise felt acutely embarrassed at being caught in such an explicit pose by the Frenchwoman.

'Colette will help you to relax. Now remember everything I said: keep absolutely still. You must not move or alter your pose in any way at all.'

Milo nodded at Colette, who pulled her short summer dress off over her head without a moment's hesitation. She was naked underneath, and Louise's thoughts flashed back to the morning when Colette had helped her with her suntan oil. She vividly remembered the attraction she had felt for the Frenchwoman then.

'Close your eyes, Loulou,' Milo commanded. 'And remember, no movement.'

Louise obeyed. She didn't dare to not comply with Milo; and besides, like a small child that believes it is invisible when its eyes are shut, some of her embarrassment disappeared when she closed her eyes.

Louise heard Colette's light steps nearby, then the couch giving under Colette's weight as she slipped on to it near Louise's feet, and a few moments later she felt the light touch of Colette's fingers on her flesh.

'That's good. I think I'll put you in the painting, too, Colette,' Milo said. 'Position yourself between Loulou's legs.'

Louise could feel Colette's weight against her legs, and then felt the soft teasing strokes of Colette's fingertips as she gently covered Louise's flesh with light caresses. Colette tenderly drifted her fingers over Louise's calves, then her knees, and then higher, to her thighs. Louise tensed when she felt the hot wet dab of Colette's tongue against her leg, just above the knee. She could feel the hot gusts of breath as Colette exhaled through her nose, and this tickled her already sensitive flesh. Louise had to fight hard not to squirm or wriggle in response to these intense sensations. She was waiting for the inevitable: the upward path which she was hoping Colette's mouth would take.

'Good, good,' murmured Milo. Louise could hear the fast strokes of his paintbrush against the canvas, a rough scrubbing sound which seemed to have increased in vigour. 'Relax, Loulou. Remember: eyes closed.'

Louise couldn't have opened her eyes, even if Milo had wanted it. Even though she was enjoying the delicate caresses with which the Frenchwoman was pleasuring her body, Louise felt a sense of shame, and could not look at Colette.

She felt Colette's hands on her inner thighs, one on either side, gently yet unmistakably pushing her legs yet further apart. Then she felt the soft brush of Colette's silken hair against her thighs, as the Frenchwoman lowered her mouth on to Louise's sex. Louise had to fight the urge to thrust her pelvis up off the couch to bring her closer to the soft, wondrous mouth that was exploring her innermost places so expertly.

Colette kissed her way across the auburn curls of Louise's pubic hair, and down one side of her reddened and swollen sex, teasing her. She slid her tongue up the length of Louise's outer lips, and then across and in, moving down the side of Louise's inner rim with a single, sweeping movement. Louise wanted to tilt her pelvis slightly, to bring Colette's mouth right on to her sex, but resisted, fearful of Milo's wrath should she disobey him.

Colette sensed her frustration, and plunged her tongue into Louise's moist opening with a sudden movement. Colette's tongue was long and amazingly agile, and Louise knew that it would not take much more of this to bring her to an orgasm. Her clitoris had hardened into a tight bud, and she willed Colette to switch her attentions to this tenderest place.

'Excellent,' said Milo, his paintbrush scuffing on the canvas with a furious intensity. Louise almost called out as Colette raised her head and took her clitoris in between her teeth, then playfully rolled it between her lips. She then started to lick Louise there in slow, deliberate strokes. Louise was lost, in both the physical sensations that she was experiencing, and the mental stimulation created by this new and overwhelming experience. Colette clearly understood how to bring another woman to orgasm. She was better than any male lover Louise had known; and Louise's orgasm racked her body with a jolting surge. She thrust her pelvis up off the couch, forcing Colette's head up with it. Louise called out, lost in her pleasure. Milo paused, and smiled, before continuing with his work.

'Milo? Milo?' Louise wandered down to the river, calling for Milo. She had been at the farmhouse for almost three weeks now, and still Milo had told her nothing about *The Venus of Collioure*. At first she had been unconcerned by his lack of response, as she was so taken by her new life and her new friends, but now she was feeling guilty that she had neglected her research for so long. Louise felt that now she must single-mindedly dedicate herself to it, ignoring all other diversions and temptations. She had waited, half-hoping that Milo would tell her about the painting of his own volition, but it had proved a forlorn hope. He was going to need a bit of prompting.

And so she decided that today she would ask him directly. After all, her time was limited. So was her money, but that had not proved to be the pressing concern that she had at first feared it might. Milo had refused to take any money from her for her food and lodgings, saying that by posing for him she had more than adequately paid her way. He had completed the portrait of her the previous day.

'Milo?' she called again. She heard a rustling in the undergrowth, and turned towards the noise. Solange emerged from the green bower beneath a tree, holding a book in her hand.

'He's not here,' Solange said.

'Do you know where he is?' Louise asked. Solange shook her head.

Louise went back to the house. There, Antoine was helping Isabelle hang some washing on the line strung between two of the olive trees; and Colette was sitting on the step of the kitchen door, peeling a fig. Louise looked round. The Citroën van was not in its usual parking place in the shade of one of the fig trees.

'Where's Milo gone?' Louise was answered by blank looks and shrugged shoulders. 'Do you know when he'll be back?' she asked.

Isabelle turned from her pegging on the washing line. 'It's anyone's guess. Sometimes he goes for a day; sometimes he's gone for weeks at a time.'

'Doesn't he tell you where he's going?' Louise asked.

'No.'

'Don't you think to ask?'

'No. It's not our business.'

'What does he do?'

'Sells his paintings, sees a lover, visits some friends? Who knows?'

Louise was exasperated, but not surprised. She had soon come to learn that Milo was impulsive and quixotic, and that he operated by his own rules.

'But he's left you stranded here,' Louise said. 'Or at least, you would be, if it wasn't for my camper van.'

'There you have it,' said Antoine with a grin. 'So we're not stranded after all.'

'But what would you do if I wasn't here with a vehicle?' she asked.

Antoine shrugged unconcernedly. 'What we normally do in these circumstances. Walk. Hitch a lift. Whatever.'

'All the way to La-Roche-Hubert?' asked Louise.

'It's not a problem. Besides, what's the rush?'

Louise knew that Antoine had a point. The pace of life here at Les Oliviers was so slow that what did it matter if it took two days to fetch the shopping?

Chapter Seven

Another week had passed, and Milo had still not returned to Les Oliviers. Louise was fretting. She felt that she was caught in a tricky predicament. She was Milo's guest, and so could not demand too much of him; on the other hand, she felt that, if she didn't demand, she would never get what she wanted out of him.

In her frustration at Milo's absence, she decided to take the opportunity of looking through his things in the house and in his studio, to see if she could find any clues to the whereabouts of *The Venus of Collioure*, if not the painting itself. She had brief pangs of guilt over whether she ought to be doing this, as it was abusing Milo's hospitality, but she quickly overrode such notions. She was sure that Milo would have no such qualms, were he in a similar situation.

Louise checked to see where the others were. Isabelle and Colette were down by the river and, from the soft calls and cries that were emanating from that direction, she figured that they were too busy with each other to bother her while she was searching. Solange was reading in the shade of the vine canopy by the kitchen, and earlier that day Antoine had said something about fixing some of the broken shutters on the house. Louise guessed that the coast was clear enough.

She started her search in Milo's studio, which, like the house itself, was never locked. She went over to the pile of canvases leaning against the wall and flicked through them quickly. Even though she had half-expected it, she was still disappointed to find that *The Venus* was not there. She looked through Milo's canvases again, taking longer to study each painting this time. She paused at one of Antoine. Unlike Milo's three female models, who regularly wandered around in the nude, Louise had not seen Antoine naked – apart from that moonlit night in the bedroom with Solange.

In Milo's painting, Antoine was lying on the large flat-topped boulder by the river that Louise knew so well. His hands were thrown above his head, and his head was turned to one side. His eyes were closed, as if he was sleeping, and Louise admired his fine profile once more. His long brown limbs were stretched out, his thighs close together and his feet crossed at the ankles. Louise's eyes were drawn to the centre of the painting, a focal point in more ways than one. Antoine was sporting an impressive erection hard up against his stomach, with the tip of his prick obscuring his belly button.

It was only on a closer inspection that Louise noticed that Antoine's wrists and ankles were bound. That put an entirely different complexion on the painting. Whereas before she had seen a man stretching like a cat in the warmth, enjoying the heat of the sun on his fine body, now she saw a powerless victim, awaiting a fate which nonetheless aroused him. Or perhaps he had been aroused against his will?

'Do you like it?' a voice asked. Louise turned. There, in the doorway of the studio, was Antoine. He was holding a hammer and was smiling at her.

'Um, yes. One for the ladies, I suppose,' Louise laughed.

Antoine laughed too. 'Or the gentlemen.'

'Oh, yes.' Louise blushed, feeling stupid. Of course Milo's erotica was for everyone, straights and gays; and not just aimed at male heterosexuals, as she had unthinkingly assumed until now.

'Do you like the pose?' Antoine asked, coming into the studio and putting the hammer down on Milo's table.

Louise nodded. The pose showed Antoine's magnificent body to its full advantage, and was certainly powerfully erotic. The dampness that Louise was feeling between her legs was confirmation of that.

'Milo put me in it. The ropes were his idea. He likes to experiment.'

Realisation slowly dawned on Louise. Of all the combinations of couplings possible here at Les Oliviers, it had never occurred to her that Milo and Antoine might be lovers, but now it seemed so obvious. Antoine confirmed it.

'It didn't take much for me to get that monster hard-on. Milo stood there at his easel, painting away and telling me what he was going to do to me after he'd finished.' Antoine laughed. 'I guess he's what you could call a prick-tease.'

'And what did he do to you?' Louise asked. She didn't have much idea of what men might do together.

'Maybe we'll show you, one day,' Antoine teased, stepping up to her and taking one of her auburn locks in his hand, laying it on his palm and inspecting it as he spoke. 'But isn't it more fun to do than to watch? Surely you must think that, after that night with me and Solange?'

Louise shifted uncomfortably. She knew that Solange had known she had been awake, but thought that it had escaped Antoine's notice. Obviously not.

Antoine advanced towards her some more, and she automatically took a step back. She felt the canvases pressing against her buttocks. Antoine came closer again, and put an arm up against the wall on either side of her, penning her in.

'Milo said I shouldn't do this, but Milo isn't here. Besides, you want it, don't you?'

Louise looked at Antoine, her pulse racing. She couldn't deny it. He had a powerful physicality which she found irresistible. Knowing that Milo had banned Antoine from making a pass at her only made this moment more delicious. She wasn't going to risk annoying Milo and jeopardising her research by flirting with Antoine; but if Antoine was to seduce her, what could she do?

Antoine bent forward to kiss her neck, and at the same time pressed himself against her. She could feel he was hard.

'He's back, he's back!'

Louise started with surprise at the shrill cry. She could hear Solange calling excitedly from up at the house. Antoine turned, and Louise slipped out from under his arms and went to the studio window. She saw the green Citroën van coming down the rough track, a tall plume of dust rising in the still air behind it. She looked at Antoine and grinned.

'Another time,' he said, shrugging his shoulders.

Together Louise and Antoine hurried up from the studio, just as the van was pulling up under the fig tree. Louise paused in the shade of the vine canopy, and watched as Milo got out of the van, scratching his head. Solange ran to him and flung her arms around him. She was swiftly followed by Isabelle and then Colette. Antoine strode up to shake Milo's hand.

'Hey, what's all the fuss?' asked Milo, pretending to be bemused by the rapturous reception he was receiving.

'We're just so happy to have you back,' said Colette, squeezing his hand.

'Anyone would think that I've been away for years,' he said, laughing. He glanced up and saw Louise standing at some distance.

'Aren't you going to come and say hello, Loulou?' Milo asked.

Louise walked slowly up to him and pecked him on the cheek, feeling mixed emotions. She was pleased Milo was back: now maybe she could get somewhere with her work. She was vaguely resentful as his return meant that now nothing more was likely to happen between her and Antoine, just as things between them had started to get interesting. And she was also angry with Milo. He had been gone for a week. He could have told her. And yet . . . She was his guest, and she was in no position to dictate what he could or couldn't do. She couldn't prevent him from gadding off for a week's jaunt, and she couldn't order him to show her *The Venus*. Louise knew she was completely impotent in these matters, and it infuriated her.

'I've brought you all back some presents,' Milo said, going round to the back of the van. 'I bought them with my winnings. They don't know how to play poker in Marseille.'

'You mean they don't know how to cheat as well as you,' Colette teased. Milo laughed and winked at her.

Squealing with excitement, the three Frenchwomen clustered around Milo to see what he had brought them. Louise wandered off. She knew that if she hung around, she might say something that she would later regret.

Some time later she became aware of a soft footfall behind her. She put down her handful of pebbles and turned around. It was Milo, barefoot as usual.

'I thought that I might find you here,' he said, sitting down next to her on the boulder.

She picked up the pebbles again and began to throw

them one by one into the deep pool. Her annoyance and frustration were signalled by the sharp jerks of her wrist as she propelled the stones towards the water.

'You didn't stay for your present.'

Louise said nothing. She knew that she was being churlish, but couldn't stop herself.

'Why are you cross with me, Loulou?' Milo asked. He seemed truly perplexed by Louise's behaviour.

'Oh Milo, isn't it obvious? I've been here for four weeks now, and you still haven't told me anything about *The Venus of Collioure*. Not a thing. I've only got a couple of months or so in France to do my research, and then I've got to go back to university.'

'Oh, Loulou, I'm sorry. It was very thoughtless of me. Mind you, I do believe that I told you that it would take some time ... But no, you are right. Four weeks is far too long.'

'So?' said Louise expectantly. 'Are you going to tell me?'

'Tomorrow,' said Milo.

'Oh, bloody hell,' said Louise, angrily throwing the rest of the pebbles into the pool and getting up. 'You're doing it again. Fobbing me off.'

Milo hurried up beside her, and held her arm to still her. 'I promise. Tomorrow I'll show you something special. It'll be a long drive, so we'll have to get up early. Monsieur Mauron in La-Roche-Hubert has agreed to lend me his car for the day. It's a smart new Peugeot and will get us there in about half the time it would take in my clapped-out old van.'

Louise was momentarily lost for words. This meant that Milo hadn't forgotten, if he had already arranged this trip in advance. She felt guilty for having judged him so peremptorily. Where was he going to take her? And what was the 'something special'? She barely dared hope that it might be her Venus.

Milo pulled her round to face him. 'Did you miss me?' he asked.

'Yes,' she said. There didn't seem much point in denying the truth. She couldn't deny how attractive he was, despite her annoyance with him about his prevarication over the painting.

'I missed you, too,' Milo whispered.

Louise was about to lean forward to kiss him, but Milo turned from her, distracted by shouts from up at the house. He slapped Louise playfully on the bottom.

'Come on. Let's go and see the others.'

Milo woke Louise at four o'clock the next morning. Bleary-eyed, she struggled from her bed and threw on some clothes. Colette and Antoine barely stirred beside her. Louise came down to the kitchen, where Milo had already got the fire on the range going. He handed her a bowl of coffee and told her to drink it quickly. As she sipped at the coffee, Milo busied himself with putting some bread, fruit and cheese into a paper bag. He saw that Louise was watching him. 'We shan't have time to stop for food on the way,' he explained. Milo still hadn't told her where they were going, and Louise was intrigued.

He went out to the van. Through the open door Louise could see that it was still dark outside. She shrugged, picked up her bag and followed Milo.

'You may want to take your cameras and notepads,' he said. Louise felt sure that his reminder could mean only one thing: they were off to see *The Venus*. She was also grateful that he had thought to remind her, for in her dopey sleeplike state she might easily have left them behind. She hauled the heavy stuffer bag out of her van and transferred it to Milo's vehicle. It was the first time she had touched her research material since the day she had packed the camper van with Liz. She had been so seduced by the indolence of Les Oliviers that she had not even thought to look at her notes.

They got to La-Roche-Hubert as dawn was breaking. Milo parked the van in a lane just off the village square, and together they walked through the silent lanes to Monsieur Mauron's house. All the lights were out, and the Peugeot was parked outside. Milo fished around on the top of the tyre of the nearside back wheel, and whispered a triumphant, 'Yes,' as he pulled out the set of keys that were hidden there.

'Thanks, Henri,' Milo muttered as he started the car up and they pulled away smoothly.

Their progress was initially very slow. Then the winding single-track country lanes gave way to larger roads, and those in turn gave way to high-speed dual carriageways. Past Aix-en-Provence, they got on the *péage*, and the Peugeot made short work of the miles. Louise admired the way that Milo handled the car. He drove at high speed, but not aggressively or dangerously; and he controlled the machine with a fluid, confident ease. Louise had never before thought that she might find the way someone drove a car to be sexy. Each time Milo reached out for the gearstick she hoped he might overshoot and touch her instead; but he never did.

Louise watched as road signs for Nîmes and later Montpellier flashed past. From her basic knowledge of French geography, she knew that they were heading southwestward, skirting the Mediterranean coast. Some time later, they passed signs for Perpignan and Spain. Still Milo would not tell Louise where they were headed, but she had already guessed. It could only be one place.

At Perpignan they came off the *péage* and headed for the coast road, moving yet further south, into the sun. Louise searched for the name she was hoping to see on all the road signs, until at last there it was: Collioure. They were heading for the small seaside port where

Gustave de Valence and the other Fauves had made their base all those years ago.

They finally arrived in the late morning. Louise felt a thrill of anticipation. Below her were the red roofs of the town, and Louise could see the glittering azure blue of the Mediterranean beyond. Milo followed the steep road down into the town, and drove through the narrow streets and then into cobbled lanes which were barely wide enough to allow the car to pass. Their progress was slowed by the number of tourists milling about, and Louise realised that the narrow lanes were pedestrianised.

'Milo, I don't think we should be driving down here,' she said nervously.

'Nonsense. I've always come this way,' he said blithely; and continued to proceed, ignoring the scowls of the people who were forced to press themselves into doorways to avoid being run over.

They eventually emerged by a row of four-storey houses facing the sea, each one painted in bright colours with contrasting shutters. Milo pulled into a side street, through a pair of high metal gates and into a courtyard.

'Here we are,' he announced, sitting back and stretching in the seat. From La-Roche-Hubert, they had been driving non-stop for five hours.

'Where are we? Apart from "in Collioure", I mean,' asked Louise.

'You'll see,' said Milo, leading her through a door which opened out on to the courtyard. They were in some kind of back room, full of storage boxes and old pieces of furniture. Milo led her through a maze of warren-like corridors until they came into a small hallway. Display panels were ranged around the walls of the hallway, and each was headed with the legend: "Gustave de Valence Museum".

Louise couldn't help feel a slight pang of disappointment: she had been hoping almost until the last minute that Milo was taking her to see *The Venus of Collioure*. She already knew from her research that the museum housed some of de Valence's lesser works, but that was all. She was still no closer to his missing masterpiece.

A uniformed man came through from another room. He was carrying a roll of tickets. He broke into a broad smile when he saw Milo, and put the tickets away in his pocket.

'Ah, Monsieur Charpentier. How delightful to see you again.'

'Hello, Georges. May I introduce my good friend Loulou? She has come all the way from England specifically to study Gustave de Valence.'

'Pleased to meet you, mademoiselle,' Georges said as he shook Louise's hand. He gestured them both through to the room from which he had just emerged.

'I'll leave you to it,' he said. 'You don't need me to show you around.'

Milo placed his hand in the small of Louise's back and guided her into the room.

'Here you are: your shangri-la. This is Gustave de Valence's studio, left exactly as it was on his death in 1929.'

Louise looked around her. She was surprised to see that the walls were wallpapered. This homely touch seemed oddly unexpected and out of place in an artist's studio. The floorboards were bare and spattered with paint, and Louise noted that the paint was still brilliantly coloured after almost a century. Two huge windows opened from the floor to the ceiling, and the shimmering reflected light poured into the room.

Just like Milo's studio, a stack of canvases leant against one of the walls. Other framed paintings were displayed on the walls. In the middle of the room, a large canvas stood on an easel. It had been de Valence's work-in-progress when he had died. Louise went up to it and studied it carefully. It was a portrait of a man sitting in an armchair, and it was unfinished. It would give her valuable clues about de Valence's later working techniques, after he had moved on from his experiment with Fauvist theories. She could still see the boldly drawn pencil outline of part of the composition; elsewhere the first layers of paint had been applied. A couple of small preparatory sketches in oils were propped against the base of the easel.

The armchair shown on the canvas faced the easel on the other side of the room. Next to the easel was a low table with tubes of oil paint, spatulas and knives, rags and bottles of turpentine, and a palette bearing dried, crusted squirts of oil paint. Hundreds of different-sized paintbrushes lay on the table, in pots on the floor and jumbled together in boxes. A single rush-seated chair stood against the wall behind the easel. Louise wondered if this was where de Valence would sit back and appraise his work. There was a newspaper on the chair. Louise picked it up to see what the headlines had been in July, 1929; but felt foolish when she saw that it was that day's issue. Moments later, the custodian came into the room, and picked up his newspaper.

'Can I take some photographs?' Louise asked him. He looked at Milo, and then nodded. 'Normally we would not permit it, mademoiselle; but considering this is a special visit, we'll make an exception.'

How kind, thought Louise. She borrowed the car keys off Milo, and went and fetched her stuffer bag. When she returned, Milo was chatting and joking with the custodian.

'I'll leave you to conduct your work in peace,' said Milo. 'I'll be back at lunchtime, and we can go and get something to eat. You can carry on after that for as long as it takes. I'm in no hurry.'

He smiled and left, as Louise busied herself with setting up her photographic equipment. Despite her disappointment at not seeing *The Venus*, she reminded herself that her dissertation encompassed Gustave de Valence's life. What better place to start her work than in his studio?

Louise finished the last of her notes at about half-past three. Milo had popped back at lunchtime, but Louise had been too engrossed in her work to break for food. She hadn't had anything to eat since some fruit at about ten that morning, but she was too busy to feel hungry.

She packed up all her equipment into the stuffer bag, and carried it back to the car. She went back inside to find Georges to thank him for all his help, and asked if he knew where Milo was.

'You might try the Hostelerie des Templiers, just around the corner by the quay.'

Louise smiled. Of course. She might have guessed that Milo would be in a bar. She walked out of the museum and into the glaring sunlight. Below her was the small pebbly beach, and to her left was a church which jutted right out into the water on a promontory. Its bell-tower was curiously bullet-shaped, and Louise remembered that Milo had said that it had been converted from a lighthouse. Louise grinned and wondered whether it was sacrilegious to think that the round tower looked decidedly phallic, complete with pink-domed roof.

To her right, she could see out across to the small harbour, and beyond the harbour stood a huge fortress with high and imposing stone walls. She followed the road round to the harbour, and as she approached she looked down on to the brightly coloured fishing boats which bobbed gently up and down on the swell, and saw shoals of small fish swimming in the clear water. She could see the tables shaded by umbrellas outside the Hostelerie des Templiers.

Entering the bar, Louise looked about, searching for Milo. She saw him sitting at a table in a corner, reading a paper. A glass of pastis and a small jug of water sat in front of him, and next to them lay an open sketch pad and a box of pastels.

'Hello,' said Louise. Milo looked up and smiled.

'Successful day's work?' he asked.

'Very,' she said, plonking herself down next to him and pulling round the sketch pad to have a better look. Milo had drawn a quick and fluid sketch of the harbour scene.

'I didn't think you'd be working today,' she said.

'Needs must,' he replied. A waiter approached, and Louise asked for a coffee and an omelette. Milo sighed, and reached for the pad. 'I'd better do another one.'

Louise wasn't sure what he meant; and as Milo busied himself with a quick sketch of the interior of the bar, Louise looked about her. The walls were covered with paintings, sketches, and drawings of all kinds and all sizes. When the waiter returned with Louise's food, Milo tore off the two sketches and handed them to him.

'The patron says it's OK,' he reassured the waiter.

Louise looked at Milo quizzically.

'I'm just following a long and honoured tradition,' he explained with a smile. 'A painting in exchange for a drink.'

Later, they walked out along the jetty that curved out into the sea and formed part of the harbour wall. Milo didn't seem particularly interested in the view until he pointed out two topless girls in a pedalo. The water was unbelievably clear, and Louise had the sudden urge to strip all her clothes off and dive into the water. However, she reckoned that genteel Collioure didn't seem quite ready for naturist bathing, and so she refrained. The heat of the sun and the semi-naked bodies parading about were certainly arousing, and she told Milo as much. He laughed.

'Come with me.' They walked back along the jetty to where the boats were tethered. Milo got on his knees and reached down to one of the boats. He undid a small length of the canvas cover which was stretched over the boat, flipped it back and then hopped down into the boat. He held his hand out to Louise.

'Milo, what are you doing?'

'Come on,' he repeated.

'We can't,' Louise said lamely.

'Who says? Now stop being so British and get in.'

At this jibe, Louise hopped down from the quayside into the boat, hoping that the owners were not about. Milo had already crawled under the canvas. Louise bobbed down and peered in. There was a space about four feet high under the cover, and Milo was arranging another canvas sheet on the wooden ribs of the boat. He beckoned her in, and she crawled under the canvas and joined him. A breeze was now blowing in from the sea, causing the boat to rock gently from side to side. Louise could hear the watery slapping of the waves against the hull. Despite the breeze, it was stifling and airless under the cover, and very hot.

'Remember you told me a while ago that you wanted to try new things?' asked Milo with a roguish smile. 'Well, how about sex, with me, on a boat?'

With that, he stripped off his shirt. Louise started to demur, but the sight of Milo's fine body as he unzipped his trousers and shuffled out of them made her stop in mid-breath. She found it hard to believe that someone who led such a dissolute lifestyle, always drinking and smoking and eating too much, could have such a fit and toned body. As far as she knew, the only exercise that Milo ever got was between the sheets. But then again, she also knew that sex was no occasional occurrence, as far as Milo was concerned. She had heard him often enough; and other times he had crept into the bed beside her to make love to one or other of his voluptuous models. Louise smiled with pleasure. Even after watching her with Colette in his studio, Milo had not shown any obvious sexual interest in her, and so she had simply assumed that she wasn't his type. But now, his burgeoning erection as he tugged off his trousers from over his ankles confirmed the opposite very clearly.

Naked, he lay back on the canvas and put his hands behind his head. 'I'm all yours,' he said.

Louise looked down at Milo, naked and prone beneath her. She had a sudden idea, prompted by the memory of Milo's portrait of Antoine and by the coil of rope next to her knees. She laughed, and whispered to him, 'I knew my Girl Guide training would come in handy one day.'

With that, she picked up the rope and lashed it around Milo's wrists. He looked on without complaint, and Louise was gratified to see his erection growing visibly. The kinky devil, she thought to herself. Then another sequence of thoughts crossed her mind: Maybe I'll leave him tied up until he tells me where *The Venus* is, or maybe I'll just have to force the information out of him . . .

She looked around the boat, wondering what she could threaten Milo with. She didn't mean him any harm, but he wouldn't know that. She saw a weathered wooden float for a fishing net, and picked it up.

'If you don't tell me where *The Venus of Collioure* is, I shall hit you with this,' she said, trying to summon up as much menace as she could.

'Go ahead,' he replied, a smile playing on his lips.

This annoyed Louise: it wasn't the reaction she expected or wanted. She figured that she didn't make a very convincing sadist, and decided to try a different tack. She bent down and slowly straddled Milo so that she was kneeling over him just above his knees. She undid the buttons down the front of her dress, one by one. Then she seductively slipped her dress off her shoulders. Under her dress she was wearing a lacy short-sleeved body. She wriggled her way out of the body, brushing against Milo every now and then. She watched with pleasure as this private striptease had an even greater effect on him. His penis was now fully erect, twitching and jerking.

'Touch it,' Milo commanded, but Louise was in control now. She smiled and shook her head.

His arousal heightened her own. She felt in the pocket of her discarded dress for her hanky, unused and still folded into a neatly ironed square. Holding it in one hand, she slid herself forward over his thighs until she was positioned over his prick. She then moved back and forth, lightly brushing her moistening sex over the tip of Milo's prick, and every time he lunged his hips upwards to try to drive his cock into her, she moved back out of his range. She could see how frustrated this was making him: all the better.

After teasing Milo like this for a few minutes, Louise finally crouched over him and, holding his penis by the base of the shaft, guided him into her as she sank down on to him. Milo moaned. She knelt forward over him, so that her breasts drifted across his chest. He responded by bending his legs at the knee. As he couldn't hold her and pull her down on to him, this movement allowed him to drive deeper into her.

This was also the movement that Louise had been waiting for. Milo's buttocks were now thrusting up off the floor of the boat, and he was taking her weight as well as his own on the soles of his feet and on his back. Louise reached down behind her, feeling the rooty swell at the base of his cock, and then the skin of his perineum, before her searching fingers came across their target: his tightly closed anus. She shook the hanky loose in her hand, and then gathered it over a finger. She inserted this finger past the taut muscle of his sphincter, all the time gently pushing and bunching up the hanky, feeding it up into him.

Milo's eyes opened wide with surprise, but he said nothing. It seemed to have a striking effect on him, as his thrusting became more urgent. Louise carefully and tenderly pushed the square of fine linen into him until it had all but disappeared, and just a small corner remained outside him. Milo licked his lips, and his breathing quickened. She knew the rush towards his orgasm had begun. As he started the final shuddering contractions, she deftly pulled the hanky free from within him. Milo roared as this extra stimulus powered him towards a massive, debilitating orgasm. She smiled with satisfaction and, working herself up and down on Milo's still-erect cock, brought herself to her climax. Then she flopped forwards on to him, and they lay still, holding each other and recovering from their love-making.

'I would never have expected that of you,' Milo said finally, when he had gathered himself sufficiently.

'It just goes to show how deceptive appearances can be,' she replied with a sweet smile. 'Now, are you going to tell me where *The Venus* is?'

Milo laughed. 'You won't get it out of me that easily.' He looked down at the discarded hanky, and laughed some more. 'I'll rephrase that: you won't get the whereabouts of *The Venus of Collioure* out of me that easily.'

'And here we have one of the finest views in Collioure.' A man's voice, loud and penetrating, interrupted Milo and Louise before she could question him any further. Louise looked down at Milo, and could barely suppress her giggles. The voice was getting closer and closer; and was accompanied by shuffling footsteps, and a few coughs; and then the tour group stopped right by their boat. Mercifully the tarpaulin just about protected Louise and Milo from view. Beneath her, Milo too was shaking with stifled laughter.

'If we pause here for a moment, we can appreciate the full splendour of the Château Royal, once the summer residence of the Kings of Majorca.'

Looking up behind her, Louise could see the feet of

the tour leader as he pointed out the finer architectural details of the château across the harbour. She hoped that no one could hear their stifled sniggers.

Louise and Milo got back to La-Roche-Hubert at just after eleven that night. Milo parked the car next to his van.

'Wouldn't it be better to park it back where we borrowed it from, outside Monsieur Mauron's house?' Louise asked.

'No, Henri won't mind,' said Milo as he opened the passenger door and helped Louise out of the car. Then he stooped and put the keys back in their hiding place under the wheel arch.

'I'd like to thank Monsieur Mauron personally,' said Louise. 'It was so kind of him to lend us the car.'

'Oh, that won't be necessary,' said Milo. 'Besides, he goes to bed very early and won't like it if we disturbed him.'

'Perhaps I could come with you to La-Roche-Hubert next time, to thank him?' Louise asked. Milo nodded and helped her bundle her stuffer bag into his van. He seemed preoccupied. As they drove off, Louise thought she could hear what sounded like shouting behind them. It was difficult to tell over the noise of the engine. She turned to see a figure chasing after the van. The man had his arms raised above his head, and was looking very agitated. Louise thought she heard the word 'Thief'. She looked at Milo.

'Don't you think that we ought to stop?' she asked.

'No. Not until he's cooled off,' said Milo.

'What? You mean that –'

'Was Monsieur Mauron? Maybe.'

'So he didn't offer to lend you his car after all? Milo, that's terrible.'

'Well, it was only for a day. The silly old fool hardly ever uses his car; it's more a status symbol for him. Just think, it would have just sat there outside his house, with the cats walking all over it and the dogs peeing against it, the local youths leaning against it and the birds shitting on it; and all the time the battery would be going flat and the brakes would be seizing. We put it to far better use, and recharged the battery for him in the process. He should thank us.'

'Oh, Milo, you are incorrigible,' Louise said laughingly.

'Loulou, I want to sleep with you tonight,' Isabelle said to Louise matter-of-factly as they were all seated around the kitchen table eating their meal a few nights later. Louise almost choked on her wine. No one else seemed to register anything out of the usual. Louise wondered if Colette had told Isabelle about the events in the studio.

Later that evening, after the meal, the coffees and the brandy, Louise allowed Isabelle to lead her up to bed. She had decided that it was time that she fully experienced lovemaking with another woman. The encounter with Colette had whetted her appetite, and she was keen to learn more. Isabelle took her into the far bedroom, where the three mattresses lay pushed together on the floor. Isabelle closed the door behind them, and went over to the clump of candles standing on the floor on one side of the bed, and lit them one by one. Louise noticed that they were stuck to the bare floorboards with gobbets of solidified wax.

Then Isabelle sat down and patted the mattress next to her. Louise obediently went over and sat by her. Her heart was in her mouth, wondering what would happen next. She was too tense and too uncertain to make a move; and besides, she wasn't sure how to.

Isabelle put her hand up and tenderly stroked Louise's hair. Her hand slid round to the back of Louise's head, and she cupped it, drawing Louise's face towards her own. Louise's lips parted in anticipation and desire. She had never kissed a woman before, although she had often wanted to. Only a few inches away from her, Isabelle paused and looked at her with a teasing smile, as if she sensed what it was that Louise wanted.

Louise's heart pounded as Isabelle lowered her lips on to her own. Louise did nothing at first, simply feeling the plump, sweet softness of Isabelle's lips. Then she began to respond, replying to Isabelle's tender, brushing kisses with her own. She raised her arms, which had been paralysed by her side, and felt for Isabelle's hair, her head, her back, her shoulders. As she drew the Frenchwoman closer still, their kisses became longer and more passionate. Louise opened her mouth a little, and gently explored Isabelle's lips and her teeth and her soft, wet tongue.

Louise thought that there was something intoxicating about this. The smell of a woman's body was so different from that of a man, but just as powerfully attractive. The two women broke from their kisses, and regarded each other wordlessly. Then Isabelle took Louise's hand, and began to kiss the palm, then nibble and kiss each finger in turn. Next she licked the tender flesh between each finger, giving Louise goose bumps. Then Isabelle drew Louise's hand downward, and placed it on her neck. Louise could feel the warmth of the other woman's flesh, and could feel the rapid rise and fall of her breathing. Isabelle pinioned Louise's hand under her own for a moment, letting her feel her heartbeat; and then Isabelle withdrew her hand, leaving Louise's where it was.

Louise understood this signal. Isabelle's invitation was unambiguous. She paused for a moment, and then slowly slid her hand down over the cotton of Isabelle's blouse. She could feel the hard ridges of her ribs under her fingers, and then the soft plump fleshiness that marked the rise of Isabelle's breast. Louise slid her hand lower, and her fingers grazed the hard point of Isabelle's nipple. She drew away, but Isabelle pressed her hand back on to her breast. She looked at Louise and nodded, and Louise could see the desire in the Frenchwoman's face. Her pupils were dilated, her lips were parted, and her breathing was becoming more rapid.

Louise spread her fingers, taking the full weight of Isabelle's breast in her hand. It was too much, too sensual, and, without thinking, she brought her other hand up to cup Isabelle's other breast through the material. The two women kissed once more, their lips desperately searching, and Louise forced Isabelle back on to the bed and hurriedly pushed up her blouse so that her breasts were fully exposed. Louise broke from their kisses to take a hard brown nipple in her mouth, feeling the plump softness of Isabelle's other breast in her hand.

From there, Louise explored every inch of the Frenchwoman's body: skimming her fingers over Isabelle's skin and softly stroking her, licking and kissing her body to taste the salty tang, gently opening her up and learning how to make another woman respond to her soft caresses. Louise needed no tuition. It came as naturally to her as lovemaking with a man; and she had the instinctive knowledge of what it was that Isabelle needed to achieve complete gratification. Louise became rapacious, greedily devouring the other woman's body, gaining pleasure from giving so much pleasure.

Through the night, the two women brought each other to new heights of sensual delight. They would doze off in a satiated sleep, before reawakening and beginning the slow, intricate business of loving each other all over again. In the other room, spurred on by the moans and sighs coming through the walls, Solange and Colette mirrored their actions, while Antoine and Milo lay nearby, looking on. Milo smiled with satisfaction, thinking how much Loulou had changed since they had first met not much more than a month ago, and how quickly she had learnt.

* * *

Days drifted by and, despite their trip to Collioure, Milo seemed no more inclined to tell Louise his secret than he had ever been. Louise wandered down to the studio, where Milo was preparing a canvas. She stood next to him, watching as he worked quickly and dextrously, stretching a length of linen over a board and pinning it down. Once he had fixed the material, he primed it with some white paint, slapping on the viscous liquid with fast strokes of a wide brush. She finally summoned up the courage to broach the subject which was dominating all her thoughts.

'Milo. I don't think I properly thanked you for taking me to Collioure and showing me Gustave's studio. It had a great effect on me. I felt so close to him, and it was so exciting to think that that was the very place where he worked, where he painted *The Venus*. But please forgive me. I need to know more. The information I collected with you on that trip was extremely valuable to me, but you still haven't answered my most important question. That question is the main reason why I came here.'

Milo looked up at Louise, and paused. He sucked thoughtfully on the end of his paintbrush.

'Ask me it again,' he said.

Louise took a deep breath. 'Do you know where *The Venus of Collioure* is?' she asked. She couldn't look at him. She so wanted him to say yes, but was so afraid that he would say no.

After a pause that seemed to last for ever, Milo spoke. 'When you first asked me that question, I didn't know you, and I didn't know whether I could trust you. I wasn't sure what your true motivation was in seeking out *The Venus of Collioure*. But now that I've come to know you, I've learnt of your genuine interest in, and I might even say love for, this painting. But I must make a few things clear before I tell you anything. You may use this information in your dissertation, but you must not reveal your sources. You must not name names, or places. I hope that you will come to understand why this has to be so.'

Louise was on tenterhooks. Milo did know. He had to know. Why else would he be talking like this?

'So, Loulou, your question is: Do I know where *The Venus of Collioure* is? And my answer is: yes and no.'

Louise looked at Milo in puzzlement. She was somewhat flummoxed by his seemingly nonsensical reply.

'Let me explain,' said Milo. 'You might want to make yourself comfortable. This could take some time. You asked at the time why it was that the custodian of the Gustave de Valence Museum knew me so well. I was only telling you the partial truth when I said that it was because I am a frequent visitor there. The main reason is that I am one of the trustees of the museum.'

'I'm impressed,' said Louise. It was undoubtedly an honour. She thought that maybe the board of trustees or whoever it was who ran the museum had decided that it would be a good move to have an artist as a trustee.

As if reading her thoughts, Milo said, 'You might be wondering why I hold such a position. Well, it's because I am Gustave de Valence's great-grandson.'

Louise reeled, as if she had been struck a hard body blow. Milo – de Valence's great-grandson? All the time, he had been keeping this critical piece of information from her, stringing her along.

'What?' was all that she could mutter in her shock. Milo led her over to the couch and gently pushed her down on to it.

'Time for a little history lesson. Gustave was born in 1880, and died in 1929 of tuberculosis. It is generally accepted that he was at his artistic prime between the years 1900 and 1910. He painted *The Venus of Collioure* in 1905, with Estelle Gachet as the model. As you may know, he had a passionate and long-lived affair with Estelle. What is not so commonly known is that they had a child, a baby boy, in 1910. That boy, their only child, was my grandfather. He grew up, married, and he too had an only child: my mother. She was born in 1942, and married Raoul Charpentier in 1963. I was born in 1965, and I too am an only child. My parents both died in a car crash, ten years ago. So that makes me the only living descendant of Gustave de Valence.'

'But . . .' Questions were crowding round in Louise's mind. 'Why didn't you tell me? Why didn't anyone mention it?'

'The others don't know. When I decided that I wanted to become an artist, it was important to me not to hitch a ride on the coat-tails of my famous forebear. I wanted my work to be judged on its own merits. I wanted to be known as Milo Charpentier, not as Gustave de Valence's great-grandson.'

'That's understandable,' said Louise. It was starting to dawn on her why she had felt familiarity on first meeting Milo. She had put it down to recognising him from the blurred photograph of Milo and Brazzini that she had seen in *New Horizons in Art*. Now she realised that she recognised him from elsewhere: from the self-portrait of Gustave de Valence that she had studied in the university library all those weeks ago. The facial features were undeniably similar; the curling brown hair was the same; the lively eyes were near-identical. Now that she had made the connection, she could mentally see the resemblance quite clearly. In fact, she felt stupid for not having made the connection before.

'Excuse me one minute,' she said to Milo. She went out to her van, and once again riffled through the large stuffer bag which contained all her research material. She pulled out a large lever-arch file with all her notes and photocopies of articles and paintings. The colour photocopies had cost her an arm and a leg, but she had to have them. She flicked through the pages until she came to the self-portrait of Gustave de Valence. Of course. It could be Milo in his hat, holding a paintbrush and rag. She opened the file and removed the photocopy. She went back to the studio, where Milo was patiently waiting. She showed him the painting, and grinned; and then held it up against his face. They were virtually the same.

'I think I'm going to have to sit down again,' said Louise. 'This is too much to take on board at once.'

Milo grinned. 'You need a drink,' he said, handing Louise a bottle of whisky. She took it gratefully and took a gulp, wincing as the strong spirit burned its way down her throat.

'There's more.'

Louise looked up at him, and whispered, '*The Venus*?'

Milo nodded. 'Gustave gave *The Venus of Collioure* to my grandfather as a christening present. Most people might find it strange, that a father should give his infant son a portrait of a nude; but Gustave knew that she was his finest work. What could be more fitting than for a child to have a loving portrait of his mother, painted by his father when at the height of his powers? The passion and emotion that the painting has conveyed to you is but the tiniest distillation of the passion and emotion that Gustave felt for Estelle. It is a love poem in oils.'

Louise nodded silently.

'My grandfather passed the painting on to my mother when she was christened. It then became a family tradition and, sure enough, when I was christened *The Venus of Collioure* came to me. She hung above my crib and then, when I was older, above my bed. Some years ago, the cord by which she was hanging finally rotted and gave way. The painting fell to the floor. Fortunately she was not harmed, although the frame suffered some damage. I took her into my studio to fix the frame, and that is why she was there when Brazzini came to visit me.

'I must congratulate you on spotting her in that photograph. It was only after the visit that I realised that she might have been visible in the photograph, but when I saw the edition of *New Horizons in Art* I felt that she was safe.' Milo tutted. 'A shame that such an interesting journal was so shoddily produced.'

'But why didn't you want anyone to know where she was?'

'I suppose because of the great personal attachment that my family had for the painting. She was no one else's business, we felt. She was ours to enjoy, and ours alone. There was also the security aspect. If it became known that we possessed such a valuable work of art, we would have been a target for every art thief between here and Timbuktu.'

'May I see her?' Louise asked.

Milo smiled forlornly. 'You forget that my initial answer to your question was both yes and no. I know roughly where she is: I do not know exactly where she is.'

'I don't understand.'

Milo sighed. 'This is hard for me to say, because I still feel a deep sense of shame.' He took a deep breath. 'In 1993, I was near-bankrupt. My paintings were not selling. I had to support myself by doing any odd job that I could find. Then I had a visit from the Comte de Grand Pressigny, an art collector. You have a lot in common with him.'

'Oh?' Louise asked, intrigued.

'He too was drawn by the power of *The Venus of Collioure*; and he too had identified her in the photograph in *New Horizons in Art* and tracked her down to me. You are the only two people to have done so. He came to me and made me an offer that I was in no position to refuse. And so, reluctantly, I sold her to him. I know she resides with him, somewhere in his château. I haven't seen her since the day I helped his men load her into the back of a van.'

Chapter Eight

Louise had nagged and nagged Milo until he had finally given in. He had agreed to take Louise to see the Comte de Grand Pressigny.

'I'll introduce you, but after that you're on your own,' he had said, grumpily.

Louise had spent the previous day, her last at Les Oliviers, wandering through the house gathering up her possessions. She had soon come to learn that the ethos of the communal living at Milo's extended to sharing each other's clothes and belongings. She was sad to leave her new close friends, but felt that it was time to move on. At last, she was going to see *The Venus of Collioure.*

It was early in the morning. Solange, Colette, Isabelle and Antoine gathered by the camper van as Louise placed her last piece of luggage in it. She slid the door shut, and went to kiss each of them farewell in turn, thinking how much she had learnt from them in the time she had spent with them. God! Somehow it seemed so much longer than six weeks to her, like some kind of fabulous, sensual, unreal dreamland; where golden, languorous days had drifted into weeks; where time had ceased to matter.

Milo seemed impatient with Louise's protracted farewells and got into the passenger seat. Louise took the hint, and went round to get behind the wheel. Doing up her seat belt, she looked down to see that Milo had a wine bottle cradled between his legs. She wound down her window to wave to the others as she drove off, and watched in her rear-view mirror as both they and the farmhouse receded and then disappeared from view. She was sad to be leaving, but her sadness was tempered by excitement. Action after so many weeks of inaction felt good. She was embarking on another stage in her voyage towards *The Venus of Collioure*.

'So, we're off on an adventure,' she said to Milo. She was well aware that he didn't particularly want to be making this journey. She had heard the others berating him in the kitchen late one night; and although it was very hard to get Milo to do something that he didn't want to, they had prevailed and now he was accompanying her. He had let it be known that it was under duress. Louise had to try her hardest to keep him in a sweet mood.

They were headed for the eastern Pyrenees, west of Perpignan; and so would retrace much of the journey they had undertaken the day Milo had taken her to Collioure. 'Wake me up at Perpignan,' Milo said, settling back into the seat, folding his arms across his chest and closing his eyes. He was making it clear that he wanted as little involvement with this venture as possible. He didn't even stir when Louise stopped at a small town to buy some food for lunch.

Some hours later, Milo woke up. Louise had remembered the route easily, and they had made good progress. Milo rubbed his eyes, looked around blearily, and groped for the bottle of wine. He then fumbled in his pocket and produced a corkscrew. He opened the bottle with practised precision and took a long, thirsty draught. Louise smiled. Despite his uncoordinated wooziness, there were some actions which would always come deftly and naturally to Milo.

They continued their journey in silence, but Milo's bad humour could not put a damper on Louise. In fact, such was her ebullience that she stopped to pick up a hitch-hiker at the side of the road, something she would not normally have done. Milo looked at her as if to say, 'What are you doing?', but Louise smiled gaily at him and waited for the young man to run up to the van. She watched his approach in the side mirror: he was wearing denim shorts and a T-shirt. The shorts were faded, holed and frayed, and the T-shirt was stretched across his broad chest as if it was several sizes too small for him. He smiled broadly as he approached the van, his even white teeth flashing out from his brown face, and his dark eyes sparkling mischievously.

'Spain?' he asked.

'We're going as far as Perpignan, if that's any use to you,' Louise said.

The young man nodded enthusiastically, opened the side door and hopped into the van. He settled in the seat behind Louise, and started to chatter away while Milo closed his eyes and maintained a stern silence. Louise could tell from the young man's heavily accented French that he was not a native speaker, and asked him where he came from.

'Barcelona. My name's Pedro.'

'I'm Loulou,' Louise said. Force of habit caused her to use Milo's pet name.

Louise looked at him in her rear-view mirror every now and then as they talked. She didn't dare risk turning round, lest she should crash the van. Besides, meeting and holding his gaze in the mirror gave their contact an unusual intimacy. He had very dark eyes: so dark that his irises and pupils merged together to appear as single large black circles. His head was crowned by a curling mop of black hair, and he had a deep, swarthy complexion.

After a while, Louise felt the fingers of one of his hands creeping forward on the headrest of her seat and gently touching her hair.

'I can't get over the colour of your hair,' he said. 'And your skin. It's so pale.'

Louise had never before thought of her pale complexion as a particular asset. All her friends back home prided themselves on getting as tanned as possible in the summer vacations, whereas she found it impossible. She could burn beautifully, but tan? Not a chance. And yet, since she had been in the South of France, her paleness had been commented on and admired many times. Strangers had stopped her in the market at La-Roche-Hubert and complimented her. She wondered if the people here found it appealing because it was so unusual.

Pedro stretched out his right arm between the two front seats and held it up against her left one, admiring the contrast between them. His dark skin was tanned darker still by the sun, and the hairs on his arm were jet black. Suddenly Louise was conscious that maybe he was thinking along the same lines as her: wondering how their bodies would look, stretched out naked next to each other. Dark on pale; roughness by smoothness; man next to woman. She blushed, and her cheeks reddened prettily. Pedro saw, and reached out to stroke her burning face. Flustered, she asked him if he was hungry.

'Very,' he replied, meeting her gaze in the mirror.

'I'll find a picnic spot,' she said, pulling off the main road. They drove a little way in silence. Then Pedro nodded at Milo, who was fast asleep and snoring gently. 'He's your boyfriend?'

'No.' Louise grinned at the thought of Milo ever actually committing himself to one person.

'Your lover, then?' said Pedro, smiling.

'Maybe,' Louise answered.

'I think so,' said Pedro.

They drove a little further in silence. Louise was keenly aware of the possible implication of what had just been said. Their conversation had touched on lovers. How long would it take for words to be converted to action?

In the distance, Louise saw the hazy blue rows of a lavender field. The low bushes were in full bloom and, as they drove nearer, she could smell the heady fragrance of the aromatic flowers on the breeze. In the middle of the field, breaking the rows, stood an ancient olive tree. Louise drew the van up at the side of the road by the field, and she and Pedro got out.

'Shall we wake him?' Pedro asked, but Louise shook her head.

'Leave him,' she said. She feared what kind of mood Milo would be in if they disturbed his rest. She did, however, ease the wine bottle out from between his thighs and hand it to Pedro. She signalled to him where the plastic beakers were stored in the back of the van. He found them, and carried them and the paper bag containing the picnic food over to the tree. Meanwhile, Louise searched as quietly as she could for the cotton throw that served as her all-purpose rug, blanket, pillow and sarong. Finding it, she joined Pedro and spread it out on the small area of grass between the gnarled trunk of the tree and the rows of lavender.

They emptied the contents of the bag out on to the throw: bread, cheese, some plump tomatoes, some olives and a cured sausage. Pedro eased the cork out of the wine bottle and poured them both a generous share of what was left. They ate in silence. Louise had read Pedro's signals as clearly as if he had whispered his need into her ear; and she knew that she too had messaged her desire to him. She knew that they were both waiting for the inevitable to happen.

Louise looked Pedro over. His legs were chunky and muscular, and she looked with interest at where the dark, thicker hairs on the insides of his thighs disappeared under the legs of his shorts. He rolled over on to his stomach, and she glimpsed through one of the many holes torn in the back of his shorts that he was not wearing any underwear beneath the denim.

She lay back on the throw and looked up into the silvery-green canopy of the tree. Ripening olives hung above her amid the leaves. Reaching to her side, she picked a stem of lavender from the nearest bush and gently crushed the flowerhead between her fingers, releasing the rich scent. Pedro rolled over, sat up and took the flower from her hand. Louise felt the electric jolt of their first physical contact. He put the lavender down, took her hand, and pressed it on to his chest and then dragged it down to the bulge of his groin.

That was all it took. Louise was swept away by a rising swell of lust. She scrabbled to her knees and knelt beside Pedro, who had thrown off his T-shirt. He lay back, gazing up at her expectantly. Holding his gaze, Louise felt for the buckle of his belt, and hurriedly undid it. She fumbled to undo the buttons of his fly, and could feel his hardness under her fingers.

Speed now governed everything. Louise did not have time for foreplay, for lover's kisses. She wanted more, and she wanted it right now. Her driving desire for the Spaniard was paramount. Pedro lifted his buttocks off the ground so that she could slide the shorts down over his hips, and down his legs. The dark hairs of Pedro's chest continued in a broad band down his stomach and spread below his belly button, where they met his dark, wiry pubic hairs. Standing proudly in the midst of these curls was his cock: dark and fleshy, circumcised and, although not the longest Louise had ever seen, it was certainly the thickest. Louise shuddered at the sight of it, wondering if she would be able to take it inside her.

Louise bent to kiss the dome of his penis, and she ran her tongue over the small slit, probing it with the tip of her tongue. Pedro moaned something in Spanish, and put his hands on her head and forced her to take more of his prick into her mouth. Louise felt the fleshy hardness passing her lips, and she opened her mouth into a wide circle to take in his girth.

Louise began to tease Pedro with her mouth, moving her head up and down, playing with her tongue, flicking and licking his warm, salty length. His moans increased in volume, and he talked to her in Spanish as his hands gripped her shoulders. She had no idea what he was saying, but she was sure that it was filthy. Suddenly Louise became aware of movement behind her. She heard the sound of twigs snapping underfoot; and, a moment later, she felt two hands on her rump, cupping her buttocks.

'Don't let me interrupt you,' Milo said, caressing her behind through the material of her dress, and then sliding the soft cotton upward. She heard the sound of a zip being undone, and moments later felt Milo hook her panties to one side and rub the swollen head of his cock against her moist and open sex. When Pedro opened his eyes and saw what was happening, he began to pump his penis more urgently into Louise's mouth.

Louise had never felt so overwhelmingly guided by carnality before. She was totally focused on two very different sensations: the feel and smell and taste of Pedro's cock thrusting rhythmically in her mouth, and the feeling of Milo's prick about to enter her from behind. Once again, she found herself not caring who might see this frantic coupling.

Milo teased her some more, rubbing his cock against her wet opening, laying his prick against her swollen lips and then brushing it against the small bead of her rock-hard clitoris, before finally pushing his cock into her. There was a moment's hesitation, as her inner lips seemed to catch against Milo's cock, and then he slid slowly and firmly into her. He plunged his full length into her, filling her completely. She began to respond to his rhythm by sucking Pedro with the same movement; and as Milo thrust forward, she allowed herself to be pushed forward over Pedro's cock. Milo held her with his hands on her hips, and she could feel her buttocks bumping into his thighs as she met each of his urgent thrusts.

Then she felt Pedro thickening in her mouth, and his grip on her shoulders tightened. Milo seemed to sense this, and speeded his thrusts. Pedro gave a low, guttural yell and slumped back on to the throw, as Louise felt the first spurts of his bitter semen spurting down the back of her throat. When he had climaxed, she gradually drew her mouth back along the length of his cock, licking him clean as she did so. Pedro removed his cock from her mouth, and rubbed the purply-red tip against her lips again; she kissed it. Pedro then rolled away from her, lying back and cupping his cock and balls in one hand as if they were painfully tender.

Milo took control. Placing a hand on her back, he pushed Louise roughly down so that her face was right on the blanket. This caused her rump to rise even higher in the air. With one hand Milo held her down in this position, and with the other he gripped her waist and bore into her with strong, powerful strokes. Then he reached down and felt round for her engorged clitoris. He began to stimulate her, rubbing her tender nub in the same rhythm with which he was fucking her. Louise was reaching overload, and she closed her eyes as her orgasm burst over her like a pulsing starburst. The contractions of her quim as she came seemed to trigger Milo's own orgasm, as he thrust into her one final, deep time. She reached behind her and felt his thighs shuddering. Milo groaned, and then collapsed over her back, his chest drenched with sweat.

* * *

Afterwards, the three lovers slept in the shade of the tree for a while, recovering from the strenuous exertions of sex. Then Louise woke the men, and they continued with their journey as if nothing unusual had happened. Louise reflected on how different Milo's lovemaking had been this time. Before, at Collioure, he had compliantly allowed her to make the running; this time he had been very much in charge. Louise wondered if it would have been any different had Pedro not been there – whether the old alpha male felt he had to assert his superiority in the presence of this young interloper.

On the outskirts of Perpignan, Louise pulled the van into a layby to let Pedro out. Leaning out through the window, she kissed him and brushed a few stray pieces of grass out of his hair.

'Thank you, Loulou,' he said.

'No, thank you,' she replied with feeling.

Milo gave directions from Perpignan, but was otherwise silent during the rest of the journey. They headed west, and gradually the road led upward, into the heavily wooded foothills of the Pyrenees. The tree-covered mountains loomed in the distance, under a wide, blue sky. Villages, fields and vineyards clustered in the river valleys and, apart from the occasional hillside village and the winding, twisting roads that led to them, the slopes were densely forested. It seemed to Louise that, in each village, almost every window displayed boxes of bright-red geraniums in bloom, and vines and creepers covered the walls of almost every house. They were passing through one such village when Milo suddenly shouted out, 'Stop!'

Louise performed an emergency stop and the van screeched to a halt, raising a cloud of dust and gravel on the narrow road. Villagers stopped what they were doing to stare.

'What is it?' Louise asked worriedly, as Milo got out of the van. She hadn't seen anything run out in front of them, and she was praying that she hadn't run over some unfortunate animal. Milo grabbed his knapsack and slung it over his shoulder.

'Follow this road for another four or five kilometres. You'll see the château up on a crest: can't miss it.'

'But . . .' Louise blurted. 'You said you'd come with me. You said you'd introduce me to the Comte.'

Milo shrugged his shoulders. 'Sorry.'

'But, Milo,' she pleaded, angry and confused. He shrugged again, and turned and walked towards the bar at the side of the road.

'How will you get home?' she shouted after him.

'Hitch,' he replied, without turning to look at her. 'And don't expect the Comte to be very forthcoming.'

Louise was furious. Infuriating and unreliable to the last, Milo had managed to have his own way after all. He didn't want to see the Comte, and so he wouldn't see the Comte: end of story. Louise sat fuming in the van. She knew it would be inadvisable to drive off while she was in this state. She began to count to ten out loud, very slowly.

Still counting, she looked over to the bar, and saw Milo go over to a young woman who was sitting in the shade of an umbrella at one of the terrace tables. Milo bent down to kiss her; and the woman looked up from her magazine, squealed with delight on recognising him, and threw her arms around his neck. They kissed passionately.

So this was why he wanted to stop, Louise thought with a resigned smile. She remembered the words of the patron in another bar: Milo was an old goat, that was for sure. Louise knew that she couldn't stay cross with Milo for long. What you saw with Milo was pretty much what you got, she thought. He made no pretence about the way he was: roguish and amoral and not entirely dependable and always, always guided by his gonads. Thinking that she should have expected as much from him on this trip, Louise shrugged, started up the van, and drove on.

After driving for another four kilometres or so, Louise saw the château, just as Milo had said she would. But it was not at all what she had been expecting. She wasn't sure where the idea had come from, but she had a definite and fixed mental image of what the Comte de Grand Pressigny's château would look like: a gracious, refined castle, perhaps dating to the sixteenth century or a little later; maybe with a moat and fairytale towers and turrets; possessing fine architectural details and clearly built by master craftsmen from the finest materials and to the highest standards.

Not so the Château de Puivent. It was perched precipitously on a rocky outcrop, towering over the small hamlet that clung to the lower reaches of the slope. Built of huge, rough-hewn blocks of stone, the massive battlements enclosed almost the entire area of the top of the crest. At one end of the battlements was a tall and impressive square tower, adjoined by a longer, slightly lower building. The battlements were punctuated by other, smaller towers; and Louise could tell that these were clearly for defence rather than decoration. The only windows were tiny slits which had enabled the archers in times gone by to defend their stronghold. There were no other buildings visible above the high walls: it seemed that the large tower and adjoining building *was* the château. Louise guessed that the buildings might date to the twelfth century, if not earlier; and she admitted to herself that her fanciful mental image of the Comte de Grand Pressigny's castle was perhaps more appropriate for the elegant châteaux of the gentle landscape of the Rhône valley than the rugged terrain of the Pyrenees.

Louise drove carefully up the narrow road that zigzagged its way round and up the rocky massif, and saw that the road terminated by one of the smaller towers in the battlements. A wooden bridge led across a deep ditch, and within the wide-arched entrance through the tower she could see the bottom of a raised portcullis. She parked her car on a small area of gravel, and walked over the bridge to the tower. Gazing around, she could now fully appreciate the strategic location of the château. It sat along a spinelike ridge, with precipitous drops on all sides.

Gazing through the entrance tower as she approached, she glimpsed yet another unexpected scene. She could see the large, square tower and associated buildings at the far end of the battlements, but the inner area between them and where she stood, which she expected to be a grassed and empty courtyard, was a garden planted with an abundance of gaily coloured flowers and plants. Islands of closely mown green lawns interrupted the bedding here and there. A gravel track, wide enough for a car, cut through the planted areas, but the greenery flopped forward across the stone chippings at every opportunity. The effect was one of lush, unrestrained fecundity; and the garden formed a great contrast to the imposing and functional fortifications which surrounded it.

On one side of the entrance tower, the door to a small room was open. A sign reading TICKETS HERE was pinned to the door. Louise went in. A man was sitting slumped in a chair, with his head thrown back. He was snoring heavily. She coughed, and the man woke with a start, and jumped up.

'Good afternoon, mademoiselle. It's been a very quiet day,' he explained. 'You're only the third visitor today. Fifty francs, please.'

Louise hadn't expected the château to be open to the public, but she realised that this could be to her advantage. It presented her with a good opportunity to look round inside the château for the elusive *Venus*. If she announced the true purpose of her visit, the Comte might simply have her turned away before she had even managed to step through the door.

'Does the Comte open his château to the public every day?' she asked as she handed over the money.

'Oh no. Just once a week. The guests wouldn't like it, otherwise.'

Guests? thought Louise. Maybe the Comte did a lot of entertaining.

The *gardien* made a quick phone call, handed Louise a thin guidebook, and then waved her through. She walked under the portcullis and into the secret garden, hidden from all prying eyes by the high walls of the battlements. She followed the gravel path until it led her to a larger gravelled area by the entrance to the main building next to the tower. Four cars were parked there: a Mercedes, a Porsche, a Ferrari and a BMW.

The large, arched door to the château was shut. Louise knocked hesitantly. Quick footsteps approached on the other side, and the door swung open. She was greeted by a ridiculously handsome man; maybe in his early thirties, she guessed. She looked him over without thinking to disguise what she was doing. He was dressed in a smart well-cut suit, and had short, dark-brown, glossy hair. His eyes were also brown, and appeared darker still, thanks to his long and thick eyelashes. When she caught his eye she blushed, realising that she had been rumbled. He, however, seemed amused by Louise's overt appraisal.

'Welcome to the Château de Puivent,' he said, standing aside to let her pass into the large, echoing hallway. 'My name is Gui, and I will be your guide on a tour of the château. Please come this way.'

She followed behind him and watched how he carried himself with confidence. Someone this good-looking should be a catwalk model, not a tour guide, she thought to herself.

Gui led her into an elegant salon. Here was another

surprise. Externally, the château had a crude rusticity, without finesse or refinement. Inside, it was decorated and furnished with sumptuous luxuriousness. Louise gawped, lost for words. The quality of the Comte's art collection also surprised her. It could rival that of any provincial art gallery. In this room alone she recognised a small Giacometti bronze figure, what looked like a Dürer engraving and a landscape in oils by Sisley. Not quite in the same league as the collections in the Louvre or the National Gallery, but extremely impressive nonetheless.

As Gui led her from room to room, Louise scanned the walls for the object of her search, but was disappointed each time. The Comte had hidden his treasure well away. They passed through several reception rooms, an elegant dining room and a music room with grand piano and a full-size concert harp.

Louise hoped that Gui wouldn't notice that she was paying such close attention to each room. He might think that she was casing the joint – which was, in effect, exactly what she was doing. Passing by one set of open double doors, she glanced in. Sitting in a high-backed armchair was a man wearing a monogrammed silk bath robe. Using a magnifying glass, he was closely studying the large tome that was balanced on his knees: Louise could see from the colour plates that it was a glossy art book about Titian. Louise guessed from her brief glimpse that he might be in his late thirties or early forties. So this must be the Comte. Behind him, the bright light streamed in through a window; and through that window Louise could see the lush flowers and the high battlements of the courtyard garden. But before she could snoop any further, Gui discreetly slipped past her and closed the doors.

Leading her on into the next room, Gui told her about the history of the château, and about the many beautiful things within it. Louise was impressed by his knowledge almost as much as she was by her surroundings: he certainly knew how to give a detailed, informative and entertaining tour.

As their slow progress through the rooms continued, Louise noted that the Comte was not concerned about displaying his impressive art collection by period or artist. A pastoral landscape hung next to a cubist still life; and quattrocento masterpieces jostled for wall space with German expressionist paintings. This seemingly arbitrary juxtaposition of styles and subject matters resulted in the creation of unexpected and surprising effects. Were this her collection, Louise would never have thought to do such a thing, but having seen it she realised that it worked.

Half an hour later, Louise groaned with disappointment when Gui announced that they had reached the last room in the tour. She had not found what she was looking for. She decided that there was nothing for it: she would have to risk being rumbled, and ask Gui directly.

'I see the Comte owns several paintings by Gustave de Valence. Do you know *The Venus of Collioure*?'

Gui smiled. 'Oh yes. I know it.'

Louise couldn't believe her luck. Gui knew the painting. That could mean only one thing. Surely now, at last, she was close to the painting, and was about to hear confirmation of all that she had hoped.

Gui continued. 'I mean, who hasn't heard of the most famous lost masterpiece of them all? All the art world is looking for it.'

Louise couldn't bear the suspense created by Gui's apparent teasing. He was going to say, 'And it's here!' any moment now.

'Of course, they're all on a fool's errand,' he continued. 'I doubt that it still exists. It was probably destroyed during the war: bombed or burnt or suffered some similar fate. Otherwise someone would have seen it by now, wouldn't they?'

Yet once more during her search for the painting, Louise experienced the lurching jar of disappointment. She was getting used to it, but it didn't make it any easier to take. But she consoled herself with the thought that, much as she was exasperated with Milo, she didn't think he would have lied to her about this, of all things. He knew how much it meant to her. He had said that the Comte de Grand Pressigny owned *The Venus of Collioure*, and that it was somewhere within the château. And after all, Gui was only an employee. It was quite likely that the Comte kept *The Venus* hidden away even from him.

Louise determined at that very moment that she would have to come back for a better look: only the next time she would go into all the rooms. It was the only way to find *The Venus*. She smiled politely at Gui as he showed her out, thanking him for the interesting tour, and started to walk down the path. When she heard the door closing heavily behind her, she walked a little further and then turned round and hurried back, trying to tread as quietly as possible on the gravel. She pressed her ear against the door and, hearing only silence, tried the great iron loop handle. It was heavy, but she felt the latch lifting on the other side. She pushed against the door with her shoulder and opened it a little way. She listened. Silence.

Louise crept back into the hall, and consulted the floor plan in the guidebook. There were at least nine rooms on this floor she hadn't yet been into, plus all the first- and second-floor rooms. In addition, there were the rooms in the tower: five on each of the five floors. Removing her sandals, she tiptoed across the hall and into the first room.

* * *

Elsewhere in the château, the Comte was sitting in his high-backed armchair. He stretched back and smiled. He liked what he saw: a Titian-haired beauty. Then he leant forward again, making fine adjustments to find the right magnification.

Louise worked methodically through the ground-floor rooms, always listening out for the approach of footsteps, but the château seemed curiously deserted. She scanned every wall, every painting, hoping to see at last her elusive *Venus*. She stopped by the double doors which Gui had so assiduously closed, and listened carefully. She heard a cough, and then a moment later the rustling sound as someone turned a page in a book. Cursing silently, she moved on. She didn't want to leave any room unchecked, but in this case she had no choice. Maybe later on she could peer in through the window that opened on to the courtyard garden. She was forced to avoid the kitchens too, as she had heard the rattle of pots and low voices within. Her search was going to prove more difficult than she had anticipated.

The Comte chuckled to himself, and leant forward to study the image on one of the video screens.

'That's it, my beauty. You have a good look around. You won't find it, though. I can guarantee you that.'

Flicking a switch to change from camera to camera, he tracked Louise on the closed-circuit TV as she crept from room to room; watching her closely as she scanned the paintings on the walls. She was clearly no common-or-garden thief. She ignored all the valuable and pocketable *objets d'art*: the Fabergé eggs, the Elizabethan miniatures, the Moghul jewels. She was intent on finding *The Venus of Collioure*. But why was such a young woman interested in that painting, and how had she tracked it down to him?

* * *

Louise consulted her plan again, and counted. Apart from the tower rooms, there were twenty-eight rooms on the first floor of the main building; the same number on the second; and four different sets of staircases leading between the floors. She stepped slowly and carefully up the spiral staircase at the far end of the building, making her way to the first floor. The staircase was gloomy, lit only by the narrow slits in the wall. It brought her out in the corner of a room with a low ceiling. The room was dominated by a massive stone fireplace, almost as high as the room itself. There was the usual array of fine furniture and art, and colourful tapestries portraying mythological scenes hung on the walls next to the paintings. She recognised one that showed Venus and Phaon, an elderly boatman. She smiled ruefully. Just her luck: she'd found a Venus, but not the right one. She noticed a small door in the opposite corner of the room, partially disguised by the tapestry that hung over it and had been cut to allow access through. She looked at the plan once more: it seemed to be a small antechamber of some sort. She went over to the door and pushed it open.

Louise caught her breath when she saw inside the room. Every inch of wall space was covered with paintings, but not the kind Louise had seen elsewhere in the château. The carnality and licentiousness on display was overwhelming. Naked women disported themselves in a variety of settings and with a variety of partners. Others pleasured themselves solitarily. All womankind was here: voluptuous older women with full, fleshy figures; younger ones, slim and lithe in the first flushes of womanhood; black women, white women, oriental women.

Louise turned slowly, looking at the paintings with astonished curiosity. What she had seen in the brochure of erotica paled in comparison with what was in front of her. But the biggest shock was still to come. As she turned to look at the wall next to the door by which she had entered, she was met by her own steady gaze: but this was no reflection in a mirror. She saw herself, lying naked among silken cushions, with Colette lying between her legs, her head buried in Louise's groin. Louise reeled, taking a couple of short steps back and groping for support. She went over to the small window and opened it. She needed air. Milo had promised her that he would keep the painting; that he wouldn't sell it. And, when she'd last seen it, her eyes had been closed in the painting. Milo had repainted them, and now she was looking out of the painting with a gaze of knowing, lascivious invitation. Milo. The bastard.

She heard a noise behind her and turned, still in mute shock. Gui was standing in the doorway.

'Hello again,' he said, with a smile. 'I'm sorry if the tour I gave you didn't satisfy you.'

Louise couldn't find any words. She didn't know what to say. Even with her usual quick-thinking, she knew she was going to have trouble talking her way out of this one.

'I . . . I . . .' she struggled.

'I'm sure the Comte would like to hear your explanation. Please come with me.'

Louise followed him, relieved that Gui had not seen her next to her portrait. To be recognised from that was the last thing she needed.

Gui led her back the way she had come, down the spiral staircase and back to the double-doored room in which she had seen the Comte. Gui opened the doors and gestured her in. The armchair was empty, and a quick glimpse around confirmed that there was no one in the room, and neither was *The Venus of Collioure*. Gui closed the doors behind her, and walked over to the chair. He picked the art book up off the seat and reshelved it among the hundreds of others that lined the walls, straightening the spines as he went past. Louise took a good look around the room as she waited for the Comte. There was a large desk, some high mahogany library steps to give access to the highest shelves, and books: thousands of books. Louise scanned the titles. Every single one was concerned with art: art history, techniques, studies of individual artists, journals, and auction catalogues. Without doubt, it was a far better-stocked history of art library than the one at Louise's university.

Gui went over to the desk and sat down behind it.

'Well. I'm waiting.'

Louise stared at him. 'What?'

'I'm waiting for you to explain why you were prying around my château.'

'You mean you . . .?'

He nodded. 'Allow me to introduce myself. Gui de Mompesson, Comte de Grand Pressigny.'

Chapter Nine

Louise was momentarily stunned into silence by Gui's revelation. Her mind whirled. Oh, shit shit *shit*, she thought. That's torn it. He's the Comte: Gui the guide is Gui the Comte. Why didn't I keep my big mouth shut earlier on? He knows I'm after *The Venus of Collioure*.

She looked at Gui, and decided that she might as well tell all. Now that he knew she was interested in de Valence's masterpiece, she had nothing to lose. And so she introduced herself; and then explained about the dawning of her curiosity about *The Venus* and how she had tracked it down to Milo; about her proposed dissertation, and her struggle with Dr Petersen; about her time at Milo's commune at Les Oliviers, and what had finally brought her here to the Château de Puivent. Gui listened to all this in silence.

When she had finished, he spoke quietly. 'I might have guessed that dear Milo wouldn't have been able to keep a secret.'

Louise looked up with a sudden jerk of her head. Of course. Milo's painting of her. Gui must surely have recognised her from it; and had he doubted that she and the model were one and the same, now that he knew she had a connection with Milo any doubt would have been eradicated. She blushed deeply with shame. What must Gui think of her? He was hardly going to take her research seriously when he knew that she had posed for an erotic and exceedingly explicit painting. She bowed her head in humiliated embarrassment.

Gui stood up and walked around the desk. Louise was painfully aware of his presence next to her. From the first moment she had met him, only a couple of hours earlier, she had been strongly attracted to him. It was a physical attraction, but there was more to it than that. She had taken to him straight away: he had been a modest and humorous guide, wearing his extensive knowledge lightly. And no wonder it had struck her that Gui carried himself with confidence. Owning this pile and all its contents would put a spring in her step, too. She wondered what he thought of her, and then winced as she guessed it was probably nothing more than annoyance and irritation.

Gui looked down at her bowed head and spoke. 'Despite your behaviour, and probably against my better judgement, something compels me to help you. Now that you are here, it would be churlish of me to turn you away. I would be pleased if you would stay here as my guest, and I will teach you all I know.' Louise looked up, feeling that he had chosen his words very carefully and deliberately. He paused for a moment, before adding, 'About *The Venus of Collioure*.'

Relieved, Louise thanked him profusely. What was it that Milo had said about the Comte not being very forthcoming? What rubbish.

The Comte reached for the phone on his desk, and a few minutes later there was a knock at the door. A woman with short straw-blonde hair entered. She had clear blue eyes and a serious expression.

Gui turned to Louise. 'This is Astrid, my manager here.'

Louise smiled at the woman, wondering what it was she managed.

'Astrid. Please show our guest to her room, and fill her in on our routine.'

Astrid nodded sombrely. 'Please come with me, miss,' she said, leading the way. Louise followed, and couldn't refrain from gawping through every open door as they ascended the main staircase to the first floor and walked along a corridor. Astrid showed her into a bedroom which was dominated by a large bed with a gathered canopy of fine silk over the head. She opened a small door that led to an en suite bathroom, and then showed Louise the bell pull by the bed for summoning the maid.

'All the information you will require is contained in here,' Astrid said, handing Louise a small leaflet printed on thick handmade paper. She nodded brusquely at Louise, and then left.

Louise sat on the bed, and looked down at the leaflet.

> Château de Puivent: an exclusive hotel for the discerning guest. Home of the Comte de Grand Pressigny, this historic château dates to the early part of the eleventh century; and, apart from the Comte's private apartments, all areas are open to our guests. We want you to feel as at ease and relaxed here as you would in your own home. Wander through the beautiful gardens, explore the stunning countryside, relax in our sauna, or while away an afternoon enjoying the Comte's extensive art collection. With a staff of sixteen, we cater for a maximum of four guests at any time, thereby assuring you the highest degree of personal attention and the finest level of service at all times. We offer a full range of recreational activities, catering for every taste; and we guarantee full satisfaction.

A hotel. So that was what the *gardien* had meant by guests. And she supposed that the man that she had mistaken for the Comte must have been a guest. Louise wondered if it was a policy of the hotel for it to be invisibly staffed. She had certainly seen no sign of any other guests or the sixteen staff members during her earlier exploration of the château.

Louise lay back on the bed, thinking of all that had happened during this very eventful day. She was still perturbed about Milo's painting. Gui had given no sign that he had recognised her as the model. Was that because he was being tactful, or because he hadn't yet made the connection? And if he hadn't yet recognised her as the model, how long would it take for him to do so? And what about the room in which the painting hung? She wondered if it was testament to the Comte's personal interest – or should she even say obsession, given the sheer quantities of erotic art held in that one small room? Or was it provided for the stimulation of the guests?

There was a knock on the door, and a young black man wearing a bellhop's uniform came in. He was carrying her suitcase. The highest levels of service, indeed: she hadn't even mentioned her luggage to anyone, but it was clearly all being taken care of.

Louise indolently watched the young man as he placed her suitcase on a low chest. He was beautiful: there was no other word for it. His hair was cropped close to his head, emphasising his elegant bone structure, and he sported a short goatee beard. His eyes were large, brown and almond-shaped, so large and dark that they looked almost as if he was wearing eyeliner. His cheekbones were fine and pronounced, and he had the most sensual lips Louise thought she had ever seen. He was tall and well-built, though he didn't appear to be too musclebound. He truly was a wonder to behold, Louise mused. She felt she could lie there and look at him all day.

'May I offer you any other service, mademoiselle?' the young man asked.

'Such as?' Louise laughed, amused by his unintentional *double entendre*.

'My speciality is sensual massage.'

Boggling with incredulity, Louise coughed back her surprise. So she had understood him correctly after all. The phrases in the hotel leaflet now took on a different meaning: 'the highest degree of personal attention and the finest level of service'; 'full range of recreational activities, catering for every taste'; 'we guarantee full satisfaction'. It was all starting to make sense to her. Louise smiled.

She was the Comte's guest, so she might as well make full use of all the facilities, she thought. And it was perfectly clear what this handsome young man was offering. Why else would he have said 'sensual'?

'Well, I am feeling pretty tired after all my travelling,' she said, stretching out on the bed and rubbing her arms as if they were sore.

'Please, let me assist you. My name is Raheem.'

'Go ahead, Raheem,' she said.

'Where would you like your massage?'

'On the bed here seems as good a place as any.' Louise couldn't believe that she was so coolly negotiating the sexual services of a man like this. She was going to make the most of it. And she had never made love to a black man before, though she had daydreamed about it often. She stood up next to him. 'Take my clothes off, Raheem.'

With the utmost care, Raheem gently undid the buttons down the front of Louise's dress. Her breath quickened, and she could feel her nipples hardening as his hands brushed against the swell of her breasts. Opening it down the front, he slipped the dress off her shoulders. She stood before him in just her panties. She hoped he liked what he saw. But then again, she thought, he was a professional, probably trained not to react.

Raheem slid her panties down over her hips, and removed them.

'Now take your clothes off,' Louise commanded.

Raheem undid his jacket and slipped it off, and then stepped out of his trousers. Underneath his uniform he was wearing nothing. As Louise had suspected, he had a fine physique: the muscles well-defined but not over-developed. Louise marvelled at the darkness of his skin, the darker pigmentation around his nipples, and the coiling mass of tight, springy pubic hairs that clustered round his groin and upper thighs, with a finer line of down that reached almost to his navel. Most of all, she marvelled at his cock. Although it was still a slumbering beast, she could see that a beast it was. He was uncircumcised, and bigger than any man she had seen before. He stood before her, waiting for her next command.

'Carry me to the bed.'

With a swift, strong movement, Raheem stepped close to her, bent to put one arm under her knees and swept her up. Louise could feel his other arm against her back, under her arm, and his hand brushing against her breast. She felt completely insubstantial in his powerful grasp: like some spectral creature. She nestled her head against his neck and breathed in his warm, spicy smell.

Raheem carried her over to the bed and gently laid her on it. Louise looked up at him and smiled, and then looked down at his cock again. She had had the desired effect on him, and his cock was stirring and stiffening, gradually coming to life. She reached out to grasp it. As she pulled his foreskin back on the very first slow stroke, she could not keep in her gasp of delighted surprise. The inner flesh of Raheem's glans, which until now had been hidden under his foreskin, was dark pink rather than the brown she had expected. She bent to kiss it, and tasted the sexy musky saltiness of his cock. Then she looked up at him.

'Massage me now, please.' Louise turned on to her

stomach on the bed, rested her chin on the backs of her hands, and closed her eyes. She heard Raheem rustling in his clothes, then the sound of a bottle being unscrewed. Then she felt his weight on the bed as he knelt over her, and placed his large capable hands on her back. His hands were wet, slick and oily, and he began to run them firmly yet tenderly over her body, never once breaking contact with her skin. She felt him drift over the sides of her breasts, and then return to applying the lazy pressure on her back.

The rhythm of Raheem's expert touch was so soothing after the rigours of her long day that Louise felt herself drifting off to sleep. She was on the point of biting the back of her hand to keep herself awake, when she felt Raheem shift his hands lower down her back and over her buttocks. He massaged these, one in either hand, with a circling motion which had the effect of parting her cheeks every now and then. Louise revelled in this sensation. Keeping one hand on her, so as not to break contact, Raheem reached for the bottle again, undid the cap with his teeth and poured a generous splash of the oil down the cleft between the fleshy globes of her buttocks. Louise gasped as she felt the warm oil dribbling down over her anus and then down into her already slick sex.

Raheem was now concentrating his efforts on the backs of her thighs, and his hands slipped every now and then down the slippery slope of her inner thighs towards her labia. He tantalised and teased and, the more Louise willed him to move to satisfy her, the more he seemed to withhold from pleasuring her. This teasing was driving Louise to distraction, and she shifted and moved under his touch, trying to direct his hands on to her sex.

She was so engrossed by Raheem that she did not notice the small lens fitted into the intricately carved wooden medallion around which the pleated material of the bed canopy was gathered. Nor had she earlier noticed the lens disguised in the frame of one of the paintings, nor the lens in the bathroom, hidden among bottles and jars on a shelf. Nor was she aware of the spyholes, two-way mirrors and hidden passages that were strategically positioned throughout the château.

Sitting in a darkened room in his private apartments at the top of the tower, Gui sat in his high-backed armchair, watching the same scene unfold from three separate viewpoints on the monitor screens on the wall. Set in the wall in a bank of three rows, the twelve large screens were capable of displaying different images from around the château; or each could show a small part of a single massive image. Gui smiled. He had sent in Raheem, his most skilled and experienced operative, and he knew that Raheem would draw the best out of this pale, Titian-haired English girl.

Gui thought back to how he had been struck by the beauty of the woman in Milo's painting that day only a few weeks previously when the talented Provençal rogue had hastened to the château, bringing a new piece of erotica to offer to him. It was Milo's finest effort yet, depicting a young woman in the throes of sensual abandon. Gui had admired her then: her pale skin and wondrous, lustrous hair; her blue eyes and the soft pinkness of her mouth. Then he had met that same young woman in the flesh. He had recognised her instantly, but had disguised his surprise at her arrival at his château.

And now that he had spent some time with her, he was even more fascinated by her: she was an intriguing mixture of innocence and worldliness. Her dedication to her research and her tenacity in pursuing her goal impressed him; but did she really believe that he would admit to owning *The Venus of Collioure,* his most prized possession and the greatest of his many secrets? Such naivety! And yet, he already knew what she was capable of in other areas, and that beneath that deceptively chaste exterior dwelt a debauched soul. Milo had told him all about his young model's desire for new experiences and her eagerness to learn; and Gui felt that here was someone who could benefit from his extensive knowledge and guidance.

It would amuse him to keep her at the château, hanging on with the promise of more information about *The Venus of Collioure.* He had not had such a young or strikingly beautiful female guest for some time, and she would provide enjoyable viewing, he felt sure. He flicked a switch on the console before him, selecting the best view of Raheem and the young Englishwoman and displaying it as a single image over the twelve large screens.

Gui watched eagerly as Raheem knelt behind Louise on the bed, his large hands almost encircling her slender waist. She was on her hands and knees, and was clearly succumbing to the powerful urges that Raheem had unleashed in her. Her back was curved like that of a female animal as she thrust her rump in the air in a wanton invitation to Raheem to enter her. Raheem took no time in responding to her rapacious demands. Gui saw him caress the full pale globes of her buttocks, before parting them and placing his massive cock on the top of her cleft. Holding his prick like some great baton, he rubbed down the length of her crack until he reached the auburn down of her pubic hair and the soft, pale-pink petals within.

This was becoming too stimulating for Gui to bear. Never taking his eyes from the screen, he fumbled with the fastener on his flies, and then unzipped them. He released his cock, and began to massage his straining penis with the exact rhythm with which Raheem was now moving within Louise.

She looks so pure and virginal, and yet she is such a slut! Gui thought excitedly. Look at her greedily take his whole length!

Gui could feel his orgasm gathering, the unmistakable

tensing at the base of his prick. He would not allow himself to come before Raheem, and so he ceased his feverish movements for a moment, lightly stroking the glistening tip of his penis instead, and fingering the sensitive flesh of his frenum. Grasping his solid shaft tightly in his hand, he slowly drew his foreskin back, and watched with narcissistic pleasure as the dome of his penis darkened from red to an angry purple as he tightened his grip. The veins bulged against his fingers. Then he looked back to the screens, and rejoined the rhythm of the frenzied coupling once more. At the very moment that Raheem's buttocks clenched and he threw back his head with the final, juddering strokes of his orgasm, Gui felt his own climax rushing up the shaft of his penis, and the thick spurts of semen shot forth and spattered over his suit.

The telephone on the bedside table rang as Louise was about to step into the shower. It was Gui.

'Louise. Please join us at eight o'clock in the grand salon. Astrid will help you dress.'

Gui put down the phone before Louise could respond. Why on earth did he think that she needed help dressing? She was sure that the meals here would be formal and impressive, and had decided to wear her trusty little black designer dress. It was a bit crumpled from being packed away in her suitcase for so long – although she had had it cleaned, soon after arriving at Les Oliviers, she hadn't worn it since that evening at the restaurant with Jean-Pierre. She didn't worry unduly, as the glory of chiffon was that the creases soon fell out. She would place it on a hanger for an hour or so and it would be perfect.

As she pulled it out of her suitcase, Louise's face fell. During her stay in Provence, clothes moths had clearly been busy in the bottom of the suitcase. Her beautiful dress was a mess of tatty holes, quite ruined.

Was that why Gui was sending Astrid to see her? Had he known about her dress? she wondered. If he had, that could mean only one thing: that he or one of his minions had been through her belongings. Anger surged through Louise. She might be his guest, but he still had to respect her privacy. But then, she thought, her anger dying away, she had hardly been respecting his privacy while she had been snooping through his château earlier that day.

Louise padded through to the bathroom, and stepped under the steaming jet of water. As she washed herself, feeling the soft firmness of her flesh beneath her soapy hands, she thought of Raheem and his tender ministrations. And then she thought of Gui. Surely he must recognise her from Milo's portrait. She flushed with shame at the thought, and then gradually overcame that shame, wondering if he would expect her to perform for him like that.

There was a dark sensuality about Gui, and Louise was extraordinarily attracted to him. The painting was like a secret between them: an intimate and private connection. She could pretend that she hadn't seen it, that she didn't know of its presence here in the château; he could pretend he didn't know she was the model. They could dance round each other, feigning ignorance and yet both fully aware of the other's knowledge. It would give their contact an extra *frisson*.

Louise's hands slipped easily over her wet flesh, caressing her breasts and then searching lower, feeling for her still-tender sex. Good as Raheem was, she was ready for more. She pleasured herself slowly, the mental image of Raheem's perfect body etched into her mind. She knew she was going to enjoy her stay here in the château, Venus or no Venus.

Elsewhere in the château, Gui too was enjoying Louise's pleasure in her own body. He flicked the RECORD button on the console, as he had done earlier during her energetic coupling with Raheem. He knew he would want to give her libidinous performance several viewings. She had undoubted potential: he could sense that there were hidden desires within her that he could easily reveal. He would have to be careful to find the right opportunity, and to introduce her gradually to his ideas.

Louise was towelling herself dry when there was a knock on the door. She pulled the fluffy towel close around her and opened it cautiously, in case it was Gui. She didn't want him to see her like this. She was relieved to see that Astrid was standing in the corridor. She was carrying a silk robe draped over one arm, and was smiling pleasantly, a great contrast to the stern-faced and briskly efficient manner with which she had dealt with Louise a few hours before.

'May I come in?' she asked.

'Oh. Of course,' said Louise, nonplussed.

'I have come to help you dress. If you'd like to put this on and come with me?' Astrid's words were phrased like a question, but seemed to Louise to be more of a command.

Louise took the robe and disappeared into the bathroom. She didn't want to change in front of this particular woman. She'd been happy to strip off in front of the female near-strangers at Les Oliviers, but that had been different.

She then followed Astrid down the corridor, along several passageways, up a flight of stairs and along another passageway. Astrid showed her into a room and Louise drew in her breath sharply. The room was a perfect square, and the four walls and the ceiling were completely covered by large sheet mirrors. Even the back of the door was mirrored: in fact, the only surface which lacked a mirror was the floor. The effect was one of enormous space; Louise could see her endlessly repeated reflection disappearing off into the distance. The room was empty, apart from two plumply upholstered and gilded chairs.

Astrid shut the door behind Louise and went over to one of the walls. Louise noticed that there were tiny mirrored handles set into the glass, and she watched as Astrid slid back a door to reveal a long row of hanging dresses.

'These are all new, and are all at your disposal,' Astrid said.

Louise walked up to the array of dresses. She pulled one out, a beautiful evening gown in ivory satin, embroidered with thousands of tiny crystal beads. She inspected the label: Versace. She was impressed, and knew without looking that every one of these dresses would be a designer item. Astrid stood next to her.

'Could I make a suggestion? I think that this dress could have been made for you.' Astrid pulled a russet-coloured silk gown out from among the other dresses. It was classically simple, a sheathlike long dress with thin straps that crossed over at the back. The colour of the material was exactly the same shade as Louise's hair. Astrid held it against her, and Louise nodded her approval. The dress was stunning; and Louise knew that, combined with her hair, the overall effect would be sensational.

Astrid crossed to the other side of the room and drew back another sliding mirrored door, revealing row after row of women's shoes.

'Imelda Marcos, eat your heart out,' Louise muttered.

'What size do you take?' Astrid asked, ignoring Louise's comment; and when Louise told her she ran her finger along a row and then picked out a pair of high-heeled shoes with delicate straps, covered with the same russet-coloured silk as the dress.

'This room is amazing,' said Louise with feeling. She

noticed other handles in the mirrors by the door and on the fourth wall, and wondered what lay behind them.

'We call it the Dressing-Up Box,' said Astrid. 'Please feel free to use it whenever you wish. There's one for the gentlemen as well. Now I must go and see to the other guests. Martine is available to prepare your hair and make-up, if you wish. You can summon her by ringing the bell or calling the receptionist on your bed-side phone.'

With that, Astrid left the room, leaving behind her a bemused and slightly amazed Louise.

A little while later, Louise was sitting silently at the grand rosewood dining table. She felt totally overawed, gauche and unsophisticated in this glittering company. She had finally met the four other guests in the grand salon: two men and two women. Gui and the two men were formally dressed in dinner jackets, and Louise recognised one of the men as the one she had mistaken for the Comte earlier that day. He was introduced to her as Philippe. The other man, younger and more talkative, was André. The two women were dressed, like Louise, in stunning gowns. The blonde woman, Marie-Thérèse, was wearing a short plum-coloured dress which exposed a generous length of finely shaped leg; and Fabienne, the dark-haired woman, was dressed in a figure-hugging sheath dress. Louise felt that their glamour was an easy, practised one; whereas she was very self-conscious and uncomfortable, feeling like a powdered and painted doll. She guessed that she must be the youngest person present by at least ten years.

The conversation between Gui and the other guests sparkled, and the livelier the talk became the more inhibited Louise became. She did not want to open her mouth for fear of embarrassing herself. She couldn't compete with the witty banter, or the talk of high finance and international business. How different from the easy, relaxed life at Les Oliviers, where she could say and do whatever she pleased. Here in the château, she felt restricted by what she thought was expected of her: genteel good manners and absolute decorum at all times. In these surroundings, how could one behave otherwise?

Louise was also beginning to doubt whether her interpretation of the information in the hotel's leaflet was correct after all. Did she just have a dirty mind, reading *doubles entendres* where none were intended? It seemed unlikely that such elegant, charming and cosmopolitan people as these would have need for such services. Louise still hadn't worked out the relationships between the four other guests. Had they come singly, or were they two couples? None of them wore wedding rings, and they gave nothing away as they talked.

Philippe, who was sitting to her right, turned to her. 'You're very quiet, Louise. Are you feeling all right?'

Gui spoke before Louise could reply. 'Louise is a little overwhelmed by us all, I fear. She is still settling in but, once she becomes accustomed to the way of life here, I'm sure she will be totally at ease.'

Marie-Thérèse turned to Gui, and spoke as if Louise was not there. 'Where did you find her?'

'She turned up on my doorstep like a lost soul. She's a student, researching into a missing masterpiece: a de Valence portrait of a reclining nude. I know Louise will prove a willing and able pupil.'

Louise looked at Gui, wondering what he meant.

'Isn't she delightful?' said Fabienne, who was sitting opposite her and looking ravishing in her slate-grey gown. 'So beautiful.'

'Isn't she?' André agreed.

Louise flushed keenly, embarrassed by all this close attention; and was pleased when the conversation took a different turn.

After the meal, the Comte and his five guests withdrew to the music room: high-ceilinged, with ornate gilded plasterwork on the wall panels and the ceiling, and equally lavishly gilded furniture. The room was dominated by an intricately carved marble fireplace. Gui went over to the grand piano and began to play a piece that Louise recognised as one of Beethoven's *Diabelli Variations*. She was surprised to hear that he played very well, phrasing the complicated piece with both drama and precision.

The others sat down to listen. André looked at Louise and patted the cushion next to him on one of the sofas. Fabienne was seated on his other side, and Louise could see that the sofa wasn't so large that she would be able to avoid being thrust against André. He might want to be sandwiched between two women, but she wasn't going to oblige. She hardly knew the man. Then she smiled at her double standards, remembering that she had hardly known Raheem, or Pedro before him, or the policeman, or the man on the ferry . . . But she couldn't behave like that at the Château de Puivent, at least not in public. It was different here, in these dignified surroundings, in such refined company; and she felt her behaviour was somehow circumscribed by the formality around her.

And so Louise pretended not to have noticed André's offer and settled into a fat armchair, kicking off her shoes and pulling her feet up under her. A liveried servant came round and offered the guests a choice of whiskies, brandies and liqueurs. Louise asked for an armagnac, and meditatively sipped the fiery liquid as she listened to Gui's skilful recital. When he had finished, he came over and sat in an armchair near Louise's. He caught her eye and smiled encouragingly at her.

As if Gui's rejoining them was her cue, Marie-Thérèse got up and walked over to the fireplace. It seemed to Louise that she was deliberately striking a pose and Louise wondered why. It was a rather odd, theatrical thing to do when everyone else was settling back into their comfortable seats and relaxing. Marie-Thérèse stood with her back to the others, seemingly intent on the decorated marble. Her straight blonde hair covered her shoulders and the upper part of her back. It was clear to Louise that Marie-Thérèse had a lovely body; the curves of her haunches were plainly visible through the sheer fabric of her short dress. André got up from the sofa and walked over to join her. Something about his manner caught Louise's attention: it was deliberate and, although Louise dismissed the idea almost as soon as she had thought it, somehow predatory.

André stood behind and slightly to one side of Marie-Thérèse. He placed his hand on her left buttock, but Marie-Thérèse did not react at all, and just carried on looking at the fireplace. So much for the refinement of her company, thought Louise, taken aback by André's actions. Blushing with embarrassment at witnessing this, Louise looked slyly around at the other guests to see how they were reacting to this bizarre turn of events. They were all watching, but their faces betrayed nothing.

André caressed Marie-Thérèse's buttock through the material of her dress, catching the fabric under his hand and gradually raising it higher and higher so that the lacy tops of her stockings were exposed. Louise watched with embarrassed fascination. She couldn't work out whether André was doing this for his own satisfaction or for that of the others. He seemed to be displaying Marie-Thérèse to them, almost like a shopowner proudly demonstrating his wares to some potential customers. Louise took another quick glance around at Gui and the other guests seated near her. They were all watching, silently but more intently than before. It seemed that this was some sort of a show. From their unsurprised reactions, it also seemed that they were expecting this. Louise certainly wasn't.

'Marie-Thérèse has a problem, don't you? Why don't you tell us all about it?' André said.

The blonde woman laughed lightly and turned to face the others. 'Well, *I* wouldn't call it a problem. It's just that other people seem to find it so. I'm an exhibitionist.'

All the time André was slowly playing with her dress, exposing her thighs and then covering her again. Marie-Thérèse acted as if nothing untoward was happening.

André continued his questioning. 'When did all this start?'

'I never really knew that I was an exhibitionist until I was on the metro one day, about four years ago. It was a hot summer's day – and you all know how hot and sticky Paris can get – and I wasn't wearing any underwear. I had a short dress on, a bit like this one, and after a while I became aware that the man sitting opposite me was staring at me. Well, staring between my legs, to be more precise. He must have been able to see everything. But instead of pulling my dress as far down as it would go, and closing my legs tight, and making myself decent, for some reason I can't quite explain, I had the sudden urge to do the exact opposite. And that's what I did. I opened my legs a little way for him, and he responded by putting his hand over his crotch. I could see that he had a growing hard-on under the material beneath his hand. I opened my legs a little further and, at the same time, I shifted slightly on the seat, surreptitiously hitching my dress right up my thighs. I don't know what else would have happened, because just then an old lady came to sit by the man, so I covered myself up. But after that first time, once I had got a taste for it, there was no stopping me.'

'Tell us more.'

'It's got me into terrible trouble. Since that first time I've been arrested, tried and found guilty of gross indecency, several times. I'm a repeat offender – I can't help myself. I love my body, and I think you all like it, too. Am I right?'

Philippe, Fabienne and André nodded vigorously.

Louise was watching Gui closely, and was disappointed to see that he nodded too. Marie-Thérèse turned and looked directly at Louise. Louise wanted to hide from her attention, but it was too late.

'Now, don't you find me sexy? Tell the truth now.'

Louise felt uncomfortable under Marie-Thérèse's close scrutiny. The Frenchwoman walked over to Louise and leant over her, a hand on either arm of her chair, pinning her in. Louise's eyes were directly on a level with Marie-Thérèse's breasts, and she knew that Louise could see the thin sheen glistening on them, created by both the heat in the room and by Marie-Thérèse's own undoubted arousal.

'How sweet. Such a shy thing, and how different from me,' Marie-Thérèse said.

If only she knew, thought Louise, but said nothing. She still felt gauche and awkward in this company.

A low wolf whistle came from Philippe, who was sitting directly behind Marie-Thérèse. Realisation spread over Louise's face, and with it a becoming flush of red. Marie-Thérèse's dress had ridden right up as she had leant over towards her, and now her rump was exposed to the others.

'They like it,' said Marie-Thérèse, looking steadily at Louise. 'Now, answer my question.'

Louise knew it was pointless to deny it. She nodded, her eyes cast down. Marie-Thérèse put her finger under Louise's chin and tilted her face up so that Louise had to look at her. She winked, and then turned to the rest of the group.

'I like to show my body to people. I think it's nice to share it. I like to show people when they're not expecting it. Sometimes I go out without any knickers on and bend over in the street to pick something up, or I'll leave the changing room curtain not quite drawn when I'm out shopping for clothes. Always accidentally, of course.' Marie-Thérèse laughed.

'I always get the same feeling as that first time with the man in the metro. The thrill, the sense of power, was amazing: it was as if I could control that man, simply by showing what I chose to show.'

Louise's cheeks were burning. Her eyes were cast to the floor, intently fixed on the intricate patterns of the Oriental carpet.

André spoke again. 'Would you like to show us?'

There was silence, apart from the occasional appreciative noise from one of the others. Curiosity got the better of her, and Louise looked up.

Marie-Thérèse stood in front of the fire. She gathered her dress by the hem, and slid it upward until she was holding it around her waist. She slowly turned, allowing the others to see her from every angle. Above her stockings she was wearing a matching G-string. Then she raised her arms and lifted the dress over her head. She now stood before the others in her underwear. Her breasts were full, and barely restrained by the black lace of her bra.

Louise's ears and cheeks were burning. This sort of behaviour here, in this setting, seemed so wrong. And yet, she couldn't stop herself from sneaking quick glances at Marie-Thérèse, every now and then.

Marie-Thérèse moved her hands to the tiny scraps of lace that held her G-string at her hips. They were tied into small bows, and she pulled these, releasing the panties, which fell from her. Her pubic hair was as blonde as the rest of her hair, and was clipped into a neat triangle. Louise was overcome by a sudden feeling of panic; that she had to get out of the stifling heat of this room and away from whatever was coming next. She was tired and wanted to sleep. She excused herself and left the room. As she closed the door behind her, she heard the others talking.

'She's shy, poor thing,' Marie-Thérèse murmured.

'We'll soon cure her of that,' Louise heard Gui reply.

Chapter Ten

Louise woke early the next morning and had already had her breakfast before the others came down from their rooms. She decided to follow the invitation in the leaflet to explore, and set out to search the château from top to bottom. This time Gui could not challenge her. After all, the permission was there in black and white. She felt more certain than ever that somewhere within the solid stone walls of the castle was *The Venus of Collioure*. She had work to do.

Louise began her search on the ground floor of the main building, going into the one last place that she had not managed to access the previous day. There were some surprised looks from the chef and his staff when she wandered into the vast kitchen area. In the far corner she noticed the entrance to the chateau cellars. These had not been shown on the plan, and she hoped with a rush of excitement that this omission might signify something. She followed the brick steps down, descending into the cobweb-festooned depths. The cellars were massive: three brick barrel-vaulted rooms, each filled with rack after rack of dusty bottles of wine. There was a damp mustiness in the air, and this was enough to tell

Louise that she needn't bother to check the area thoroughly. She knew that there was no way that Gui would risk keeping a fragile masterpiece in such hostile conditions. The damp and the dust and the mould in this environment would attack and destroy an oil painting within weeks.

She moved on with her search. She quickly scanned the other ground-floor rooms that she had been in before, as a double check; and then she began on the first floor. There were some nine or ten bedrooms, all of which were empty; but two of which had clearly been recently vacated, given the crumpled bed linen and the distinctive smell of sex in the air. She reached down to feel the sheets on one of the beds, and they were still warm. She wondered who had slept where, the previous night.

Louise came to the door of the room Astrid had taken her to the previous day: the Dressing-Up Box. She opened the door and stepped into the mirrored room. She already knew that *The Venus* was not to be found in here, but she couldn't resist the temptation to have a better look at all the fabulous dresses that she had seen so briefly – and maybe even try some of them on. She slid back the door and looked once more at the sparkling array of designer outfits: Donna Karan, Jean-Paul Gaultier, Nicole-Farhi, Vivienne Westwood, John Galliano. Just about every famous designer and every famous label she could think of was there. This was like a dream come true.

One dress drew her attention. She carefully slid it from its hanger and removed its protective covering. It was a vampish fifties-style fishtail gown, strapless and sequinned and totally over the top. She loved it. She quickly stripped off her clothes, stepped into the gown and drew it up around her. Louise went over to the other wardrobe and selected a matching pair of shoes, and then paraded round the room. She turned this way and that, admiring her reflection. She looked fantastic, but there was no way she was going to allow anyone to see her dressed like this. It was neither subtle nor her style. She flicked through the other dresses on the rack, wondering what other treasures were hanging there.

After trying on some ten or fifteen gowns, Louise had to admit to herself that she was getting bored. She would never have believed it possible, but the lure of designer dresses palled somewhat when she was faced with such a surfeit of them. She pulled on her own clothes again, deciding that, even though they were far cheaper, they were also far more comfortable and practical.

She was about to leave the room when it occurred to her that she hadn't yet investigated the other two wardrobes. She went over to the one in the third long mirrored wall, and opened it. Thinking it would contain yet more designer dresses, she was surprised by the contents. The wardrobe was filled with what she knew might be described as 'specialist' wear: silk and satin, leather and lace, rubber and latex; all were there. She pulled out an outfit: a maid's uniform comprising a short black skirt and a white lace apron, complete with white lace headband. There were nurses' outfits, schoolgirls' outfits, buckled bondage outfits and a huge range of lingerie.

Louise looked around guiltily, before pulling a red lacy basque off a hanger. She looked at the label. It was her size. This was another kind of clothing that she had never worn before. She stripped off again, more quickly this time, and slipped into the basque. It took her a few minutes to lace up the front panel, pulling the laces as tightly as she could to cinch in her already slender waist.

Louise looked in the mirror again, and liked what she saw. She was amazed by the transformation that such a small article of clothing could effect. Her breasts were forced right up, giving her a full cleavage; and they were barely held by the cups of the basque. She could just see the faint pink of the tops of her areolae showing above the red lacy material. As she moved, the constriction of the basque was such that her breasts trembled and wobbled with every step. Even an underwired and deep-plunged bra hadn't been able to do this for her before. She gazed down and brought her hands to her breasts, idly dreaming that her hands were Gui's.

She decided that the image was not yet complete, and searched for some matching knickers. She found some that were so small they were little more then a scrap of string at the back, and put them on. Red stockings were next, clipped on to the suspenders that hung down from the bottom of the basque. Then Louise went over to the shoe wardrobe and pulled out a pair of red wet-look leather shoes with four-inch stiletto heels. There were shoes with higher heels, but she didn't think that she would be able to balance in them.

She stood back and admired the view. Her figure had been transformed by the basque into an almost cartoon-like caricature of a woman: all voluptuous curves and a tiny waist. The four-inch heels made her legs seem supermodel-length; and the red spelt out one thing. Slut. She wondered what effect it would have on Gui, as it was certainly having an effect on her. She could feel herself becoming aroused by the narcissistic pleasure of looking at her own image in the mirror.

She decided to see what wonders were contained in the last wardrobe: the one next to the door. She slid back the mirrored door. The space was shelved, and each shelf contained a vast selection of sex toys. Louise didn't doubt that it would rival that offered behind the blacked-out windows of any high-street sex shop back home. She studied the contents with fascination. There were dildoes – single dildoes, double-ended dildoes, double-ended dildoes with a flexible section in the middle. There were a huge variety of rings and clips and other items for which Louise could not even guess a purpose. Then there were the vibrators; they came in all sorts of colours, some ridged and some smooth, some shaped like massive penises and others with strange, additional protuberances.

Louise was fascinated. She had never seen a vibrator before, let alone felt one. She gazed around, and smiled when she saw some packets of batteries stacked to one side of the vibrators. She picked up a red plastic vibrator, shaped like a penis with prominent veins, and tried to grip it in her palm. Its girth was too great to let her fingers meet her thumb. She wondered how it turned on, and guessed from the lack of an obvious switch that it might operate like the torch she kept in her camper van. She screwed the base in and, sure enough, the vibrator whirred into life.

'Red suits you.' Gui's voice suddenly interrupted her close inspection of the buzzing appliance, and she threw down the vibrator as if it had scalded her. Louise turned round, flushed with shame, angry and embarrassed to have been caught – and especially to have been caught by Gui.

He smiled. 'It's always important to accessorise, isn't it?' he said, looking at the vibrator.

'Ha, ha, very funny,' she snapped. 'Do you always go round sneaking up on people?'

'No, as it happens, I don't. I was passing along the corridor and heard a noise in here.' Then Gui's voice took on a sudden, steely edge. 'But I might remind you, Louise, that I can go any damn where I please.' He glared at her, and for the first time Louise had a hint that there might be a darker side to her host.

'I'm sorry,' she apologised. She tried to cover herself as best she could; but Gui was standing between her and her pile of clothes on the floor.

'You look stunning,' he said, brazenly casting his gaze up and down her full length. 'I would never have thought that scarlet on a redhead would work, but you have proved me wrong. I have to admit that I am quite fascinated by your hair colour: it's very unusual, and so striking. And especially so for you to be that colour all over.'

Louise looked at him, frowning. Did he mean what she understood him to mean? She looked down: she was covered by the tiny knickers, albeit only just.

Gui continued. 'It has been my experience that virtually every redheaded woman I've ever known does not have matching pubic hair. Normally because most redheads are such thanks to a bottle rather than their genes. You are a rare and fascinating exception.'

'How the hell do you know that?' Louise stormed.

'Let's just say a little bird told me,' Gui said smiling.

Louise thought quickly, and then nodded. 'Raheem. The sneaky little sod. Does he go telling tales on all your guests, spreading round their intimate secrets?'

'You're wrong, Louise. It wasn't Raheem. I saw for myself.'

Louise looked at him incomprehendingly. The door had been firmly closed while she had been getting changed.

Gui took her by the arm and led her gently into the middle of the room, until they were standing beneath the light fitting which sat in the middle of the mirrored ceiling.

'Look up carefully,' he instructed.

She looked up at the fitting, squinting at the four bright bulbs.

'Next to the bulbs. See those tiny lenses?' Gui asked.

It dawned on Louise. 'Cameras?' she muttered. Suddenly she had forgotten about her anger and her near-nakedness.

Gui nodded. 'Once you know to look for them, you'll find them everywhere, throughout the château.'

'Including in my room,' she said, nodding her head. She silently apologised to Raheem. 'But why?'

'I would have thought that was obvious, Louise. I'm a voyeur, and this hotel is my personal fiefdom, set up and run purely for my own benefit.' He laughed. 'Despite what you guests might think.'

Louise was intrigued, both by the contents of Gui's admission and by the openness with which it was expressed. There had been no sense of shame in what he had said; no fear of her disapproval.

'So you just watch?' she asked.

'I watch, and I learn, and I teach.'

'You teach?' she asked, even more intrigued.

'In that way, I can participate by proxy. With the cumulative benefit of my considerable experience, I have a lot to pass on. Only to the right pupils, though. Such knowledge would be wasted on the majority of people.'

These words electrified Louise. What Gui seemed to be offering her was exactly what she was searching for.

'And I understand that you are keen to learn.'

Louise's face darkened. How could he know that?

Gui seemed to sense her thoughts. 'Milo told me all that you'd said to him, about how you had just broken free from a stultifying relationship and were seeking new experiences. Most commendable.'

Louise exploded. 'Milo. That shit. First he sells you that painting of me – which he promised me he wouldn't part with, or even show anyone else; and now I find that he's also told you my innermost secrets. Has that man got no scruples, no morals at all?'

'Come now, Louise. You know him well enough by now. This shouldn't come as a surprise to you. I might add, however, that he didn't breathe so much as a word to me about your interest in *The Venus of Collioure*.'

'That does surprise me,' Louise said bitterly.

Stepping over her clothes where they lay on the floor, Gui went over to the first wardrobe and drew out a beautiful silk kimono.

'Put this on,' he said, 'and come with me.'

Louise obeyed and silently followed Gui along the corridors and up the narrow stone staircase that led to his private apartments at the top of the tower. She hoped that she wouldn't bump into anyone else on the way there, as she was very aware of her distinct lack of clothing. He turned a key in the door and she followed him into an elegant and surprisingly spacious hallway. Four closed doors opened off it, two on the left and two on the right.

A man in a butler's suit appeared in the vestibule through one of the doors. The absence of any expression on his face when he saw Louise made her wonder whether Gui entertained kimono-clad women in his apartments on a regular basis.

'It's all right Bertrand, I shan't be needing you,' Gui said, and the man nodded, and went back into the room.

'In here, Louise,' said Gui, opening one of the doors for her and showing her in. 'This is what I call my control centre.'

The room was empty of furniture apart from a large centrally placed desk bearing a console, and a high-backed leather armchair. There was a closed door on the opposite side of the room. Louise gawped at the equipment on display: the banks of screens on the wall, the console, the headphones, the video camera on a tripod and the binoculars. It seemed bizarrely fantastic and unreal, more like something out of a spy movie than real life. She almost expected to see a large bald man stroking a white cat seated in the high-backed chair in front of the console, and told Gui so.

He laughed. 'I've got many ambitions, but world domination isn't one of them.'

Louise nodded, still silently viewing the impressive range of technology before her.

Gui sensed her wonderment. 'When you have the desire to watch, you make sure that you have the best equipment,' he said simply. 'Here. Look.'

He leant over the console and flicked a few switches. Immediately the twelve great screens on the wall burst into life, eerily glowing in the low light of the room. Gui flicked another switch, and the twelve screens combined to show a single writhing image. It took Louise a little while to decipher the vast scene in front of her. She blushed when she realised that it was a close-up view of André and Fabienne on a bed, their limbs wrapped around each other.

Gui adjusted yet another switch and sound burst forth from the speakers mounted on either side of the screens. Fabienne's moans were increasing in both frequency and volume, as she thrashed her head from side to side. Gui smiled.

'You see, I get to learn my guests' innermost secrets this way,' Gui said. 'André worships women. There's no other way of describing it: he simply cannot get enough of them. Like me, he is a voyeur, though perhaps it's fair to say that he's not quite as dedicated to the cause as I am.' Gui laughed. 'Fabienne is insatiable: what you might call a nymphomaniac, so she and André go very well together. You know all about Marie-Thérèse's particular penchant; and as for Philippe – well, let's just say that he's got a problem.'

'I don't think you should be telling me all this,' said Louise uncomfortably; wondering, nevertheless, what Philippe's problem comprised.

'Nonsense. If you are to be my protégée, this information is vital.'

Louise smiled. Gui had confirmed her suspicions and his intentions.

'You have a go,' said Gui. 'This button selects the camera.'

Louise was unsure, but Gui nodded at her encouragingly. She pressed the button and the images flashed before her: the grand salon, the kitchens, her bedroom, even the gardens. When the view came round to André and Fabienne once more, she watched for a while.

Gui watched her as she watched the screens. After a while, he spoke.

'As a student of the history of art, I expect that you are used to giving things your closest attention. Detailed observation is everything, as is a developed sense of aestheticism.'

Louise frowned. Gui might be right in theory, but she didn't think his ideas were necessarily right in practice. Dr Petersen certainly didn't seem to have much in the way of a developed sense of aestheticism.

Gui was clearly warming to his theme. 'It is so much better when you can take pleasure in what you see, don't you think? I see you like to watch. But how do you like to be watched?'

Louise looked at him. He had struck a chord. She thought about the whole business of watching and being watched. Gui's voyeurism excited her. She knew that he had seen the portrait of her being pleasured by Colette; and that he had watched her with Raheem. And he knew that she knew this, which gave an extra twist to their relationship.

And then there was her proposed exhibitionism. At university, she and Tom had fucked in public places, where they might have been discovered at any moment: but they hadn't been. On the ferry, she had had sex with an anonymous soldier while crew members looked on from a distance. But that didn't affect her, as she didn't know them and they didn't know her. They were just people whose paths had collided for a half-hour or so, never to meet again. The prospect of becoming involved in an exhibitionist relationship with people she knew, while Gui looked on, was very different.

And yet, the more she thought about it, the more the idea appealed to her. She liked the thought of behaving so provocatively, and not just for her partner's pleasure.

She thought back to the way that Marie-Thérèse had displayed herself, and had to admit that, if she thought about it, she would like to do that, too. Now here was her chance.

She mulled all this over, then looked at Gui and nodded. 'I'm going to Fabienne's room now. I want you to watch me.'

Louise did not go straight to Fabienne's room, however. First she went back to the Dressing-Up Box. She threw off the kimono and undid the tight laces of the basque, breathing a sigh of relief at the release. She slipped off the red knickers and kicked off the shoes. Then she went over to the wardrobe with the specialist clothes. First she slipped on a lacy black G-string. Then she searched. She knew what she was looking for, and she was sure that she would find what she was after in the well-stocked wardrobe. Sure enough, she soon pulled out a short, sleeveless black rubber dress. She gradually eased herself into the tight shiny dress, wriggling and tugging to pull it up over her hips, then over her breasts, and then feeding one arm after the other in through the straps. Once it was on there was a great deal of adjusting to be done. The rubber stuck to her like a limpet, and she had to yank and tug to straighten up the hem and the neckline and to smooth out the last of the wrinkles.

When she had finished, she regarded herself coolly in the mirror. The rubber hugged her every curve, shining seductively. She felt that the dress almost cried out to be touched, such was the sensual appeal of the material. Louise smiled. That would do. Apart from one final thing: she bent down and picked up the vibrator off the floor.

She walked slowly and purposefully to Fabienne's room. She paused by the door, knocked and went straight in, without waiting for an answer. Startled, André looked up. She had interrupted him just as he was doing up the belt on his jeans. He whistled when he saw Louise. She looked beyond him into the room, where Fabienne lay spread naked on the bed. She looked up at Louise, and smiled.

'Come in,' Fabienne purred.

Louise placed the vibrator on a table by the wall. She knew that both pairs of eyes were avidly watching her every move.

'You've ... changed since last night,' André murmured, clearly impressed by what he saw.

'Let's just say I've taken some advice,' said Louise.

Fabienne rolled over on to her stomach and cupped her chin in her hands, making it clear that she was ready to watch. This pleased Louise. Being the centre of attention was what she craved, above all. She knew this now.

Louise started to move her hands over her dress, feeling her body through the tautly stretched fabric. She moved slowly, giving André and Fabienne ample opportunity to regard her. The jut of her nipples through the material was clear, and she saw that André's eyes were riveted to them. She would give him what he needed. She stopped and turned to face him. 'Help me take my dress off?' she asked. 'Then you can see better.'

She watched with mounting pleasure as he hurried to stand up, and then she raised her arms, and nodded at him. He needed no more bidding, and grasped the hem of the dress, slowly pulling the clinging material up over her hips. André stopped when he caught sight of her G-string. 'Oh God,' he muttered, and dropped to his knees in front of her. 'Let me look, please,' he said, an edge of desperation in his voice. He knelt beside her; his head was close to her groin.

'Show me,' he whispered. She smiled, and nodded. He put his hands on her hips and slowly turned her round, breathing roughly. He stared intently at her bottom, the firm rounded cheeks and the thin lacy thong between them.

'Bend, please,' André asked, and Louise slowly bent from her waist, her bottom tightening and the lace-covered swell of her mound becoming visible between her legs. 'Enough,' he whispered, and she straightened up again. André slowly turned her to face him again. He nuzzled against the tiny scrap of material, breathing in her warm, sweet smell. Then he looked up. 'Can I?' he asked.

Louise gloried in this, the power her body gave her over him, and nodded her assent.

André gently slipped a finger under the front of the black lacy panel. Louise let out a gentle moan. Slowly, he pulled the material to one side, revealing the fine auburn tuft between her legs. Again, he nuzzled against her. Louise felt the hotness of his breath against her most sensitive parts, and felt the tightening knot of want that she knew was moistening and swelling her, readying her.

'André, would you like to watch me touch myself?' Louise asked. Almost choked with lust, André nodded vigorously. She put her hand on his shoulder to steady herself as she stepped out of her lacy underwear.

Still with her dress hiked up around her waist, Louise started to run her hands over her thighs, which were slightly parted. André was transfixed, kneeling in front of her like a supplicant. He could see her clitoris, prominent now, and the clear wetness that glistened on it, indicating her arousal. She brought her hands closer to her pussy, teasing expertly. She circled her clitoris with her thumb, applying light pressure every now and then, while her fingers held her lips apart so that André could see right into her. Then she slowly started to slide her fingers over her vagina, slick with her juices. Louise knew that, barely six inches from her, André could feel the heat she was generating.

She felt him breathe in, and knew that he was taking in her perfume, the unmistakable scent of an aroused woman. To be so closely observed, to be the exact focus of all André's senses, to see him transfixed by her as a starving man before an opulent banquet, she felt the aphrodisiac of power washing over her once again. She suddenly knew exactly what it was that Marie-Thérèse meant, the previous night, when she had talked about the power her body gave her.

André watched, his breath coming in short agitated leaps, as Louise slowly slid her middle finger deep into herself. It disappeared, right up to the knuckle, and then reappeared anointed in clear sticky juices, and André was watching so intently she knew that his cock would be swollen and hard, trapped in his jeans and twitching for release, that he was aching to come, but she wouldn't let him – not now. This was her show. Louise moaned as she steadily worked the finger in and out, and then added a second and then a third finger, her pace quickening as she did so.

'I need something bigger,' she whispered urgently, and André looked round. She knew that he wasn't going to offer his services, as this was too good for him to miss, watching only six inches from her beautiful sex. His eyes lit on the vibrator lying where Louise had placed it on the table, and he hurried over and picked it up. She took it from him, and he knelt in front of her again. This was so good. She would show him something he wouldn't forget in a hurry.

She twisted the base of the vibrator, and it buzzed and jerked into life. It had a powerful motion, and Louise could feel the tremors pulsing through her hand. She held it near the base, placed the tip of the red penis against her wet opening, and slowly began to push. She moaned, much louder this time, as the vibrator started to disappear into her. She knew that André could see her lips parting and stretching to accommodate the juddering monster.

'Oh God, that's good,' Louise groaned, with her head thrown back. Her hair swayed gently, echoing the shudders that racked through her body.

André obviously couldn't wait any longer, and fumbled in his jeans to release his prick. Looking down, Louise saw that Fabienne had moved from the bed and now was kneeling next to him. Without a word, Fabienne took André's cock and started to masturbate him, slowly and expertly, while watching intently as Louise pleasured herself.

Louise saw the sudden rising surge of André's approaching orgasm and, unable to hold it back, he groaned as thick threads of semen shot up into the air and landed on her hand while she worked the vibrator in and out. She reached down with her other hand, scooped up his cream on a finger, and slowly inserted the finger into her mouth, sucking it clean. It tasted good: salty and rich. In addition to feeling her sex engorged and stretched by a huge, vibrating plastic penis, and her clitoris tight and pulsing – in addition to the two rapt onlookers who knelt in front of her – this final sensation brought her to overload. She thrashed and shook as a crashing orgasm swept over her clitoris and outward to the rest of her body, down to the very tips of her fingers and her toes. Her knees almost buckled under her, but she somehow controlled herself.

After the waves of sensation had ceased, Louise stood still, and slowly withdrew the vibrator. She looked down at André and Fabienne as she raised it to her mouth and licked her musky juices, now mingling with André's. Then she let the vibrator drop to the floor. She smiled and placed her hand on Fabienne's head, as if blessing her.

Then she looked up, searching for the camera lenses that she knew were concealed somewhere in the room.

She spotted one amongst the crystals of a small chandelier, and winked at it. She hoped that Gui had enjoyed the show as much as she had.

Louise settled into this new existence at the château almost as easily as she had fallen into the one at Les Oliviers. And, as had happened at Les Oliviers, she gradually thought less and less about her research. She was so wrapped up in learning from Gui, and her explorations in exhibitionism found the perfect foil in his obsessive voyeurism.

She quickly came to know the staff and the other guests intimately: apart from Philippe, that was. He behaved distantly towards her, and seemed to actively avoid her. She could not work out why this should be, as she had not knowingly offended him.

Gui set her a variety of tasks which she undertook with enthusiasm. She learnt many new techniques and positions of lovemaking, always performed with an eye to the camera lenses or the others watching in the room. Under Gui's patient tuition, she became even bolder, more imaginative and more demanding in her lovemaking. But she was frustrated by one thing: Gui's interest went no further than voyeurism. He would tell her in explicit detail what he required of her; and sometimes would even fit her with a tiny earpiece so that he could convey his instructions to her as she undertook her duties, but he was never there with her. He never came into the room to watch or participate, as André and Marie-Thérèse and Fabienne did. He was always a distant observer, sitting in front of his flickering screens; or thumbing through the photographs that he instructed the hotel photographer to take. His seeming disinterest in her made Louise behave increasingly wantonly, hoping to tempt him into participation, but she did not succeed.

* * *

Louise had a nasty shock one day when she saw the day's date on a newspaper. She had been at the château for four weeks, and her time in France was fast running out. She realised that her behaviour in ignoring her research was the equivalent of an ostrich burying its head in the sand. She had to go back to university and, if she went back without sufficient material for her dissertation, her future would be in jeopardy. A bad degree result would seriously affect her job prospects.

Over the next week, Louise reapplied herself to her research. It frustrated her that, just as Milo had, Gui seemed to be delaying her as best he could. He talked to her at length about the other de Valence paintings that he owned, and made oblique references to *The Venus*; but he came no closer to revealing it to her. Louise made full studies of the other de Valence paintings in Gui's collection in the rest of the château. They were much fuller studies than she wanted to make, but in the absence of *The Venus of Collioure* she felt that they would have to make do, as they were peripherally connected with her dissertation topic.

Finally, Louise decided to have it out with Gui. Once again, she climbed the narrow stone staircase leading to his apartments.

She knocked briskly. Bertrand opened the door, and seemed to detect something of her pent-up anger, as he politely explained to her that the apartments were strictly private and that he would inform the Comte that she wished to see him, and that she should go down to the grand salon and await him there. Louise was about to go when she heard Gui's voice calling out behind Bertrand. She was then ushered into the vestibule. Gui was standing in one of the doorways. He beckoned her towards him.

'What is it, Louise?' he asked.

'*The Venus of Collioure*. If you haven't got her, or if you have got her but aren't going to let me see her, I might as well leave. I can't waste my time here.' Bold words but, in truth, Louise hadn't a clue what she would do or where she would go next if the Comte called her bluff. The trail for *The Venus* ran cold at the château.

'How demanding of you,' he said. 'Very well. Come with me.'

He led her into a spacious, elegantly furnished living room. On one wall was a large embroidered hanging, obviously masking something beneath.

'Draw it back,' he said to her. She walked over and pulled the draped hanging down. Underneath, in an ornate gilded frame, was Estelle Gachet, lying on her red bed, with a rug on the floor and a discarded shoe nearby. *The Venus of Collioure*. But not *The Venus of Collioure* that Louise had been searching for.

'Nice try, Gui,' said Louise bitterly. It was a fake, and not a very convincing one at that. The paint was applied too thinly, too tentatively; and the colours were not nearly pure or vibrant enough to be those of a genuine de Valence. Stepping closer, Louise could see that some of the paint was still drying; and then she saw the tiny initials in the corner: MC.

'I'm impressed by the speed with which you spotted that. Barely a pause.' Gui said. 'Let's just say it was a little test. Milo was very amused when I asked him to prepare this for you.'

'I'm not going to play your games any more,' Louise said bluntly. 'I'm wasting my time here.'

'Oh, I wouldn't say that,' said Gui consolingly. 'Won't you admit that you've learnt something from me?'

'Maybe, but it's not what I came here for.'

'Perhaps this will help you,' Gui said, going over to a walnut writing desk and opening one of the drawers. He pulled out an old card-backed artist's portfolio, tied up with faded red ribbon. He handed it to Louise.

'Open it,' he said.

It took Louise a little while to undo the knotted ribbon

She was curious, and her trepidation made her fumble-fingered. When she finally succeeded, she lifted the stiff board back. Beneath was a single sheet of thick paper. Louise could see that it had been ripped out of a sketchbook. On it, in pencil, was a sketch of a woman. The woman was Estelle Gachet, and the sketch was undoubtedly the preparatory sketch for *The Venus of Collioure*.

Louise looked up. She hadn't expected this. Until now, she hadn't known of its existence.

'My God. Where did you get it from?' she asked.

'That would be telling,' Gui teased. 'You may study it for as long as you wish.'

Louise was now more sure than ever that Gui also possessed the finished Venus. She still believed what Milo had told her, and this sketch seemed to corroborate it. She could imagine Gui, the compulsive collector, acquiring it so that he could compare it with the finished masterpiece.

There was a knock at the door, and Bertrand entered the room.

'There's a slight problem downstairs, sir. Astrid has noticed that one of the alarm sensors appears to be behaving erratically.'

'I'll be right down. Come with me, Bertrand,' Gui replied. He turned to Louise.

'Will you be all right here for a few moments?' he asked her. She nodded. Once she heard the door to the stairway closing, she put down the portfolio, and hurried into the hallway. There were still two other doors off the vestibule that she hadn't been through: two rooms in which *The Venus of Collioure* might hang. The first door led into a compact bathroom. It was undoubtedly a man's bathroom, with dark-blue tiles and matching dark-blue towels, and chrome fittings and accessories. The second led into a small kitchen. It was modestly fitted and bore no decoration or ornamentation. The table was spread with newspaper, and Bertrand had clearly been interrupted from a session of shoe polishing.

Louise cursed, and then remembered the other door in the control centre. That must be Gui's bedroom. She hurried into the control centre and was reaching for the door handle when she heard footsteps approaching up the stone staircase, and so darted back into the living room, plonked herself on one of the sofas and tried to look as nonchalant as possible as she studied the sketch.

'False alarm,' said Gui, entering the room. Louise tried to act coolly, but she had a nagging suspicion that Gui knew what she had been doing. Gui confirmed this by reaching in his pocket and bringing out a slim, high-tech video monitor. He switched it on and Louise could see the grainy image of them both in the living room. As she moved, so did her image on the small screen.

'That door is always kept locked, by the way,' he said, patting his pocket. 'And I have the only key.'

Chapter Eleven

Louise had gone for a walk. She felt the atmosphere at the château was becoming a little too claustrophobic for her liking, and so she set off one morning down the rough track on the far side of the crest on which the château sat. She had a bottle of water with her, and a book. She was going to find a quiet, relaxing spot and have a read. She wanted to put Gui and *The Venus of Collioure* and all the goings-on at the château out of her mind for a little while.

Louise could see that the path headed off up into the wooded mountains. It was a narrow, stony track, probably used by shepherds and few others, she thought, and it passed through the dense woods of dark pine trees and paler-leaved deciduous trees. The smell of the resin oozing from the trunks of the pine trees was intensified by the heat, creating an intoxicatingly strong perfume. A large striped butterfly flitted past in the dappled shade, and Louise wished that she had an identification guide with her. She thought that it might be some kind of swallowtail, but wasn't sure. She watched as it found another, similarly marked butterfly, and they fluttered around each other, upward and out of sight.

After walking for about an hour, during which the path had ascended a ridge, descended into another valley and risen once more up another mountainside, Louise saw that the path opened out into a small, sloping meadow. The grass was long, uncut and ungrazed, and the wispy grass flowers nodded in the breeze. Louise walked through the meadow, marvelling at the variety of flowering plants growing there. She stooped to inspect the intricate flowers of an orchid, and then sat down in the grass and opened her book.

She couldn't concentrate on it for long, though. She could hear buzzards calling overhead, and put the book down and watched the spiralling birds of prey and the distinctive silhouettes of swallows as they dashed and swooped high above her. The view from the meadow was spectacular: the mountains beyond were forested, dotted here and there by small meadows similar to the one in which she was sitting. The sky was as brilliantly blue as it had been since she had first arrived in France, and there were a few large fluffy clouds in the distance. She watched as the shadows cast by the clouds slowly travelled over the land beneath them. She could hardly imagine anywhere more perfect. She lay back in among the fragrant grasses and flowers, and closed her eyes.

Some time later, Louise became aware of the distant clanking of bells. She looked up, but could see nothing. She could hear four or five distinct tones, and they seemed gradually to be getting louder. She closed her eyes and dozed on. Later, she heard a man's voice calling out, and then some sharp yells and whistles. The bells sounded very close now. She turned her head and looked down to where the path she had used opened out into the meadow. A Jersey cow appeared, and then another, and another. The lead cow had a thick leather collar around its neck, from which hung a gently clanking iron bell.

Louise watched as the herd entered the meadow,

spread out and began to graze contentedly on the rich grass. She could see that six of the cows wore bells, but not the rest. She rested her head on the sweet grass again and closed her eyes, idly trying to work out why that should be. The clanking of one of the bells got louder and louder, but Louise did not stir. She liked cows: their gentle inquisitiveness; their large eyes framed by long curling lashes; and their slow, deliberate movements.

One of the cows approached. She could hear its snuffling breath and the tearing noise as it grazed on the grass, and then felt the warm, wet dab of its nose as it sniffed her arm. Then she heard the man's voice again.

'Shoo, shoo, you great oaf.'

Still lying with her eyes shut, Louise wasn't sure if the man was addressing her or the cow. Then she heard a hard thwack, and knew that the man had hit the cow on the rump to drive it away from her.

'Oh, what have we here?' the man said to himself. Louise lay still, pretending to be asleep. She was curious to know what the man would do. 'Mademoiselle?' he said. She did not reply. 'Mademoiselle?' he repeated, a tinge of concern in his voice.

Louise realised that this was probably an odd sight, a strange woman lying in the middle of a meadow miles from anywhere. To reassure him that the scene was not as alarming as it might appear, Louise shifted languorously, as if enjoying a good dream. She moaned, for good effect.

'My very own sleeping beauty,' the man said. She felt him kneel beside her. His knees brushed against her waist. He leant over her: even with her eyes closed, she could tell that he had blocked the sun, and she could feel his hot breath on her skin.

'Wake up,' he whispered in her ear. She didn't stir.

He shook her gently by the arm. 'Wake up,' he repeated. She shifted again, and moaned some more.

Then she had an idea that might give her cowherd some encouragement. 'Marc,' she moaned. 'Oh Marc.' Then she writhed, slowly and sinuously, as if enjoying a dream of a lover's touch. She gently gyrated her hips and brought her hand to her breast. 'Marc, touch me,' she moaned.

It seemed to do the job. The man gently lifted her hand from her breast and placed it by her side. Then she felt him quickly and deftly begin to unbutton her dress, starting at the neckline. His hands brushed against the swell of her breasts, and Louise cried out again: only this time it was no pretence. Her body was responding to primal urges within her, unleashed by the rough hands of the cowherd.

All through that afternoon, Louise moaned and writhed in the sun, enjoying the sensual embrace of her dream lover. Not once did she wake for him: not when he undressed her or caressed her or explored her body. The cowherd thought she was a deep sleeper; but Louise had rarely been more wakeful. Even when he slid inside her and gradually worked them both to slow, powerful orgasms, she did not wake.

Louise got back to the château as the sun was setting behind the western mountains. She was tired out by all the exercise and fresh air, not to mention her other exertions. She went up to her room and rang the bell. Violette, one of the maids, appeared at her door almost instantly.

'You rang, mademoiselle?'

'Violette. I think I would like to spend an hour or so in the sauna. Would you go and prepare it for me, please?'

The maid silently curtsied her acknowledgement of Louise's order, and left. Louise slipped off her dress and went into the bathroom, wondering whether Gui was watching. She turned on the shower and stepped under the powerful jet of hot water. She turned her face to the source of the water, feeling it beating down on her face. Then she reached for the soap, and took a brisk shower. This was no time for luxuriating: the sauna was the place for relaxation.

She towelled herself off roughly and put on one of the huge fluffy bathrobes. Then she padded barefoot along the corridor and into the tower. The sauna was situated on the floor directly beneath Gui's private apartments, and comprised a large pine-panelled sauna and an adjoining room with a shower and two deep plunge pools: one full of cold water for a refreshing, quick immersion and the other more welcoming with warm water. Thick piles of towels lay around the shower room, ready for use.

Louise opened the door into the sauna and was greeted by an impenetrable wall of steam. She couldn't even see to the other side of the room. She quickly closed the door behind her to conserve the steamy atmosphere, and groped her way to the bench seat against the opposite wall. The air was stifling, hot and damp, but once she became accustomed to it she began to enjoy the feeling of taking the thick air into her lungs. She sat back against the warm pine panelling, undid the belt of her robe and slipped it off her shoulders. Then she got up and shuffled her way towards the brazier. She reached down for the large cast-iron ladle hanging over the side of a pail of water on the floor, and scooped up some water and dribbled it over the glowing coals.

Louise knew that they were fake, and the brazier was powered by electricity, but the coals still glowed and sizzled and spat effectively, giving off fresh clouds of thick steam. She groped her way back to her seat, and folded her bathrobe double before sitting down on it: her buttocks weren't well upholstered enough on their own to prevent her from feeling the hard slats of the bench.

'Did you have a good day?' a voice asked out of the mist.

Louise gave a little gasp of surprise. She had thought she was alone in the sauna. She peered across the room, trying to see through the swathes of steam that curled and rolled through the misty air, and gradually was able to make out another shape against the opposite wall.

'Philippe?' she asked. The shape got up and approached her. She was relieved to see that he had a small white towel around his waist. She, however, was naked. She thought she would appear too gauche if she were suddenly to scrabble beneath her and put on her robe, so she covered herself as best she could, by casually laying one hand over her lap and covering her breasts with the other.

Philippe came and sat next to her. 'Your modesty is very becoming,' he said. She blushed, but knew that her face would already be so red from the sweltering heat in the sauna that Philippe would not be able to see her blushes. She couldn't help looking down at his body: it was trim and well kept, suggesting a healthy athleticism.

'How are you finding it here at the château?' Philippe asked.

'Fine, thanks,' Louise replied. She felt awkward.

'You seem to be taking it all in your stride. I take it that Gui has filled you in on what we are all doing here?'

She nodded again.

'I almost envy the others their appetites. I was sent here by my doctor.' Philippe frowned and looked down at his hands, which were folded in his lap.

Louise didn't know what to say. She remembered that Gui had mentioned something about Philippe having a 'problem'. She had wondered about it then, but now she wasn't entirely sure that she wanted to know what it was.

Philippe continued. 'He told me that I am a very

unusual case. A thirty-eight-year-old male virgin. He said he'd never met one before.'

Louise couldn't repress the laughter that burst out of her. She had thought that he was going to regale her with some sad story of a sexual hang-up or malfunction. But virginity? That was hardly a medical matter, she thought, and was more likely to be cured by opportunity than medicine.

Philippe looked at her with hurt eyes. 'I'm sorry that you find it funny.'

Louise felt guilty. She hadn't meant to seem rude. She reached over and touched his arm. 'I'm sorry. It's just that I'm a bit surprised, to be honest.'

'Why should you be surprised?' Philippe asked.

'Well,' said Louise. She wanted to bolster his confidence. 'A good-looking man like you. I'd have thought you'd get lots of offers.' She wasn't being overly flattering: Philippe was a handsome man.

'I do. I just don't know what to do with them.'

'You're kidding?'

Philippe shook his head.

'You mean, no one's ever thought to show you?'

He shook his head again. 'And the longer I've left it, the more of a hang-up I've got about it. That's why my doctor sent me here. He said, if I get used to being around naked women, and to seeing other people making love, I might get the confidence up eventually to do something about it.'

'Has it succeeded?' Louise asked. By now, she had completely forgotten her own nakedness – she was so wrapped up with Philippe's predicament. She had turned on the bench seat and was facing him, her arm still resting on his.

'Not yet,' Philippe replied. His eyes flitted over her body, and then he looked away, as if embarrassed.

'Don't be shy,' said Louise. 'You can look. I saw you looking at Marie-Thérèse, that night. You can look at me, too.' She put her hand on his cheek and drew his head around so that he was facing her. His eyes were fixed on hers, and she could feel him trembling. She was filled with an overwhelming sense of tenderness and pity for this poor man. No wonder he had seemed to avoid her and she had rarely seen him about.

'Look at me,' she whispered to him. Philippe lowered his eyes slowly down her body.

'Do you like what you see?' she asked. He nodded. Louise pushed her hair back, so that he could see her shoulders and breasts more clearly, and took one of his hands from his lap. He pulled back against her grip when he realised what she was going to do.

'It's all right,' she soothed. 'Feel. It's nice; smooth and soft. You don't need to be afraid.'

She placed his quivering hand on her right breast, holding it there with her own. Philippe looked so startled that Louise thought he might get up and run away at any moment.

'Does it feel nice?' she asked. He nodded dumbly. She could feel her nipple puckering under the warm flesh of his palm.

'Let me tell you what a woman likes. She likes to be kissed,' said Louise, leaning towards Philippe and softly grazing his lips with her own. 'She likes to be kissed all over her body.'

She turned and lay back on the bench seat, looking up at him. 'Try it.'

Philippe sat stock-still, as if struck by lightning. She could see his erection growing under his towel.

'Try anything you want, Philippe. Or, if you can't think what to do, ask me, and I'll teach you.' Louise closed her eyes. This was a new sensation. She herself had been taught often enough over the past few months, led into new sexual experiences; but she had never been the tutor. Not until now. To take a raw, uninitiated man into previously uncharted realms of sensual abandon was an experience she had never even dreamt of, never thinking it would be possible. And somehow here she was, with a thirty-eight-year-old man who needed tutoring in all the ways of giving and gaining sexual fulfilment.

And he was making a very promising start. Louise could feel his hands exploring her body, followed by tiny, tentative kisses. Describing what she wanted, showing him techniques and responding fully to his ministrations, Louise gradually introduced Philippe into the art of love. She showed him what she could do for his body, how she could tease and manipulate; and what he could do for hers. She taught him about foreplay, how the build-up to lovemaking is as important as the culmination. She guided his hands over her body, showing him her innermost and most intimate places, inviting him to look and touch and taste and smell.

Philippe proved a keen student, and Louise barely noticed as the minutes passed into hours. Occasionally she would break free to throw more water on to the brazier, although by now she couldn't tell where the steam settling on her skin ended and her own sweat and juices began. Gradually, Louise became aware that the balance of the relationship seemed to have shifted away from a student–teacher one: either that or he was a natural, learning quickly and acting intuitively.

'I want to fuck you,' he eventually whispered in her ear. He was ready.

'Yes,' she sighed, as she felt him press against her sex. Philippe needed no encouragement or direction. He moved fluidly, moving inside her with a natural rhythm, smothering her with kisses and whispering obscenities in her ear. Louise was slightly surprised at this, but guessed that all the stimulation of the last couple of hours must have proved overwhelming for him; that, and the frustration of thirty-eight years of celibacy.

With one hand he reached down and caressed her

clitoris, while he grasped her breast in the other and fondled it. All the time, he was plunging into her and rearing back like some magnificent beast. Louise could feel his excitement rising, and knew that he was trembling to control his orgasm, holding it back until she had reached hers. She felt it building inexorably within her, and then she collapsed against him, grasping him as she shuddered under the force of her climax. He looked down at her and allowed his own orgasm to follow, thrusting into her as he closed his eyes and threw back his head. He finally collapsed on to her, shuddering with relief as he held her and kissed her and thanked her.

Louise knew Philippe would prove an excellent lover. His consideration in holding himself back for her showed that. And she felt pleased with herself, knowing she could take all the credit for tutoring him so successfully.

Louise bumped into Gui on the stairs later that evening. He invited her up to his apartments for a pre-dinner glass of wine.

'You're looking very pleased with yourself,' he said to her, as he poured her drink into a fine crystal glass.

'Like the cat that got the cream,' Louise replied. 'And you can interpret that any way you want.'

'Ah,' smiled Gui. 'I take it that you have had another encounter.'

Louise couldn't resist the temptation to crow. 'You could say that. Two, in fact. And I guess you missed them, poor old Gui. For all your high-tech gadgetry, I bet that even you haven't managed to put the surrounding countryside under surveillance; or found a lens that can cope with the steamy conditions in the sauna.'

Gui shook his head. 'Unfortunately not. But the sauna *is* wired for sound. Sometimes I like to close my eyes and listen. You might think it an odd admission for a voyeur to make, but I find that the mental pictures that my imagination can summon up for me are often sufficient for my purposes. And besides, voyeurism isn't specifically about watching other people: it's about witnessing other people. And I witnessed your exploits with Philippe with great interest.'

Louise felt that the wind had slightly been taken from her sails. She rallied quickly. 'You heard his admission, then?'

'Oh, yes,' said Gui, smiling.

'And you heard how I was able to help him?'

'Oh, yes.'

'So what did you think of that?' she asked, sitting back smugly.

'I thought it was most amusing.'

This was not the reaction Louise was expecting. 'What? Amusing?'

'Louise, for all your professed worldliness, for all that you have told me you have learnt this summer, you are still very naive. You fell for one of the oldest tricks in the book.'

'But . . . you told me that he's got a problem,' Louise countered limply.

'And so he has. Philippe is totally without scruples. His problem is that he will say or do whatever is necessary to get a woman into bed with him. He's a compulsive liar.'

'What . . .?' Louise muttered in disbelief.

Gui nodded his confirmation. 'Dear old Philippe has been coming here with his virginity problem for the last fifteen years at least. He's found numerous kind ladies who have been touched by his distress, helped him in his hour of need, and relieved him of his most tiresome burden. You might want to talk to Fabienne. I believe she rendered him the exact same service just last week.'

Gui laughed, and Louise couldn't help but join in.

'The silly sod. He didn't have to go through all that

rigmarole. He could have just asked me weeks ago, and I'd have happily obliged.'

'Ah, but then the seduction would not have been nearly as sweet.'

'Sometimes I don't think I'm ever going to get the hang of this,' Louise murmured.

'I think you pretty much have already, Louise. You've proved yourself a most willing and able student. And such studiousness deserves a reward.'

Louise had hoped that her reward would finally be *The Venus of Collioure*, but she was not surprised when de Valence's masterpiece was not forthcoming. She was feeling jaded and restless. She would soon have to leave France to go back for the start of the new university term, and she had failed utterly in her dissertation research. She had finally and reluctantly accepted the conclusion that the Comte had been playing with her. He was not going to show her *The Venus of Collioure*, no matter how hard she tried to persuade him.

Once she had come to terms with that conclusion, she decided to stay on with Gui at his castle purely for the enjoyment. After all, it wasn't every day that she got the chance to stay in a luxurious château as the guest of a French aristocrat. She would deal with the problem of finding a new dissertation topic once she got back to university; and doubtless she would have to suffer Dr Petersen's smug I-told-you-soing; but until then she was going to enjoy herself as best she could for the short period that she had left in the Pyrenees.

She was woken a few mornings later by the sound of banging and hammering outside her window. Bleary-eyed, she went to the window and drew back the muslin curtains that were billowing into the room in the early-morning breeze. In the courtyard garden below her, men were busily starting to erect a length of scaffolding along a stretch of the battlement wall. She mentioned this over breakfast to Raheem, as he poured her coffee.

'It's for tomorrow's pageant, mademoiselle. It's held here every year, to commemorate the local peasant revolt of 1188 and the successful defence of the castle led by the lady of the house, while her husband was away at the Crusades. I think you'll enjoy it. It starts at lunchtime and goes on all day and into the night, and everyone joins in.'

Later that morning, Louise changed into her bikini and pulled a long T-shirt over it. She wandered out into the gardens to watch the progress of the work. She had no great interest in the erection of scaffolding: it was the scaffolders who interested her more. The workmen had stripped off their tops in the blazing heat of the sun, and presented a fine display of bronzed and muscular masculinity. Louise thought with a wry smile how different this view was from that of English workmen, boiled beetroot red in the sun, with beer bellies and bum cracks on full display. She was standing idly gazing at them when Paul, another member of the hotel staff, appeared at her shoulder, and asked if he could get her anything. Louise thought for a moment, and then requested a sun lounger. She also asked him to bring down her book from her bedside table.

Paul swiftly complied, and produced no ordinary sun lounger, but a teak chair with brass fittings, complete with footrest, armrests, headrests and a plump, cotton-covered cushion. He also brought out a low table to go next to the chair, an umbrella to shade her, a crystal jug of water and a matching glass, her suntan lotion and her sunglasses. Louise shook her head. She was trying to get used to the pampered existence here, but it still took her breath away sometimes. Ask and ye shall get, tenfold, she thought to herself.

She settled down into the chair, stretching her legs out and watching the scaffolders over the top of her book.

She could tell that they were aware of her scrutiny, as they started to compete against each other in acts of daredevilry, agility and strength. She watched as they tossed the metal poles to each other as if they weighed no more than bamboo ones; they climbed up the scaffolding without using the ladders; and they balanced seemingly on tiptoes on the edge of the poles, reaching out with both hands and with no safety harness to protect them from the long drop below.

When the wind was blowing in her direction, she overheard one of the men commenting to another about her. Louise smiled to herself. The coarseness of what he said made him not so different from his English counterparts, after all. He was a fine specimen, with bleached blond hair and baggy knee-length shorts, and his appearance reminded her of that of a surfer. She was pleased that she triggered such thoughts in him, and hoped that she was having a similar effect on the others.

As Louise looked across at the workman, she caught his eye. He paused, and started to pull down his shorts. Louise watched, laughing to herself in amused disbelief. She hadn't expected French workmen to be as keen on mooning as their English counterparts. But the scaffolder was wearing pants underneath: stretchy cotton ones that incongruously reminded her of an Edwardian gentleman's bathing trunks. The pants came down his thighs a little way, and the material clung to his buttocks and his groin. He threw his shorts down to the ground below him, and she heard him telling the others how hot he was. So was she.

Louise sat up and pulled the T-shirt off over her head. Then she reached for her bottle of suntan lotion, and squeezed a generous dollop on to her palm. She proceeded to slowly cover herself with the lotion, rubbing it into her arms, neck and chest until it had completely disappeared. She spent a disproportionately long time attending to her breasts. This was as much for her own enjoyment as for that of the men. Then she drew first one leg up and then the other, applying the lotion with a sensual massaging motion. She knew that the men were watching her, and she allowed her hand to drift up her inner thigh until it was brushing against the tiny strip of her bikini bottoms. She could hear muttered and crudely appreciative comments drifting across to her on the breeze.

Pleased with herself, Louise then rolled over on to her stomach, and picked up her book once more. That would have cheered up their working day, she thought. She heard approaching footsteps. She pulled down her sunglasses and peered over her shoulder. One of the men was walking purposefully towards her. It was her surfer-scaffolder. Louise watched his approach, making it clear that she was sizing him up; and that wasn't hard to do, as his clinging pants didn't leave much to the imagination.

'Excuse me, mademoiselle. I couldn't help noticing that you haven't done your back, and you might burn. May I help?' he asked politely.

She smiled at him. Very different from the crudeness of expression he had been employing a little earlier. 'That would be nice,' she replied, lying down again. She closed her eyes as he popped open the lid of the lotion, and seconds later she felt his hands on her back. Despite the thick, warm slickness of the lotion, she could still feel the roughness of his palms against her skin. But it didn't hurt: to the contrary, she found it arousing. He gently massaged the lotion along her spine, then fanned his hands out over her back, all the time working with a light pressure.

'Mademoiselle? I think it would be easier if I could undo your top,' he said after a few minutes.

'Fine,' Louise replied, her eyes still shut. She had been hoping that this might happen.

She felt his fingers fumbling with the fine cord which

she had knotted into a bow on her back. He found the loose end and pulled, and the tension of the cord under her breasts was released. He then undid the other cord around her neck, and gently laid the loose ends on the cushion by her face. She reached up and pulled the bikini top out from under her, and tossed it to one side.

The man began to massage more lotion into her back. This time he spread his hands further round to the side, allowing his fingers to slide over the swell of her breasts.

'You might find it easier if you straddle me,' she said, her eyes still closed.

The man instantly did as he was told, and she could feel the warm, coarse hairiness of his thighs brushing against her legs as he knelt over her. He bent close to her, and she felt the cotton-covered bulge of his groin pressing against the curve of her buttocks. All that separated them were two thin pieces of material. The man pressed against her, and Louise reacted wantonly, arching her buttocks up against him. But despite her tuition under the Comte, even Louise was not yet enough of an exhibitionist to proceed any further in front of such an audience.

'Thank you. That will do,' she said, her eyes still closed. The man complied silently, getting up off the chair and replacing the bottle on the table. Louise watched over her shoulder as he departed, and saw him walk away, not towards the scaffolding, but to the loos. She had a pretty good idea of what he was going to do in there, and smiled. She liked having that effect on men.

Louise lay in the sun, dozing and reading, for the rest of the morning, listening to the hollow metallic clanks of the scaffolding and the men's ribald comments.

'I enjoyed that show. And so did the others,' a familiar voice said. She looked up, and saw Gui smiling down at her. He was wearing a loose cotton shirt and chinos, and had his hands in his pockets. It was, for him, an unusually casual attitude.

'Always happy to oblige.'

'I've come to ask you a favour,' Gui said, moving round to sit on the end of the lounger. Louise reached for her bikini top and put it back on before turning to talk to him.

'Fire away.'

'I gather that Raheem briefly told you about the pageant. Let me elaborate. We hold it annually, and all the locals join in. Everyone gets dressed up in period costumes. It starts with a procession down in the village, and then the villagers march up to re-enact the storming of the château. We have a brief scurry – fireworks going off, water being poured over the battlements in the place of boiling oil, lots of shouting and yelling – that sort of thing, and then Lady Blanche comes to the battlements and appeases the rioters with a little speech. Then we open up the gates and everyone pours in – not to sack the place but for the evening feast here in the courtyard garden. I provide it as a little thank-you to the villagers.'

Louise wondered what for, but said nothing.

'What I wanted to ask you, Louise, was if you would be willing to play Lady Blanche for me this year? Marie-Thérèse and Fabienne have already played the role in previous pageants, and I would be honoured if you would accept the role this year.'

Louise was a bit taken aback, but felt that she could not refuse. She was Gui's guest, after all. It was the least she could do to repay him. 'But what about the speech? I don't have to make it up, do I?' she asked nervously.

He patted her leg comfortingly. 'No, don't worry. I've got it written down. It's the same speech every year, and it's short. It has to be, because everyone knows that the gates open as soon as you finish, and when the gates open the wine starts flowing. You'll probably find that, if you look down, you'll see that they'll be mouthing the words along with you, egging you to get on with it.'

'OK,' said Louise, wondering what she was letting herself in for.

The next day, she was starting to get an idea. The drumming and blowing of trumpets in the village below started early in the morning, and provided the aural backdrop as Astrid took her to the Dressing-Up Box and fitted her into her Lady Blanche costume. It wasn't strictly accurate for the period it was supposed to represent, but Louise felt that it would be churlish to point this out. The spirit of the thing was what mattered. It looked medieval, which was close enough, give or take a few hundred years. Astrid helped her into a long embroidered blouse which had a simple drawstring at the scooped neck, and over that went a magnificent green velvet gown, which laced up below her breasts. It was topped by a massive headdress: a pointed cone like a witch's hat, covered in matching velvet with a trail of lace protruding from the end. Louise wasn't sure if a headdress like this had ever existed in the annals of history, but it was certainly dramatic enough for her part.

Astrid took the costume away to make a few adjustments, and Gui came by with a copy of the speech. He was right: it was short, barely ten lines long. Louise looked out of her bedroom window as she paced back and forth, trying to memorise it. Trestle tables were being set out on the gravel parking space below her window, and a huge bonfire was being constructed near to the entrance tower.

At lunchtime, Astrid returned with the costume and helped Louise to fit into it. Louise then made her way down to the courtyard garden, where Gui was waiting for her. He was dressed in a short green tunic which came down as far as the top of his buttocks, and he wore matching-coloured leggings. The tight material of the leggings revealed the firm musculature of Gui's calves and thighs, and Louise couldn't keep her eyes from travelling further upward to his codpiece: it was large, bright red, festooned with ribbons, and positively demanded attention.

Gui complemented her on her appearance and led her over to the scaffolding. He climbed up the ladder behind her. 'You'll get a good view from here. You'll also be the centre of attention.' Gui laughed. 'Well, for a few moments, at least.'

'I know, I know,' laughed Louise. 'To paraphrase a certain French king: "*Après moi le vin*".'

The banging of the drums got louder, and Louise could hear raucous shouts and yells welling up from the village on the lower reaches of the slope. She felt slightly giddy looking over the drop on the other side of the battlements: apart from where it was broken by the narrow path along the base of the wall, the drop was almost vertical.

'Don't forget: you make the speech when the guy in the black cloak challenges you from the path below. Then the gates open and the fun begins.' Gui turned and climbed back down the ladder, leaving her alone on the scaffolding.

Louise watched as the snake of tiny figures gradually wound its way up the twisting road to the château. She could see that almost everyone had got into the spirit of the occasion, with a gaudy variety of home-made costumes. Some of the men were carrying long spears and others had swords and shields. The noise was unbelievable. As well as the shouting and yelling, some people were singing, and others were banging drums and blowing on horns. A small band brought up the rear. They were playing *La Marseillaise* to help get the people into the revolutionary spirit. Anachronisms seemed to be the order of the day here. Louise grinned. First the costumes, and now the music. She wondered what else might be out of period: peasants with mobile phones and pacemakers, fillings and filofaxes?

The crowd swarmed around the entrance tower, and Louise could hear but not see the ruckus. There was a furious pounding against the gate, and Louise wasn't so sure that it would be able to withstand it. Further along the scaffolding, men were pouring large drums of water over the battlements, and she could hear the yells as the people below got a good soaking. Rockets shot up from near the bonfire. It was all very impressive.

The crowd surged along the path and paused under the wall, and a sea of upturned faces regarded Louise expectantly. Right on cue, at the front of the gathering a tall man in an imposing black cloak roared a challenge at her. She replied, managing to deliver her speech word-perfect, much to her relief. She heard the portcullis being winched up and the heavy gates being thrown back, and the crowd cheered as they ran back towards the gate.

Louise watched them swarming into the château gardens, crowding round the tables with the food and wine, and gathering round the ox which was roasting on a spit over the glowing embers of the bonfire. She carefully climbed down the ladder and joined the throng, wandering among the revellers in the walled garden. She was chatting to a group of villagers when she felt a light touch on her arm. She turned, and there at her elbow was Gui.

'I want to show you something. Come with me.'

Gui led her away from the noise and into the peace of the château. She followed him once more up the staircase to his apartments. He showed her into the control centre, and closed the door behind him. Louise wondered what it was that Gui had in mind. Maybe he was going to show her more of the athletic exploits of his guests, captured live and in flagrante as they brought their sexual fantasies to life. But no, she had seen André,

Fabienne and Philippe talking by the ox-roast, and Marie-Thérèse had been among the crowd, lifting her skirts to a chorus of appreciative cheers. Perhaps Gui had their performances on tape instead.

But, instead of going to the console as she expected, Gui walked over to the door on the other side of the room, behind which, Louise guessed by a process of elimination, was his bedroom. It had to be: it was the only room in the entire château she had not yet been into.

'Take your shoes off,' he said, kicking off his own mock-medieval leather ones and revealing his tanned feet. Louise obeyed. She saw with pleasure that Gui had what she called Botticelli toes: like the people depicted in Botticelli's paintings, his second toe was longer than his big toe. This gave his feet an elegant, refined appearance, very unlike her own.

'Come here,' he said. Louise followed, curious. He stopped her in front of the closed door, and turned her round. He took off her headdress. 'Let me put this on you instead,' he said, placing a strip of black velvet over her eyes. It was one of his games, but she couldn't join in whole-heartedly. She couldn't summon up the energy to complain either, to tell him that she didn't feel like it. So she stood and allowed him to fasten the blindfold without demur.

Once he had tested it, she heard Gui unlock the door with a key and then he led her into the room. She faltered when she felt a roughness under her feet, but Gui gently led her on a few more paces. Then he stopped her in her tracks, swivelled her around and straightened her, pulling her shoulders back and placing his hand under her chin to draw it up. It was as if he was preparing her for something. Then he undid the tie at the back of her head, and drew away the blindfold.

'Open your eyes,' he said.

Louise opened her eyes and took in the scene in front

of her. Gui's bedroom was decorated in a sparse, simple style, very much at odds with the decor of the rest of the château. The walls were painted a pale oatmeal colour, and the floor was covered with coir matting. A large futon was spread on the floor, and a low table stood next to it. There were no curtains on the windows, and the light flooded in. A single plain glass vase containing some white arum lilies was the only decoration in the room. Louise took the scene in. She had somehow expected a self-confessed voyeur's bedroom to be very different: full of mirrors and video cameras, perhaps.

'I don't understand,' she said.

Gui stepped up to her and gently brushed her hair away from her face. 'I've never invited anyone in here before. I wanted you to understand how special I think you are.'

Louise felt her stomach give a little leap at his words. She had long wanted to hear him say something like this, but had thought that she was just another diversion, another amusement to him, and nothing more. She looked up at him, almost holding her breath in anticipation as he lowered his head to kiss her.

Kissing her sweetly, Gui pulled Louise down on to the futon with him. For the first time, her hands explored his body, feeling the firm muscles under his tunic and leggings. His eyes, normally so watchful, were closed. Louise looked at the long dark lashes against his skin, and couldn't resist the temptation to kiss his eyelids, so gently that her lips barely brushed his skin. Gui reached up and gathered her hair in his hands, rubbing it across his face and breathing her in.

'Come here, my Titian beauty,' he said, drawing her to him. Louise could feel her breasts pressing against Gui's broad chest, and his strong arms encircling her. She could also feel a hardness rubbing against her from beneath the padded softness of his codpiece.

As they kissed, she could feel his hands feeling for the

drawstring at the neck of her blouse. Gradually, Gui managed to undress her, while still kissing her. Louise marvelled at his skill and dexterity, as he broke free from their passionate kisses only once, in order to lift her dress over her head. Naked, Louise pushed Gui back on to the bed and straddled him. He lay there and gazed up at her with a look of lust and wonderment, and Louise sat back on her haunches and basked in his appreciation of her.

'I wouldn't have thought it possible, but you are even more beautiful in the flesh,' he murmured, reaching up to cup her trembling breasts. She gasped with pleasure as he kneaded them, playing her taut pink nipples between his fingers, nipping and teasing.

Then Louise pulled off Gui's costume, her hands working quickly to uncover his body. He was built like a Greek statue, every muscle finely delineated. There was not an ounce of surplus fat on him. She thought that she could look at his body for hours. She didn't even need to touch it – just to lie next to him and gaze over his flawless physique would be enough for her. But the opportunity to do more was hers, and Louise wasn't going to squander it. She lay next to him, exploring his body with her fingers, feeling the different textures of his skin, his lips, his muscles and his hair. Taking deep breaths through her nose, she smelt his hair, his neck, and even his armpits, drawing in his unique aroma. She bent over him and covered his body with tiny, grazing kisses; her hair drifting in curling copper tresses over his flesh as her head moved lower and lower, over his downy-haired thighs, down his muscular calves, down his long, slender feet.

She thought of her lovemaking as a form of worship, too. He was so perfect, in every way, that she didn't want this moment to end.

Gui had been lying still, enjoying her caresses; but as she kissed her way up his inner thigh, he pulled her up by the shoulders until she was lying on top of him. His prick was pressing into her stomach, and she could feel it throbbing against her.

'Not that, this,' he whispered, and Louise could feel him moving and adjusting and positioning himself, and then she gasped as he moved into her. They made love with a ferocious passion, Louise straddling him and riding him, while bending forward from the waist to kiss him. The intensity of the sensations as he thrust up into her was almost painful, he was so deep inside her. She had wanted this for so long.

Sweat-drenched, they brought each other to greater and greater heights of ecstasy, until at last they toppled over into the free fall of their simultaneous orgasms. Gui moaned distractedly, looking up at her with an expression of pure desire. Louise could feel her sex contracting powerfully around him as she came.

Louise looked down at Gui and kissed him tenderly.

'So you don't just watch, after all,' she laughed.

She pushed herself up and off him, and rolled to his side, reaching for the glass and bottle of mineral water on the low table. She poured a glassful, took a deep swig and then offered him the glass. She watched him fondly, and then lay back and looked down at her own prone and sweat-covered body. Slowly she raised her glance to the wall beyond the bottom of the bed; the wall to which her back had been turned when Gui had unmasked her.

Colour: a bright, vivid, glowing sheet of sumptuous colour covered almost the whole wall. Louise leapt up like an Olympic sprinter bursting out of the blocks. She stared at the wall. Speechless, she turned to face Gui, who lay back on the futon below her, laughing.

Eventually, Louise recovered herself enough to be able to speak.

'Bastard. You bastard,' she muttered, a huge smile stretched across her face.

It was *The Venus of Collioure*.

Chapter Twelve

Louise spent the next three days closeted in Gui's bedroom, photographing, videoing and documenting the painting. She concentrated especially on the areas of the painting that had been hidden by the three people in the old photograph, taking detail shot after detail shot. At times, she would stand back from her work and simply admire the masterpiece before her. It was stunning: the colours so vibrant and the lines so vigorously drawn that the painting seemed to reverberate with life. Now that Louise had studied the painting more closely, she was sure that she could see something of Milo in the face that gazed down at her with such languid eroticism. Estelle Gachet's great-grandson certainly seemed to have inherited something of her unabashed sensuality.

Gui had sworn Louise to secrecy, and she couldn't even tell the other guests or the chateau staff what it was that she was so diligently studying in the Comte's private apartments. Louise was sure that they would all have thought up far racier explanations for her prolonged incarceration up there, and would be bored and disappointed with the true reason.

On the fourth day after Gui's revelation, it was time

for Louise to leave the Château de Puivent and all it contained. She had completed her studies, and the new university term started in three days. There was just time to make the long journey back to England and get unpacked before being thrown into the busy schedule of lectures, seminars and studying.

For the third and final time that summer, Louise readied to pack her camper van. Raheem and Bertrand helped her to carry her luggage and equipment down from the château to where she had parked the van by the entrance tower, many weeks beforehand. She oversaw the two men as they loaded the van for her. She had already made her farewells with Gui. She had found it poignantly difficult, as she was far fonder of him than she cared to admit. She also felt a sad certainty that, despite what he had told her in his bedroom that one time they had made love, he would quickly forget her once she had gone.

As Raheem was putting the last of her belongings into the van, she tried the ignition. The engine was as dead as a dodo, and Louise knew with a sinking feeling that it was more than a flat battery. The *gardien* wandered over from the gatehouse and looked under the bonnet with her. He drew in his breath sharply, and tutted and sniffed, making noises that Louise took to be the Gallic equivalent of 'Sounds expensive, mate'. He offered to call up Michel, the mechanic from the nearest garage. Louise waited fretfully for Michel's arrival; and then waited some more for his diagnosis. It didn't take him very long to ascertain that the starter motor was broken, and he told her that it would take him a fortnight at least to get a replacement part. Louise was becoming more and more perturbed by the possibility of a delay, as she knew that there were steep fines for late registration at university, and she could scarcely afford to incur a penalty.

Louise looked up from her discussions under the

bonnet with Michel and saw with dismay that Gui was approaching from the château. She had hoped to leave without having to see him again, as she had found their previous parting very painful. Gui asked what the problem was, and Louise explained the situation to him. He nodded, and gave some quick instructions to Michel which she didn't catch.

Gui suggested they go for a walk. Preoccupied by her predicament, Louise frowned at Gui's suggestion. The last thing she felt like was a walk. Gui took her gently by the arm and led her away from the van. Louise looked back over her shoulder in agitation.

'How am I going to get home? I can't afford to hire a car, and I've got far too much stuff to be able to carry it all with me on the train,' she fretted.

'I have a proposal to put to you,' said Gui, in a low, calming voice. 'Leave your belongings here. Take your clothes and your research material, of course – but leave everything else. That includes the van.'

'Oh, you sweetheart. Would you freight my belongings on to me in England? Or send someone over with them in the van when it's fixed?' Louise asked. She would have to worry about paying for all this later.

'No,' said Gui.

Louise's face fell. Gui continued. 'I've a better idea. Leave them here, and come back for them next year, after you've graduated.'

'But . . .' Louise didn't think that she could cope for a year without her trusty vehicle.

'I have a proposition to put to you. I've been very impressed by you, Louise.'

She looked at him questioningly.

'And not just by the enthusiasm with which you embraced my special interest. I'm impressed by your research, and by your studiousness. You worked by your initiative, and you wouldn't be put off, despite the various setbacks that you encountered, and it brought you the final result that you wanted. Your conversations with me about Gustave de Valence have shown me that you have a rare understanding of his work; and I am certain that this extends to your other studies. I would like you to come back here to the Château de Puivent after you graduate next year and work for me.'

Louise hesitated. Being one of Gui's specialist sex operatives wasn't quite the career she had planned out for herself, enjoyable as her experiences at the château had been.

Gui clearly understood the turn her thoughts had taken. 'No, you idiot!' he laughed. 'Not that. As the curator of my art collection.'

'What?' Not for the first time, Gui had caused her to be lost for words.

'I think you heard,' he said, smiling.

'But . . .' Louise struggled for words. His suggestion was so unexpected. 'What if I get a poor degree? You wouldn't want me then.'

'You won't. Especially with your peach of a dissertation.' He winked at her.

Louise couldn't believe her luck. A dream summer had ended in the offer of a dream job.

And so a little while later, for the second time in a day, Louise said her reluctant goodbyes to everyone at the château. She was heartened by the thought that the partings were now *au revoir* rather than a final farewell. She would be back in less than a year, after all.

Gui dropped her at the train station, but Louise asked that he didn't come to see her off on the platform, as she found this particular goodbye the hardest of all. He had kissed her on the cheek and squeezed her hand, and she still felt the memory of his touch on her skin as she boarded the train.

As the train pulled away, Louise sat back and looked around her. She was surprised by how empty the train was: in her carriage there were only two other people an old couple, both asleep, their heads nodding in time with the clackety rhythm of the wheels on the rails. Sleep seemed like a good idea. It was going to be a long journey.

Louise's thoughts drifted back to all she had seen and done over the summer; and to all she had learnt. She had come looking for new experiences, and had certainly had plenty of those. She had been taken under the wings of two very different men; and both had educated her in more ways than one. Even if she hadn't tracked down *The Venus of Collioure*, it would still have been worthwhile.

She gazed out at the beautiful scenery passing by. The sun was shining as intensely as ever, its rays almost burning her skin through the thick glass of the railway carriage. Louise lay back in her seat and drifted off to sleep. When she awoke again, the carriage was empty. She wasn't sure how long she had been asleep for. She had been having an erotic dream. In it, Marie-Thérèse had been exhibiting herself to several shaven-headed soldiers in full uniform, while Louise pointed out Marie-Thérèse's finer points to the eager squaddies, much like an auctioneer at a slave market. Louise shifted lazily on the warm fabric of the carriage seat, thinking about sex. The heat she was experiencing was not solely from an external source.

The steady rhythm of the train gradually slowed, and then finally it came to a halt. The train had stopped in a stretch of woodland, and Louise looked out at the lush, inviting greenery. It looked fresh and cool in the woods, very different from the airless fug within the carriage.

An announcement came over the train tannoy: 'Due to engineering works on the line, the train will be stationary for the next ten minutes. We apologise for any inconvenience.'

Louise didn't mind in the slightest. She was in no rush. She gazed out of the window, past the railway track running parallel to the train, and off into the trees.

She watched as a deer walked unconcernedly along one of the woodland paths, browsing on the fresh tips of the low branches. After a while, the deer ambled off, and Louise closed her eyes again, recapturing the charged moments from her dream. As she did so, she slipped her hands down and pulled up the hem of her skirt. After all, she was alone and no one was going to see.

She opened her legs wide and pulled her knickers to one side. She reached down and touched herself gently, then with more deliberate movements. Spreading her lips with one hand, she began to stroke her inflamed clitoris in the slow, steady rhythm that she knew would eventually bring her to an orgasm. She thought of the squaddies, picturing them stepping up to Marie-Thérèse and exploring the Frenchwoman's body with their hands, much as she was exploring her own.

With her eyes still shut, she heard another train drawing near. It slowed down as it approached. Louise did not open her eyes. There must be passengers on board, but she was past caring who saw and, besides, what could they do? In another few minutes her train would draw her away from them for ever. Let them look all they liked. She listened as the other train drew alongside, the screeching of the brakes signalling its gradual halt. She was already aroused by her fantasy, but knowing that someone might be seated at the window in another carriage right next to her own charged Louise even more. She spread her legs yet further, and increased the speed with which she was caressing her clitoris. That was not enough for her though, and with her other hand she slid a finger into her throbbing sex, trying to fill herself and satiate her desire.

Louise could not resist the temptation to see if anyone was watching her. Thinking that someone might be was erotic enough, but it would be even more erotic to know so. She opened her eyes just the tiniest fraction, just enough that she could see out from under her long lashes without giving herself away. She almost jumped when she saw the man sitting not three feet away from her in the other carriage. He was so close that, were it not for the glass between them, she felt she could reach out and touch him. His head was turned towards her, and his eyes were fixed on her hands as she pleasured herself. Louise could see that he, too, was alone in his carriage, and she hoped that this might embolden him.

Louise decided to put on a show for him. Pretending to be still unaware of the man's presence, still with her eyes shut, she unbuttoned the front of her dress and pulled it aside. Taking her pink-tipped breasts in her hands, she caressed them, enjoying the sensation of their soft fullness. Then she slid one hand back to her pulsing vagina, and slipped three fingers inside herself, arching her back up to press her clitoris against the palm of her hand.

Louise did not have to wait long for the man to take advantage of his lonely situation in his carriage. She watched stealthily as he fumbled with the buttons on his jeans, and pulled out his cock. It was already hard and long. He began to pump it back and forth in his hand, all the time watching Louise intently, his tongue snaking out over his lips every now and then.

Louise could feel the rising swell of her orgasm building deep within her. She played her fingers around inside herself, then fluttered them out around her tender, swollen labia and her stiff clitoris. She was aching for release; aching so badly that it was almost painful. She glanced at the man again. He was standing now, facing the window and working his penis with a concentrated fury. Then there was a sudden jolt of the carriage and Louise was jerked forward and then back again in her seat. Her train started to inch slowly away. She opened her eyes wide in surprise, and then looked at the man. On meeting her gaze, the man bucked and hunched forward and a jet of milky semen spurted from his penis and splashed against the window. Louise watched as her carriage slowly moved past the man's, leaving him behind. She leant back in the seat and slowly strummed her throbbing clitoris to its climax, thinking of the anonymous man who had shared his orgasm with her.

Louise was finding it hard to adjust to being back in England after her Provençal summer. It was late September, and already she could feel the cool tinge of autumn in the air. The skies above her were grey and clouded, so different from the piercingly bright light to which she had become accustomed over the summer.

Louise had decided to live out of the university halls of residence for her third year, and was renting a house in the town centre, together with Liz, Fran and Charlotte. She arrived late the night before term was due to begin, and her three friends greeted her as if she had been away for years rather than a few months. It seemed hard to believe that it was barely three months since she had last seen them, for so much had happened to her in the intervening period. Louise knew that she had changed irrevocably, and wondered whether that change would show. Her friends pumped her for the details of her trip, wanting to know first and foremost what Frenchmen were like in bed. Louise smiled wryly to herself. She could tell them all about Frenchwomen as well, she thought, but decided that it could wait. It was probably best to break them in gently.

The next morning, Louise received a letter in the post from Dr Petersen, asking her to report to his office at nine o'clock that very day. She felt sure that none of her fellow third-year students would have received such a summons, and she had a good idea what it was that Dr Petersen wanted to talk to her about.

She knocked on the door of his office, and heard a terse 'Come' from the other side. Smiling, she opened the door. Dr Petersen scowled at her. She had forgotten what a sour-face he was, and thought with a wicked smirk that a summer with Milo or the Comte would sort him out.

'Miss Sherringham,' he said, barely deigning to acknowledge her. 'Take a seat.'

Louise settled on to the uncomfortable wooden chair facing his desk. She felt totally at ease. In fact, she was almost looking forward to what was going to come.

'Now. I would be grateful if you would tell me how your research proceeded this summer. I take it that you had complete success in your mission?' he asked, his voice barbed with sarcasm.

Louise smiled happily. 'Yes, thanks for asking. I did.'

Dr Petersen looked up sharply. 'I'm sorry?'

'I said, "Yes, I did." My research was a complete success.'

'I am correct in thinking that your topic is still, let me see . . .' Dr Petersen shuffled through some papers on his desk, before picking one up and reading from it. '"Lost and Found: The Search for *The Venus of Collioure*"?'

'Yes, you are.'

'And am I correct in understanding that you are claiming to have been successful in your search? That you have found *The Venus of Collioure*?'

'Yes, you are,' said Louise. She was enjoying this.

'Well, that's quite a claim to make, Louise. You realise that you will have to produce watertight supporting evidence, if not the painting itself, for your research to be taken seriously?' Dr Petersen could not keep the annoyance from his voice.

'Yes, I do.'

'So would you kindly show me what this evidence comprises? I take it that you have not brought the painting back with you from France.'

He's still snide as ever, Louise thought to herself. 'Well, at eight feet by six feet in its frame, that might have proved a little difficult,' she replied flippantly. 'But

I can certainly show you my evidence.' She reached for her bag and pulled out the folder which contained the large colour and black-and-white photographs she had taken of *The Venus*. She handed the folder to Dr Petersen.

He couldn't prevent his eyebrows from darting upward in surprise when he saw the first photograph: a large colour print that Gui had taken of Louise standing next to the painting. Dr Petersen pulled the print from its protective cover, reached into his inside jacket pocket and put on his half-moon glasses. He held the photograph very close, almost under his nose, and scanned it carefully. Then he opened one of his desk drawers, and took out a large magnifying glass. After a couple of minutes of close scrutiny, he put the print down on the desk and silently turned to the next photograph: a colour detail of the nude's head and shoulders. He gave this a similar period of close attention, before turning to the next detail shot of de Valence's signature in the bottom right-hand corner of the painting. It took Dr Petersen a full twenty minutes to peruse the entire folder. He then picked up the first colour print again and once more looked at it very closely. Louise could tell that he was finding it difficult to say what he was thinking, to admit that he could not fault her evidence. She was elated. She had never before seen Dr Petersen at a loss for words.

'I also have a video tape that I made of *The Venus of Collioure*; and over a hundred colour transparencies of the painting, both full views and detail shots. They are all available to you.'

Dr Petersen finally spoke. 'I, um, would like to take these away for closer scrutiny. That doesn't necessarily mean that I accept your claim.'

Louise knew deep down inside that Petersen realised that this was the real thing, but he couldn't bring himself to admit it. How could a painting of de Valence's originality and genius not be immediately apparent for what it was? This was no fake, no feeble copy. The mark of genius was written large across the canvas.

'Not that I believe this is the original for a moment, but where did you find this painting?' he asked.

Louise looked at him, almost with pity. This wretched man had done his best to try to stop her in her search, and now that she had succeeded he was begrudging her any praise. At least he was consistent. Louise could not prevent herself from crowing.

'Ah. That's for me to know and for you to find out. After all I, a mere student, managed to track it down, so I'm sure that it will be easy for you to do the same.'

Dr Petersen was silent. He picked up the colour prints again and studied them. He shook his head.

'The video tape, please, Miss Sherringham. And the transparencies.'

Louise happily handed them over. It had all been worth it, just to see the expression on Petersen's face.

Chapter Thirteen

Nine months had passed. Louise had worked hard, both on her coursework and on her dissertation. She had spoken to Gui several times on the phone, keeping him informed about the progress of her work. Each time they had spoken, he had reiterated the absolute necessity for secrecy concerning the whereabouts of the painting.

Despite her initial elation at Dr Petersen's reaction to her evidence concerning the existence of *The Venus of Collioure,* now Louise was worried. It was late May; she had just submitted her dissertation; and she had been called in to see Dr Petersen again. He had told her with a barely concealed smile that, even with the mass of evidence that she had accumulated and researched and presented, it would be very hard for the examiners to pass her dissertation.

'What we see in these photographs and slides and on the video could, after all, be a very skilful fake. Without seeing the painting itself, we will not be able to verify your claim. You should have understood this from the start of your research. I fear you have wasted both your own time and ours.'

Dr Petersen could not disguise his jubilant pleasure. Louise knew how intensely he disliked her, and that he considered her downfall a just retribution for going against his wishes by pursuing this project.

Leaving his office, Louise tried to put a brave face on the little bombshell she had just received. After all, the job with the Comte was hers, even if she failed her finals. And yet her pride in her work and her knowledge that she was right made it hard to take this criticism from Dr Petersen. She didn't want to fall at this last, irritating hurdle; but she knew that she had to admit that he had a point. Without the painting itself to inspect, no self-respecting art academic could unequivocally accept her evidence. Gui had sworn her to secrecy, and made her promise not to reveal her sources or the whereabouts of the painting. No matter what, Louise knew that she could not break that promise. There was nothing she could do.

Three weeks later, Louise's final exams were over, and she was waiting for her viva, the spoken examination during which she knew she would have to defend her work on *The Venus of Collioure*. She was facing the prospect with a hopeless fatalism. She knew she would be in for a drubbing, and that it would most likely be orchestrated by Dr Petersen.

The day before her viva, Louise received a telegram. It bore no signature, and read:

Urgent! James Bower Gallery, Knightsbridge,
London. Tonight, 8 p.m.

Louise smiled. Milo, the old rogue. He must have organised an exhibition and forgotten to send her an invitation to the preview, hence this panicky last-minute effort. She had spent the last few days going over her dissertation with a fine-tooth comb, undertaking some last-minute revision of the more abstruse details, and she was getting pretty sick of it. She was glad of a distraction, and so decided to obey the summons.

Arriving at the gallery, she was surprised to see that, although all the lights were blazing inside, there appeared to be no one there. Perhaps she was the first to arrive. Or perhaps the guests were in one of the rooms at the back of the building.

She tried the door, but it was locked. She rang the bell, and waited. A smartly dressed woman hurried to the door and let her in.

'Miss Sherringham. We've been expecting you. Please come this way.'

Louise was struck by the echoing silence in the gallery. Very odd. She must be the first to arrive after all. She gazed at the paintings displayed on the walls as she followed the woman through the various rooms in the gallery. She recognised some of the erotic scenes from the brochure that she had perused so closely all that time ago. None of the paintings were by Milo, however.

The woman stopped by a door in the back gallery. She opened the door, and gestured Louise inside.

Louise stepped in, her eyes trying to adjust to the dim light. A figure was standing in the corner.

'Milo?' she asked.

'No, it's me,' a familiar voice replied.

'Gui! What on earth are you doing here?' Louise asked in astonishment.

'Accompanying my second-favourite nude on a foreign trip,' he said, flipping on a light switch and gesturing at the wall behind him. There was *The Venus of Collioure* in all her naked and savage glory.

'But . . .?'

'Well, I figured that your examiners might want the chance to study her in the flesh, so to speak.'

Louise was totally dumbfounded. Gui must think something of her if he was willing to bring his most prized and secret possession all this way, and to expose her to the full scrutiny of curious and ambitious art historians.

'But . . .'

'You can bring your examiners down here tomorrow afternoon. I've checked: yours is the final viva of the day; and if you tell your examiners what's waiting for them, I'm sure they'll be more than happy to accompany you.'

'How on earth did you manage to find that out?' Louise asked.

'Over the past few months, Bernice and I have become good friends on the telephone. She really is a most helpful secretary: an asset to your department.'

Louise grinned. Bernice had not uttered a single word of this to Louise; no mean undertaking for the most indiscreet and gossip-loving member of the departmental staff. Poor Bernice must have been bursting with the knowledge, but unwillingly unable to share it.

The significance of Gui's action started to dawn on Louise, and with it came rising elation. She knew that, faced with *The Venus of Collioure*, there was no way that Dr Petersen could discredit her now; and she knew that she would stagger the examiners with her discovery. She also knew that none of this mattered in the slightest, as in a month's time she would be spending the first of many more golden days with Gui in France. She fell into Gui's welcoming arms, and kissed him with a fervour and passion that took them both by surprise.

'But how on earth did you manage to get her into the country?' she finally asked, pulling away from him for a moment. 'How did you get an export licence in France? And then the import duties on this side of the Channel! They must have been phenomenal for such a valuable work of art.'

'That was the easiest part of all.' Gui laughed. 'You don't need an export licence for a mere copy, do you?

That's what the officials in Paris decided it was, and I wasn't going to disabuse them. Those petty bureaucrats issuing the licences wouldn't know a genuine de Valence if it got up and bit them on the arse.'

Louise laughed.

'But we would, wouldn't we?' Gui continued, with a wink. 'And, luckily for me, the nice officer from Customs and Excise at Dover with whom I dealt was a bit of an art buff. He was very interested in the painting – he knew a little of the story of the infamous, long-missing *Venus of Collioure*. So, when I showed him the official French certification that proved beyond doubt that my painting was a worthless fake, he was more than happy to believe it. After all, it couldn't possibly be the genuine lost masterpiece, could it?'

Louise laughed again, and silenced Gui with a kiss.

BLACK LACE NEW BOOKS

Published in September

DARKER THAN LOVE
Kristina Lloyd
£5.99

It's 1875 and the morals of Queen Victoria have no hold over London's debauched elite. Young and naive Clarissa is eager to meet Lord Marldon, the man to whom she is betrothed. She knows he is handsome, dark and sophisticated. He is, in fact, depraved and louche with a taste for sexual excess.

ISBN 0 352 33279 4

RISKY BUSINESS
Lisette Allen
£5.99

Liam is a hard-working journalist fighting a battle against injustice. Rebecca is a spoilt rich girl used to having her own way. Their lives collide when they are thrown into a dangerous intimacy with each other. His rugged charm is about to turn her world upside-down.

ISBN 0 352 33280 8

DARK OBSESSION
Fredrica Alleyn
£7.99

Ambitious young interior designer Annabel Moss is delighted when a new assignment takes her to the country estate of Lord and Lady Corbett-Wynne. The grandeur of the house and the impeccable family credentials are a façade for shockingly salacious practices. Lord James, Lady Marina, their family and their subservient staff maintain a veneer of respectability over some highly esoteric sexual practices and Annabel is drawn into a world of decadence where anything is allowed as long as a respectable appearance prevails.

ISBN 0 352 33281 6

Published in October

SEARCHING FOR VENUS
Ella Broussard
£5.99

Art history student Louise decides to travel to rural France to track down a lost painting – the sensuous *Venus of Collioure* – whose disappearance is one of the mysteries of the art world. She is about to embark on another quest: one which will bring her sexual fulfilment with a number of dashing Frenchmen!

ISBN 0 352 33284 0

UNDERCOVER SECRETS
Zoe le Verdier
£5.99

Anna Caplin is a TV reporter. When her boss offers her the chance to infiltrate a secret medical institute, she grabs the opportunity – not realising the institute specialises in human sexual response. It isn't long before Anna finds herself involved in some highly unorthodox situations with Doctor Galloway – the institute's director.

ISBN 0 352 33285 9

To be published in November

FORBIDDEN FRUIT
Susie Raymond
£5.99

Beth is thirty-eight. Jonathan is sixteen. An affair between them is unthinkable. Or is it? To Jonathan, Beth is much more exciting than girls his own age. She's a real woman: sexy, sophisticated and experienced. And Beth can't get the image of his fit young body out of her mind. Although she knows she shouldn't encourage him, the temptation is irresistible. What will happen when they have tasted the forbidden fruit?

ISBN 0 352 33306 5

HOSTAGE TO FANTASY
Louisa Francis
£5.99

Bridie Flanagan is a spirited young Irish woman living a harsh life in outback Australia at the turn of the century. A reversal of fortune enables her to travel to the thriving city of Melbourne and become a lady. But rugged bushranger Lucas Martin is in pursuit of her; he wants her money and she wants his body. Can they reach a civilised agreement?

ISBN 0 352 33305 7

If you would like a complete list of plot summaries of Black Lace titles, please fill out the questionnaire overleaf or send a stamped addressed envelope to:

BLACK LACE BOOKLIST

All books are priced £4.99 unless another price is given.

Black Lace books with a contemporary setting

ODALISQUE	Fleur Reynolds ISBN 0 352 32887 8	☐
VIRTUOSO	Katrina Vincenzi ISBN 0 352 32907 6	☐
THE SILKEN CAGE	Sophie Danson ISBN 0 352 32928 9	☐
RIVER OF SECRETS	Saskia Hope & Georgia Angelis ISBN 0 352 32925 4	☐
SUMMER OF ENLIGHTENMENT	Cheryl Mildenhall ISBN 0 352 32937 8	☐
MOON OF DESIRE	Sophie Danson ISBN 0 352 32911 4	☐
A BOUQUET OF BLACK ORCHIDS	Roxanne Carr ISBN 0 352 32939 4	☐
THE TUTOR	Portia Da Costa ISBN 0 352 32946 7	☐
THE HOUSE IN NEW ORLEANS	Fleur Reynolds ISBN 0 352 32951 3	☐
WICKED WORK	Pamela Kyle ISBN 0 352 32958 0	☐
DREAM LOVER	Katrina Vincenzi ISBN 0 352 32956 4	☐
UNFINISHED BUSINESS	Sarah Hope-Walker ISBN 0 352 32983 1	☐
THE DEVIL INSIDE	Portia Da Costa ISBN 0 352 32993 9	☐
HEALING PASSION	Sylvie Ouellette ISBN 0 352 32998 X	☐
THE STALLION	Georgina Brown ISBN 0 352 33005 8	☐

RUDE AWAKENING	Pamela Kyle ISBN 0 352 33036 8	☐
EYE OF THE STORM	Georgina Brown ISBN 0 352 33044 9	☐
GEMINI HEAT	Portia Da Costa ISBN 0 352 32912 2	☐
ODYSSEY	Katrina Vincenzi-Thyne ISBN 0 352 33111 9	☐
PULLING POWER	Cheryl Mildenhall ISBN 0 352 33139 9	☐
PALAZZO	Jan Smith ISBN 0 352 33156 9	☐
THE GALLERY	Fredrica Alleyn ISBN 0 352 33148 8	☐
AVENGING ANGELS	Roxanne Carr ISBN 0 352 33147 X	☐
COUNTRY MATTERS	Tesni Morgan ISBN 0 352 33174 7	☐
GINGER ROOT	Robyn Russell ISBN 0 352 33152 6	☐
DANGEROUS CONSEQUENCES	Pamela Rochford ISBN 0 352 33185 2	☐
THE NAME OF AN ANGEL £6.99	Laura Thornton ISBN 0 352 33205 0	☐
SILENT SEDUCTION	Tanya Bishop ISBN 0 352 33193 3	☐
BONDED	Fleur Reynolds ISBN 0 352 33192 5	☐
THE STRANGER	Portia Da Costa ISBN 0 352 33211 5	☐
CONTEST OF WILLS £5.99	Louisa Francis ISBN 0 352 33223 9	☐
BY ANY MEANS £5.99	Cheryl Mildenhall ISBN 0 352 33221 2	☐
MÉNAGE £5.99	Emma Holly ISBN 0 352 33231 X	☐
THE SUCCUBUS £5.99	Zoe le Verdier ISBN 0 352 33230 1	☐
FEMININE WILES £7.99	Karina Moore ISBN 0 352 33235 2	☐

AN ACT OF LOVE £5.99 | Ella Broussard ISBN 0 352 33240 9 | □
THE SEVEN-YEAR LIST £5.99 | Zoe le Verdier ISBN 0 352 33254 9 | □
MASQUE OF PASSION £5.99 | Tesni Morgan ISBN 0 352 33259 X | □
DRAWN TOGETHER £5.99 | Robyn Russell ISBN 0 352 33269 7 | □
DRAMATIC AFFAIRS £5.99 | Fredrica Alleyn ISBN 0 352 33289 1 | □

Black Lace books with an historical setting

THE CAPTIVE FLESH	Cleo Cordell ISBN 0 352 32872 X	□
THE SENSES BEJEWELLED	Cleo Cordell ISBN 0 352 32904 1	□
HANDMAIDEN OF PALMYRA	Fleur Reynolds ISBN 0 352 32919 X	□
JULIET RISING	Cleo Cordell ISBN 0 352 32938 6	□
ELENA'S CONQUEST	Lisette Allen ISBN 0 352 32950 5	□
PATH OF THE TIGER	Cleo Cordell ISBN 0 352 32959 9	□
BELLA'S BLADE	Georgia Angelis ISBN 0 352 32965 3	□
WESTERN STAR	Roxanne Carr ISBN 0 352 32969 6	□
CRIMSON BUCCANEER	Cleo Cordell ISBN 0 352 32987 4	□
LA BASQUIASE	Angel Strand ISBN 0 352 32988 2	□
THE LURE OF SATYRIA	Cheryl Mildenhall ISBN 0 352 32994 7	□
THE INTIMATE EYE	Georgia Angelis ISBN 0 352 33004 X	□
THE AMULET	Lisette Allen ISBN 0 352 33019 8	□
CONQUERED	Fleur Reynolds ISBN 0 352 33025 2	□

JEWEL OF XANADU	Roxanne Carr ISBN 0 352 33037 6	☐
THE MISTRESS	Vivienne LaFay ISBN 0 352 33057 0	☐
LORD WRAXALL'S FANCY	Anna Lieff Saxby ISBN 0 352 33080 5	☐
FORBIDDEN CRUSADE	Juliet Hastings ISBN 0 352 33079 1	☐
TO TAKE A QUEEN	Jan Smith ISBN 0 352 33098 8	☐
ÎLE DE PARADIS	Mercedes Kelly ISBN 0 352 33121 6	☐
NADYA'S QUEST	Lisette Allen ISBN 0 352 33135 6	☐
DESIRE UNDER CAPRICORN	Louisa Francis ISBN 0 352 33136 4	☐
THE HAND OF AMUN	Juliet Hastings ISBN 0 352 33144 5	☐
THE LION LOVER	Mercedes Kelly ISBN 0 352 33162 3	☐
A VOLCANIC AFFAIR	Xanthia Rhodes ISBN 0 352 33184 4	☐
FRENCH MANNERS	Olivia Christie ISBN 0 352 33214 X	☐
ARTISTIC LICENCE	Vivienne LaFay ISBN 0 352 33210 7	☐
INVITATION TO SIN £6.99	Charlotte Royal ISBN 0 352 33217 4	☐
ELENA'S DESTINY	Lisette Allen ISBN 0 352 33218 2	☐
LAKE OF LOST LOVE £5.99	Mercedes Kelly ISBN 0 352 33220 4	☐
UNHALLOWED RITES £5.99	Martine Marquand ISBN 0 352 33222 0	☐
THE CAPTIVATION £5.99	Natasha Rostova ISBN 0 352 33234 4	☐
A DANGEROUS LADY £5.99	Lucinda Carrington ISBN 0 352 33236 0	☐
PLEASURE'S DAUGHTER £5.99	Sedalia Johnson ISBN 0 352 33237 9	☐

SAVAGE SURRENDER £5.99	Deanna Ashford ISBN 0 352 33253 0	☐
CIRCO EROTICA £5.99	Mercedes Kelly ISBN 0 352 33257 3	☐
BARBARIAN GEISHA £5.99	Charlotte Royal ISBN 0 352 33267 0	☐

Black Lace anthologies

PAST PASSIONS £6.99	ISBN 0 352 33159 3	☐
PANDORA'S BOX 2 £4.99	ISBN 0 352 33151 8	☐
PANDORA'S BOX 3 £5.99	ISBN 0 352 33274 3	☐
SUGAR AND SPICE £7.99	ISBN 0 352 33227 1	☐

Black Lace non-fiction

WOMAN, SEX AND ASTROLOGY £5.99	Sarah Bartlett ISBN 0 352 33262 X	☐

-------✂-------------------

Please send me the books I have ticked above.

Name ....

Address ....

....

....

.... Post Code ....

Send to: **Cash Sales, Black Lace Books, Thames Wharf Studios, Rainville Road, London W6 9HT.**

US customers: for prices and details of how to order books for delivery by mail, call 1-800-805-1083.

Please enclose a cheque or postal order, made payable to **Virgin Publishing Ltd**, to the value of the books you have ordered plus postage and packing costs as follows:

UK and BFPO – £1.00 for the first book, 50p for each subsequent book.

Overseas (including Republic of Ireland) – £2.00 for the first book, £1.00 each subsequent book.

If you would prefer to pay by VISA or ACCESS/MASTERCARD, please write your card number and expiry date here:

....

Please allow up to 28 days for delivery.

Signature ....

-------✂-------------------